# Praise for *The Fire and the Light*
## Book One of The Souls of Aredyrah Series

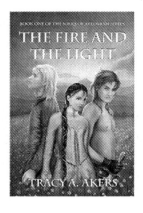

*"The Fire and the Light* is a spellbinder, a book to treasure, a novel of rare power and originality, brimming with, yes, fire and light. Its fascinating multi-layered plot examines, in mythological terms, a societal system webbed in isolationism and superstition. Sensitive and richly-textured, the lives of its vividly-realized characters achieve compelling dimension as they struggle to break free of the prejudices and lies that have distorted their existence…Here's a classic in the making."

~William F. Nolan, award-winning author
of the *Logan's Run* series

*"The Fire and the Light* is a fast-paced and intriguing story that wears its message of tolerance and compassion lightly."

~Kate Constable, author of the
*Chanters of Tremaris* series

"…fast-paced, interesting, and fun for readers of all ages."

~Leslie Halpern, author of *Dreams on Film*

"…the plot is compelling…it could teach young readers valuable lessons about the cruelty of prejudice and the consequences of the lust for power."

~Marlene Y. Satter, *ForeWord Clarion Review*

**Awards**

BOOK TWO
THE SOULS OF AREDYRAH SERIES

# THE SEARCH FOR
# THE
# UNNAMED ONE

TRACY A. AKERS

*For Brit & Rigel —*
*Welcome to my*
*imagination !*

*Tracy A. Akers*

*Aisling Press, Tampa Florida*

AISLING PRESS
Published by Oculus Media Group
Oculus Media Group, LLC (USA)
Tampa, FL 33543

Printing History
Aisling Press trade paperback edition / July 2007

Cover Design: Annah Hutchings; © Tracy A. Akers
Interior Character Illustrations: Annah Hutchings © Tracy A. Akers
Editor: Julia Gabell

Publisher's Cataloging-in-Publication Data
(Prepared by The Donohue Group, Inc.)

Akers, Tracy A.
    The search for the unnamed one / Tracy A. Akers.

        p. ; cm. – (The souls of the Aredyrah series ; Bk. Two)
        ISBN-13: 978-1-934677-04-9; ISBN-10: 1-934677-04-3
        ISBN-13: 978-0-9778875-1-4 (series); ISBN-10: 0-9778875-1-0 (series)

    1. Prophecies—Fiction. 2. Cousins—Fiction. 3. Fantasy fiction. 4. Bildungsromans.
    I. Title

PS3601.K47 S43 2007
813./6

2007920556

PRINTED IN THE UNITED STATES OF AMERICA

10  9  8  7  6  5  4  3  2  1

*for the believers*
*(you know who you are)*

# Acknowledgments

Thanks to my husband for his immeasurable support. Without him, the story of Aredyrah would probably still be a manuscript waiting for a publisher. To all my friends and family members: Thanks for putting up with me. You may think I "eat and drink Aredyrah," but the size of my hips indicates there's more to the menu. Special thanks to Alina Kolluri for her friendship, inspiration, and suggestions to the storyline; to my teachers for sharing their wisdom, most notably Judy Candis, and fellow writers Jessi Dickinson, Belea Keeney, Elvira Weaver, and Audrey Jacobs. To Debbie Smith, thanks for renewing our friendship and for the amazing referral. And to all of my Ringer friends: Had we not met, none of this wonderful craziness would have happened. Thanks for reintroducing me to my right brain.

Thanks to my amazing artist, Annah Hutchings, for once again adding her magic; to Cameron and author William F. Nolan for their confidence in my work and willingness to tell others about it; to my new publisher, Bo Savino, for her friendship and complete lack of hesitation regarding the publication of this book; to my editor, Julie Gabell, for her generosity of spirit and the extra polish she gave my manuscript; to Sylvia Hemmerly, for her belief in me and the invaluable advice she has given me regarding publishing and marketing; to my brother, Grady Orr, who designed my website and keeps it updated; to Elspeth Williams who gave up two weeks of her summer vacation to proofread my manuscript; to Cathy Wheeler and Melanie Gasbarro for their support and encouragement, (and their relentless search for typos within the pages;) to David Williams for always being on hand to share his expertise on the ancient world; and to middle-school reading coach Ann Shanks for being my cheerleader.

Last, but not least, I would like to thank all of the readers who have taken the time to write me, passed the book onto a friend, or who have simply told someone else about it. Also, thanks to all of the book store managers, school teachers, reading coaches, media specialists, conference and convention organizers, library staff members, and media representatives who have invited me to share my world with their students, patrons, and readers. You are all, each and every one of you, vital to keeping this story alive. The world of Aredyrah thanks you.

# Aredyrah

# Table of Contents

# Introduction

by
William F. Nolan

The heartening thing about writing in any genre is that there is always room for new talent. The door to creativity is never closed. If an individual, man or woman, has a talent for putting words on paper, and works hard at his or her craft, readers will respond favorably. This is true of all genres, from romance to westerns, from sports to sci-fi, from hard-boiled to high fantasy.

Tracy Akers writes High Fantasy. She is a new voice to be heard, a new talent to discover and savor. With the first two books in her "Souls of Aredyrah" series, she has firmly established her place in the popular genre of High Fantasy. If you enjoy reading about mystical realms, magic potions, and handsome princes, of legendary gods and wicked kings, of conflict and sacrifice, then Tracy Akers is for you.

She delivers fully-realized characters and genuine emotion. In the volume you hold in your hands, book two of her ongoing series, the stakes are high for Reiv, her teenaged protagonist. He achieves vivid life in these pages, and the reader shares his defeats and his ultimate triumphs.

Here is High Fantasy written with vigor and imagination, providing readers with new worlds to experience, new challenges, new romance. Here is a zest for life!

There are several characters who figure in the action of this new novel, and each is presented in deeply humanistic terms. The reader gets to know each of them

1

in the course of a stirring narrative, and each has a pivotal role to play in the special world created by Tracy Akers.

Yes, indeed, there is always room for a dedicated new writer in the vast landscape of popular literature—and Tracy Akers now stands alongside so many others who continue to give readers the thrills that only proven talent can provide.

High Fantasy. High Talent. Welcome to Aredyrah.

William F. Nolan
Author of the *Logan's Run* series

# 1

# Phantom

The air in the catacombs was thick and damp and filled with the odor of human waste and lingering decay. Whyn pulled the stench through his nostrils and into his lungs, his belly tightening with a desire that tingled to his toes. It was not the same desire he felt for Cinnia, his wife, nor for any woman who had ever pleased him. This was different, and yet the effect it had on him was as powerful as an aphrodisiac.

Whyn stared at the slender back of the Priestess who walked but steps ahead of him. She possessed a beauty unlike any woman he had ever seen, and an ugliness he found equally attractive. She seemed to float on air, her long white hair swaying at her back, the hem of her pastel gown trailing behind her. As Whyn gazed at her, he realized the ache in his belly was for her, but it was not like that of a man for a woman. It was more like that of a soul craving sustenance. Until recently, he had only thought of the Priestess as an authority figure; even now he feared her more than longed for her. But for some reason the need to drink her in was overwhelming. It was as though she were a separate part of himself, and he had only to fill himself with her to find fulfillment.

He glanced past her toward the light in the corridor ahead. A grizzled old man shuffled several paces in front of them,

3

leading them through the twisting darkness. The lantern in the man's hand swayed, its golden orb casting eerie shadows upon the walls. One by one grimy doors came into view. Wide eyes watched through tiny, barred windows, only to melt into blackness as the lantern passed.

A hand clawed toward the light, the pale face behind it momentarily revealed. "Mercy, good Prince," a woman's voice rasped.

Whyn kept his eyes forward, daring not to look at the woman, nor to acknowledge her plea. She was only a Jecta, and no doubt an insurgent bent on the destruction of Tearia.

"Does this place pain your heart, my young Prince?" the Priestess asked, pausing to face him.

"No, Priestess," Whyn replied. "It lifts my spirits."

The Priestess smiled, her porcelain skin and gold-painted features reflecting her satisfaction through the darkness. She flashed her eyes toward the old man. "You. Leave us," she ordered.

The man turned and nodded, then bowed his way back down the corridor from which they had come, taking the lantern with him.

Whyn and the Priestess stood in the dimness. The only light to guide them now was an occasional torch bracketed to the wall. Wynn struggled to focus on his surroundings, listening to the sound of his own rapid breathing and the melancholy drip of water somewhere in the distance.

The Priestess brushed past him. Clutching a shoulder bag close to her body, she ducked into a passage that branched from the main artery. She motioned Whyn in and led him in the direction of what looked like a distant orifice, its circular glow like that of a red eclipse on a starless night. As Whyn followed at her back, it seemed to him that the Priestess was a beautiful phantom lit from within, leading him to a mysterious world to which he would soon be privy.

Moans and hushed whispers wafted from the endless line of cells that they passed. How many people were imprisoned in this place? Whyn wondered. Hundreds, it seemed. But he knew there would soon be thousands…or perhaps there would be none. After the Purge, there would no longer be any need to keep prisoners, no longer any need to waste the food and manpower on them. Now with Whyn's father, the King of Tearia, dead, there was nothing to stop the Priestess from her magnificent plan.

The air became steamy, the stench more pungent. The orifice loomed larger now, but still seemed very distant. No longer did it look like the glow of a moon, but more like the mouth of a great furnace, its door rimmed by the flames that burned behind it. Sweat dripped down Whyn's neck and slid over his chest, leaving the thin, golden material of his tunic plastered against his skin. A chill raced through him. Strange how he could feel both hot and cold at the same time. It was as though his flesh had been set afire while at the same time his insides had been turned to ice.

"Here is where we will find answers to the Prophecy," the Priestess said, halting before a door much like any other.

Whyn stopped, his eyes gazing toward the red circle of light at the far end of the corridor. He felt an overwhelming urge to continue toward it, as though it was somehow beckoning him.

"You will not be going to that place today," the Priestess said, recognizing the longing in his eyes.

Whyn nodded and turned his attention to the door before them. A flicker of candlelight could be seen beyond the barred window, a luxury none of the other prisoners were allowed.

"Who is kept in this place?" he asked.

"The last of the Memory Keepers," the Priestess said. She pulled a key from a peg on the wall, turned it in the lock with a *click*, then pushed the door open and entered the cell.

Whyn followed and surveyed his surroundings. The room glittered with candles, revealing tomes and parchments stacked against walls and littering the small wooden table at the room's center. In the far corner rested a pallet of straw covered by a tattered blanket. An old woman lay upon it, her bony frame pulled into the fetal position.

"Tenzy, raise yourself," the Priestess commanded. "I do not give you light to sleep by."

The old woman stirred and blinked herself awake, then raised her frail body from the floor. Pulling her ratty shawl around her shoulders, she eyed Whyn with interest. For a moment it seemed as though she recognized him, but there was no way she could have. He had never been to this place, and she had surely never been within the sunlit walls of Tearia.

"The light," Tenzy whispered, staring hard at Whyn's face.

"Yes, fool woman," the Priestess hissed. "I give you light to find answers within these parchments, not to sleep by."

The woman's eyes darted toward the Priestess, then back at Whyn. Her face grew hard. "My error, Priestess. No light here," she said.

"That can be arranged," the Priestess said. "Let me catch you sleeping one more time when you should be working and you will find yourself in the darkness like the rest."

The old woman cackled. "Who would find your precious answers then? You? Or perhaps this pretty boy-thing of yours?" She moved toward the table and shuffled her hands through a pile of parchments, stacking some into piles, rolling others into scrolls.

"Watch your words," the Priestess warned.

"Or what?" Tenzy retorted. "There is nothing more you can do to me, and there is very little more I can do for you. You asked me to find evidence of the Prophecy, and I have found none. As I told you before, there is no longer any trace of it. Your Red King of old saw that no record survived, certainly none written by the hand of those of us you call Jecta. What more would you have me do?"

"I would have you look at this," the Priestess said, pulling a tome from the bag at her shoulder. She tossed it onto the table.

A startled gasp escaped the old woman's throat. She ran her fingers over the cracked leather cover of the book, her eyes drinking in the symbols tooled into the grain.

"So you recognize it," the Priestess said.

"Aye, that I do," the old woman whispered.

"Then you should have no trouble translating it from its abominable language into one I can understand."

"This is an ancient book...written in an ancient language. My memory fails me these days. I may not be able to—"

"Do not play games with me," the Priestess snapped. "You *will* interpret it, and you have three days time in which to do it. If I do not have satisfaction from you by then, I shall seal your books up and you with them."

"Just as well," Tenzy said. "I have grown weary of this existence."

"Perhaps you would feel differently if another was sealed up with you."

Tenzy flinched.

"Test me one more time and the pages of your precious books will forever bear the stench of you and your kin's rotting flesh."

"My kin are all dead," Tenzy said.

"So you say," the Priestess replied. She turned and walked toward the door. "Perhaps a crooked child would sway you." She smiled cruelly.

Tenzy pursed her lips. "I will do what I can."

"Three days, no more," the Priestess said, and with that she swept out, ordering Whyn to follow.

# 2

# Patience, Prince

The Shell Seekers were gathered on the south side of the hill, their encampment of brightly-colored tents barely hidden from the towering stone walls of Tearia on the other side of it. As tents were raised, sundries unpacked, and wares prepared for Market, small parties began to make their way from the camp toward the selling grounds beyond. Market was held but two days out of the month, and was the only time the Jecta were allowed to sell their goods near the city. It was a profitable event, especially for the Shell Seekers. The elite citizens of Tearia were always eager to trade coin for the spoils of the sea, a place no sensible person dared enter. But even though the Shell Seeker wares were highly coveted, the Shell Seekers themselves were still considered Jecta.

Reiv paced back and forth by the cart that contained his group's supplies. It was a transporter made of wood and bamboo poles, pulled by the labor of man, not horse, and laden with every imaginable craft and sundry. It had taken hours to pack it for the journey to Market. Now it seemed to be taking even longer to unpack it.

"Gods, let us get *on* with it," Reiv grumbled.

"Patience, Prince," Jensa said. "We have a system and you had best learn to follow it or it will take us longer still." She eased her pale eyes in his direction, her brow raised in open amusement.

"I have asked you not to call me that," Reiv said. "You know I am Prince no longer. I am Shell Seeker now."

Torin, Jensa's older brother, smirked. "You will never be one of us," he said. "Your skin is too tender."

Reiv curled his lip as he envisioned his burn-scarred fist crashing through Torin's perfect teeth. But he knew his damaged hands didn't have the strength to stun Torin, much less knock out a tooth.

Reiv was new to the Shell Seekers' ways, but was determined to fit in. Torin, however, would have nothing of it; he hated the thought of residing with a Tearian, and made certain that everyone knew it. It had been only weeks since Reiv had moved in with them, invited by Jensa when he left Pobu to make a new life for himself. But while Torin resented Reiv's heritage, and Jensa patiently tolerated it, their little brother Kerrik thought having a prince under their roof the greatest thing in the world.

"You two are so mean to each other," Kerrik said as he rounded the cart and stood before them. "That's not how families are supposed to act."

"Family—ha!" Torin scoffed. "Since when is he—"

"Let's put our differences aside today, shall we?" Jensa said. "You and Reiv will not have to look at each other for two days. I, for one, will welcome the respite from your constant bickering."

"I don't see why Reiv can't work Market with us," Kerrik said. "I'll see that he stays out of trouble."

"I told you," Jensa said. "Reiv is going to Pobu to spend some time with Dayn and Alicine."

"Oooh, Alicine." Kerrik grinned. "That's who Reiv *really* wants to see."

"Silence for once," Torin said, stooping to work a knot on a strap that straddled the mound of supplies on the cart. "Now help me get these ropes untied."

"Oh, you never let me say anything," Kerrik grumbled. He marched back to the cart, his twisted right foot kicking up the sand.

"You may say anything of significance," Torin said. "Reiv's personal life does not fall into that category."

"How about your personal life," Kerrik said. "Are you going to see Mya?"

"Of course I'm going to see her. Her husband recently passed. I must offer my condolences."

"But you always saw her before, even when Eben wasn't dead. I thought—"

"Enough, Kerrik," Torin ordered.

Reiv chortled. "So Torin does like girls after all."

"What's that supposed to mean?" Torin rose from his stooped position by the cart.

"Well," Reiv said, "it seems to me that a man as handsome as you—well, handsome to the girls anyway—would show a little more interest in them. I had begun to think your attentions turned in the other direction. I had even thought to sleep with one eye open, just in case."

Torin puffed up immediately and stormed in Reiv's direction. Jensa leapt between them, easily stopping the older and much stronger Torin in his tracks.

"Enough of this!" she said. "You both have work to do. Now get on with it."

Torin clenched his jaw while Reiv grinned a grin of supreme satisfaction. His comment had clearly touched a nerve in the man's tough hide.

After some time, an eternity in Reiv's eyes, the tent was unloaded and raised, sundries pulled out and stored, and the remaining supplies secured to the cart for the trip to the selling grounds a short distance away. Though the Jecta were allowed to sell their wares there, camping near the walls was strictly forbidden. Tearian Guards were assigned to patrol the grounds at night, and for that reason valuable merchandise was never displayed until morning.

"Are we finished or not?" Reiv asked, tapping his foot with impatience.

"Yes...yes," Jensa said. Then she ducked into the tent.

Reiv followed. "You said you would take me to Pobu as soon as we were unpacked. We are unpacked."

Jensa shuffled through a crate, pulling out bits of deadwood and two flints. "Pile these outside the tent," she said, handing him the wood. "And get a fire going. I need to start us a meal."

"A meal?" Reiv cried. "But you said—"

"I said I would get you to Pobu as soon as things were settled here. We have not eaten in hours. Shall I send Torin to unload without my help *and* with an empty belly?"

"I would not care." Reiv said.

"Well, I would," Jensa replied. "Besides, I'm hungry and you are, too, whether you admit it or not."

Kerrik bounded into the tent. "I'm starving. It was High Sun *hours* ago." He rummaged through a sack and pulled out a chunk of palm nut.

"Just one, Kerrik," Jensa said. "And it wasn't hours ago."

Kerrik thrust the bag in Reiv's direction. "Want one?" he asked.

"No. I am sick of those things."

"You used to like them," Kerrik said. He tossed the bag back where he found it, munching on the nut.

Reiv trudged out of the tent and threw the wood to the ground, then started the fire with a bit of dry grass and the flints. Jensa joined him shortly thereafter, holding four skewers with limp, silvery fish impaled on them. She handed one to Reiv and the other to Kerrik, while she held the remaining two over the flames. The fish were not big; the largest were to be sold at Market, though only for a pittance. Tearian law limited how much profit they could make. The vast waters belonged to the royal family, and it was only by their grace that the Shell Seekers were allowed to sell the spoils of the sea at all.

Torin walked up and grabbed one of the skewers from Jensa. He held it over the flames for a moment more, then plopped onto the ground and pulled out a small knife. Slicing the fish down the middle, he picked out its entrails and began to eat.

"That is practically raw," Jensa scolded. "Do you want to get worms?"

"I have things to do in case you haven't noticed," Torin said. "We arrived later than we should have. Most of the others have already set up, and we won't likely get a good spot if we dawdle here. Besides, I'm not going to have the help I usually do, thanks to him." He shot Reiv a look, then continued tearing into the fish.

But Reiv refused the bait; arguing with Torin would only prolong his departure for Pobu, and it was already taking long enough. He pulled his fish off the flames and sat cross-legged in the sand as he used his thumb to split the fish.

"You, too?" Jensa shook her head. "I see I will have two bellies to medicate."

"Tearians eat raw fish all the time," Reiv said. "It is considered a delicacy."

"Humph," she said. "The only thing delicate about it is the feeling in the gut that follows."

Reiv rolled his eyes and dug his teeth into the fish, chewing quickly and swallowing it down in gulps. He tossed the remains onto the fire and went to wipe his greasy hands down his tunic. But then he thought better of it. He had worked too hard to make himself look presentable that morning. He raked his hands through the sand, then rose and folded his arms across his chest.

"So, are we ready to go then?"

"Do you mind if I finish mine first?" Jensa asked with annoyance.

Reiv sighed.

"You might as well grab some palm nut while you're waiting," she said. "That fish won't hold you for long."

"She's right, you know," Torin said. "You're going to need all the strength you can muster when you face Alicine today." He laughed.

"You find that amusing, do you?" Reiv said. "Well I think I can handle one girl, and a rather small one at that."

"You didn't do such a good job of handling her before," Kerrik piped in.

"What do you know about it?" Reiv asked.

"I know you ran away because of her."

"I did no such thing!"

"Oh yes you did," Torin interjected. "Hopefully when you run away from her *this* time, you'll run in the opposite direction of Meirla."

"Gods...enough!" Jensa said, rising. "Come Reiv. I can stand no more of this. Let us get you to Pobu before I am forced to kill the both of you."

Reiv nodded and turned to leave, but Kerrik called for him to stop. Reiv complied grudgingly. "What is it, Kerrik?" he said.

"Do you have the bracelet for Alicine?" Kerrik asked.

"Yes, in my money pouch."

"And some coin in case you want to buy her something?"

"Yes, yes."

"You'd better let me check your kohl," Kerrik said.

Reiv heaved a sigh and leaned down to give Kerrik a closer look at the black design painted around his eyes.

"Looks good," Kerrik said. "Your hair, too. Those cockles look really nice wound in your red hair like that. I don't know about the tunic, though. It doesn't look like something a Shell Seeker would wear. But the necklaces make up for it I guess."

"Thank you. May I go now?"

"I'm only trying to help," Kerrik said. "You do want to get her back, don't you?"

"Since when is a seven-year-old an expert on women?"

"Since I started paying attention."

# 3

# Painted Faces

The Jecta city of Pobu was a dismal-looking place from a distance, its brown buildings huddled against an even browner countryside. The population that lived there didn't have the luxury of spending their hard-earned coin on adornment. They were barely able to put food in their mouths, much less color into their lives.

Pobu was only a short distance east of the Shell Seeker encampment, not a far walk, but Jensa insisted she escort Reiv there nonetheless. There were too many disgruntled Jecta who resented his past life as a prince. Strangely enough, Torin had agreed, and he rarely showed any interest in Reiv's well being.

Reiv and Jensa reached the courtyard past the main entrance to the city and headed though an alley that led them to a side street. They saw few residents; most had already gone to the Market grounds to make preparations for the following day. Although the Shell Seekers were always the most popular vendors, the Tearian patrons were still willing to pick through Jecta wares looking for a bargain. Tearians were far too lazy to create their own crafts. They despised the Jecta, but didn't mind paying a bit of coin for a particularly nice piece of pottery or a trinket or two.

Reiv and Jensa arrived at the hut of the Spirit Keeper, a dwelling much like any other except it was surrounded by a flowering garden of medicinal herbs. Nannaven, the Spirit Keeper's given name, was a wise old healer who had taken in Reiv, Dayn, and Alicine when they were banished from Tearia for alleged thievery. But Reiv had experienced difficulties adjusting to Pobu, rejected not only by the residents who despised him, but also by Alicine who had spurned his advances. The shame and humiliation he felt after the incident with Alicine had been the catalyst he needed to leave Pobu. But neither she nor Dayn had taken his abandonment of them lightly. Reiv could not really blame them. Dayn and Alicine were, after all, from a place far away, a place that until recently Reiv had not even known existed. As fate would have it, Dayn had turned out to be Reiv's cousin as well as his friend. Reiv could only hope that Dayn still considered him as such, and that Alicine had forgiven him for the eagerness of his hands upon her.

After they arrived at Nannaven's door, Jensa departed, claiming the need to help her brothers finish setting up the booth. The strange expression on her face left Reiv curious as to whether there was another reason as well. He knew Dayn would want to see Jensa, her beauty could be mesmerizing, and she had openly befriended him. But her departure with Reiv three weeks earlier had clearly stung him. Since that day, Reiv had begun to notice that Jensa always asked about Dayn whenever Torin returned from Pobu with news. This day, however, she made no mention of Dayn, and disappeared into the streets without another word.

Standing before Nannaven's door, Reiv felt a rush of nausea. He knew it wasn't from the nearly-raw fish he had eaten. He hadn't seen Dayn and Alicine in almost a month, and the last time they had spoken there was much anger between them. More than anything, Reiv wanted to make things right, to make things the way they had been before.

He pulled in a steadying breath and rapped on the door. It swung open immediately and there stood Dayn, his blue eyes alight with excitement. A grin stretched across Dayn's face as he looked Reiv up and down. He burst into sudden laughter and threw his arms around Reiv, grabbing him in a fierce hug. At first Reiv felt uncomfortable at the closeness of his cousin, but he soon found himself laughing and hugging Dayn back with equal enthusiasm.

Dayn ushered him inside and poured them each a mug of cool tea, then motioned for Reiv to join him at the table. They sat across from each other and leaned across the tabletop, anxious to spill all the news.

"I can't get over the sight of you," Dayn said. "You've changed so much."

Reiv looked down at himself and smiled. "I think being a Shell Seeker suits me. You are looking well, too. Much more Jecta-like, I might add."

It was true. Dayn had given up his tunic and trousers for a kilt-like wrap around his hips. His chest was bare and tan, and his arms much more muscular. His pale hair was shoulder-length now, and was pulled back and bound at his neck. Somehow it made him look older than his sixteen years.

"I realized my desire for conformity is stronger than my need for modesty," Dayn said. "But I'm not so sure about piercing holes in my body like the others here do." He glanced at Reiv's hands. "You're not wearing your gloves."

Reiv looked at the mottled hands wrapped around his own mug and realized he was not. He had not worn the gloves in weeks now and had grown so accustomed to it, he had quite forgotten Dayn had never seen the scars before. It seemed years since he had refused to show them to anyone.

"I cannot hunt for shells with gloves on and no one there seems to care what my hands look like anyway. Even I do not care so much anymore. But you know, they seem to have gotten better since I have been with the Shell Seekers. It must be the seawater. They say it has healing properties."

Dayn grinned and tilted his head. "What's that on your eyes? I mean...is it permanent?"

Reiv laughed, realizing the black pattern that outlined them must appear strange to his cousin. "No, it is kohl, not tattoo. It protects them from the glare." A gleam came to his eyes, further accentuating their violet color against the black outline of the kohl. "The girls there really seem to like it." He winked, and they both laughed.

"Speaking of girls," Reiv said, craning his neck, "where is Alicine?"

"She's out tending to some patients, but hopefully she'll be home soon. Nannaven had some mysterious errand to run and left Alicine to finish up the rounds. She looks forward to seeing you, cousin."

Reiv noticed that Dayn's eyes had shifted at that last remark, but his heart could not help but leap. "It will be nice to see her, too. I hope she is well."

"Yes, she's well."

"And does she still wish to go back home to Kirador?"

"Yes, but she doesn't talk of it as much lately. I keep hoping she'll grow happy here, but sometimes she just seems so sad." Dayn shook his head slowly. "I don't know how to make her happy, Reiv."

Reiv nodded, but said not a word. As he considered what Dayn had just said, the thought occurred to him that maybe there was something else that Alicine needed in order to be happy. Perhaps *he* was the source of her sadness...because they had parted with harsh words...because she missed him and didn't really think him so bad. His fingers slid to the money pouch at his side, reminding him of the shell bracelet tucked inside. He had worked hard to craft it, hoping Alicine would accept it as a token of his affection, praying she would consider a future with him now that he had made something of himself as a Shell Seeker. His thoughts were interrupted as the door suddenly pushed open and Alicine swept into the room.

She stopped and stared at him, her face awash with unreadable emotion. Her lips struggled to form a smile, but seemed to waver as though conflicted.

Reiv smiled. "Hello, Alicine," he said.

"Hello," she responded, but her tone was somewhat cooler than he had hoped. No doubt she was not as forgiving as Dayn had implied.

"You look different," she said.

Reiv grinned sheepishly. "Yes, I suppose I do. You look well."

"Thank you," she said. She walked over and sat across from him at the table, staring at the tabletop as though afraid to meet his gaze. She no longer wore the form-fitting sarong he had last seen her in, but was attired in a modest tunic dress the color of dark umber, tied at the waist with a belt of patterned cloth. Her black hair was pulled back and braided in one long plait, much as she had worn it the day they first met. Her eyes moved to his hands.

"They look better," she said, nodding in their direction.

Reiv held them up and rotated them back and forth. "Yes, I was telling Dayn that I think the sea does them good."

"Does it do you good as well?" she asked.

"Yes," Reiv replied, "it does."

"So you like it there?"

"Very much."

"You'll not be coming back then?"

"No, Alicine, I will not be coming back, at least not to live, but I was wondering—"

"What's that on your eyes?"

"Oh, it is kohl. All Shell Seekers wear it. Jensa came up with the design. The first day I refused it and—"

Alicine cut him short. "So I suppose that is what you are now—a Shell Seeker?"

"Well, yes," he said.

"So what will you be doing next, tattooing your body and piercing your ears?"

"Jecta paint their faces, too," Dayn interjected. "Besides, Reiv says the girls like him with the kohl and—" His face went lax as Alicine's hostile glare shot his way.

"Well," Alicine said to Reiv, "as long as the girls *there* like it."

"Am I to take it, then, that you do not?" Reiv asked.

Alicine rolled her eyes and turned her head aside with indifference. "No, not really, but what does it matter what I think?"

Reiv's face flushed with anger mixed with humiliation. He pushed up from the table. "What do you mean by that?"

"What I mean is, you clearly have no need of a life here with us. Obviously Jensa has much more to offer."

Reiv leaned across the table, resting his hands upon it as he eyed Alicine darkly. "You know why I left. Why are you throwing this up in my face? You know there is no future for me here. Do you want me to return to a place where I am neither wanted nor appreciated?"

Angry blotches rushed to Alicine's cheeks. "I don't care what you do! Stay in Meirla for all I care. Stay there and take a Shell Seeker wife and have Shell Seeker children and live happily ever after surrounded by their scanty clothes and painted faces."

"Well as long as I have your permission! You know, maybe I will do that very thing right now. Would that make you happy?" He stormed toward the door.

Then it was Alicine's turn to leap from the table. "What's that supposed to mean?" she shouted.

"You know full well what it means!" he shouted back.

"I only know that you walked out the door and left me and Dayn behind and now you're doing it again."

Dayn rose. "Alicine, enough..."

But she persisted. "Well, Reiv, as long as you have Jensa and the other girls, then that's all that matters."

"I do not have to listen to this," Reiv said. He swung the door open violently, then turned his head toward Dayn. "I will see you later, Dayn." Then he bolted into the street.

# 4

# Loyalties Lie

Mahon walked toward the palace, fully prepared to offer his condolences to Whyn, who had summoned him there. As Commander of the Guard, Mahon had been busy organizing security for Market and had only just learned of the King's death. The formal announcement of Sedric's passing had not yet been made public. The family would grieve in private this evening, withholding formal announcements until morning. Though Mahon was the husband of Brina, sister of the Queen, he had no doubt that he was the last family member to be informed of the King's demise. Mahon and Brina had not shared a bed-chamber for sixteen years now, and while he had the royal family's sympathies, he knew he did not have their respect.

As Mahon approached the palace, he could not help but wonder why he had been ordered to keep his meeting with Whyn a secret from Brina. He did not normally share information with her about his duties; they barely spoke to one another other as it was. No doubt the Prince's summons had something to do with Reiv, Whyn's twin who had been banished from Tearia. Reiv was a Jecta now, impure and discarded because of the damage to his hands; but that was not why Mahon despised him. It was Reiv who had driven the latest nail into the coffin of Mahon's marriage. During Reiv's recent banishment to Pobu, Mahon had dutifully supported it, but Brina had fought it with all her heart and soul. She had always loved Reiv as though he were her own son. But he was not.

Mahon played over and over in his mind the uneasy rumors that had been circulating in the streets. The thought of them made the hairs stand up on the back of his neck. Reiv had become the topic of much misguided speculation, and it was causing concern for both the Temple and the Throne. Mahon ground his teeth, resentful of the fact that he had to deal not only with Brina, but with the whispers that proclaimed Reiv to be The Unnamed One, the hero of some outlandish prophecy.

As much as Mahon wanted to blame his recent problems on Reiv, he knew the boy wasn't the only reason for his and Brina's estrangement. It had begun sixteen years prior, at the death of their infant son, Keefe. Mahon closed his eyes, fighting to suppress the memory, but it did little good. He could not shake the image of his only child's face, nor the mark upon the child's neck. The birthmark had required that Keefe be weeded out; it was law. What else could a man do? Of course he felt guilty for it, yet he could not understand why he alone had borne the brunt of it for all these years. It was Brina, not he, who had killed Keefe, strangled him with her own hands, she said. But then Mahon had met Dayn, and it was as though every truth about Keefe he had ever known was a lie.

A voice sounded in Mahon's head, sending a stab of pain to his chest. *Are you Mahon?* it asked.

"Silence from you!" Mahon hissed. He quickened his pace, as if by doing so he could leave the voice on the trail behind him. But the voice persisted.

*Are you Mahon?*

"Yes," Mahon growled. "And you are Dayn. Now leave me in peace."

But Mahon knew there would never be peace until his own questions were answered. And now there were several. Dayn was about the same age Keefe would have been; he had a similar birthmark on his neck. That could be coincidence, of course, but what about the uncanny resemblance between Dayn and Whyn? The boys looked enough alike to be brothers, or cousins. Ever since Mahon's brief encounter with Dayn, he could not see Whyn without thinking of Dayn, could not hear Whyn's voice without thinking of Dayn. Mahon knew it did no good to dwell on things he could not change, but Dayn had asked him questions, questions that made him even more suspicious. And "Are you Mahon?" was one of them.

He squared his shoulders and hustled up the steps to the entrance of the palace. There he was met by two guards who pushed open the towering doors. Mahon made his way across the polished marble floor, the sword at his side clanking to the rhythm of his feet as he moved through the foyer toward the receiving room. More guards stood posted, their bodies snapping to brisk attention as he swept past them and through the portal to the room beyond.

Whyn could be seen seated in a high-backed chair centered on the dais against the far wall. His blond head was held high as he waited for Mahon to make his way across the cavernous room. As Mahon approached, he could not help but notice the determined expression on Whyn's boyish face, a look that did not indicate the emotions of a grieving son, but more like that of a vengeful one.

Mahon stopped and bowed before his new King, his hands firmly at his sides, his head lowered almost to his knees. "My Lord," he said. "My condolences for the passing of your father. May the gods bless Tearia and her King."

Mahon stared at his feet, waiting for a response, but for a long while it seemed as though none was coming. Then Mahon sensed Whyn rise and heard his footsteps as they stepped down the dais and moved in his direction.

"Rise, Mahon," Whyn ordered. "We have no time for condolences. We have duties to attend to."

Mahon rose and surveyed Whyn's face. Although there was no sound of grief in his nephew's voice, nor any hint of sorrow in his features, Whyn's skin seemed paler than usual and there were hints of dark circles under his pale blue eyes. Surely he was hiding his emotions in an attempted display of strength. He had, after all, been by his father's side for months. The ordeal had clearly taken its toll.

"My duty is always to Tearia and her King," Mahon said.

"And to her gods," Whyn added.

"Of course."

"The Priestess has made a demand of me. I am, therefore, making it of you."

"Anything, my Lord."

"I wish for you to post spies at Market today. And send more into Pobu."

"Spies are already in place, and have been for quite some time."

"Double them," Whyn said.

"Consider it done. What is it you would have them seek?"

"The Unnamed One."

Mahon kept his expression in check. "What do you wish to know of him?"

"I wish to know that he is dead."

Mahon felt the blood drain from his face and hoped Whyn did not notice. "My Lord, forgive me, but he is your brother. Surely your family—"

"He is my brother no longer, just as he is your nephew no longer. Do I sense from your response that you still feel loyalty to him?"

"No, of course not."

"But your loyalty does lie with Brina, as it always has, and she loves him as her own, an emotion she rarely spared for me."

"I do not wish to dispute you, but I know Brina has always loved you equally," Mahon said.

"While I doubt she maintains as much affection for me, her love for Reiv has always been strong." Whyn eyed Mahon suspiciously. "Will your wife's duty to her renegade nephew hinder her husband's duty to his King?"

"No—no, of course not! I will do right by the Throne as I always have. I am your servant."

"Then you will send spies throughout the Market grounds and Pobu today. There can be no obvious display of arms. You have informants within the Jecta population, do you not?"

"Yes, Lord. Many. Most are eager to earn a bit of coin. They have more loyalty to their bellies than to their friends. That is why there are so many detained Jecta as of late. You know the rumors about the insurgency."

"I am well aware. That is another reason to double our efforts for information within Pobu. Have them find the Unnamed One and report to you alone. He is to be disposed of only on your order."

"On *my* order?"

"Of course. It would not look well for it to be on mine; people have not forgotten he was once my brother and King-heir. But once this so-called Unnamed One is disposed of, the traitorous whispers in our streets will cease. Then we will take care of the Jecta filth once and for all."

"What do you have planned for them?" Mahon asked.

"There is to be a new Purge. The Priestess has ordered it. The Goddess has ordered it."

"A new Purge? You mean…"

"You know exactly what I mean. It will take some time to get the plans sorted out and our forces in shape. The Guard has grown weak, Mahon. Too weak if we are to be successful in this endeavor."

"I have always abided by the expectations of my King," Mahon said defensively. "The state of the Guard is, and always has been, representative of those expectations."

"Those expectations of which you speak were those of a weak King. But Tearia has a weak King no longer. Things are different now and preparations need to be made. You will contact your spies and proceed with your duty."

Mahon stood speechless, unable to utter a single syllable as the realization of what was happening scurried through his mind.

"Do not let your emotions get in the way of this, Mahon, or you will regret it."

"Of course not. I will do as you command."

"How long do you think it will take to locate Reiv?" Whyn asked.

"I do not know. I have received no word of him in weeks, though I have made no inquiries. He was to fade, and that is what he has done."

"What of Brina? Has she had contact with him?"

"No—no my Lord. Not since Reiv was banished from Tearia. True, she paid him visits when he was still housed within the walls, but she has had no contact with him since. Her loyalty lies with you."

Whyn narrowed his eyes. "How can you be so certain where her loyalties lie, Mahon? She abandoned her loyalty to you easy enough."

Fear for Brina's safety mushroomed in Mahon's throat. "I—I give you my word that she has not left the city."

"I suggest you exercise caution when giving your word. No one has been able to locate Brina to inform her of my father's passing." Whyn laughed. "And you thought *you* were the last to know."

Mahon felt his breath stall. Gods, where could she have gone? Surely not to Pobu. She could not have slipped passed the gates so easily. But then again, with the hustle and bustle of Market preparations...

"I will locate her immediately, my Lord."

Whyn nodded. "You had best get a rein on your wife, Mahon. I can risk no information reaching Reiv's ears. If Brina is found outside the gates, I can only assume she has been meeting with my brother. Of course that would make her an excellent source of information."

"She has not been meeting him, I assure you," Mahon said. "Your spies must find him quickly, though I doubt it will be too difficult. Reiv does tend to stand out, even amongst the dark-hairs of Pobu. I expect a prompt report, Mahon, and I want to know where Brina has been."

"It will be done." Mahon bowed as Whyn returned to his chair and slouched upon it.

"Leave me," Whyn said with a flick of his hand.

Mahon rose and turned, then walked from the room as quickly as he was able. He could feel the sweat of fear beading on his face, just as he could feel the cold grip of disaster clutching at his chest. Who was that young man he had just faced? Certainly not the good-hearted nephew he had known for the past sixteen years. It was as though Whyn was a stranger to him now. But of even more concern to Mahon was the nagging question of his own conscience.

Mahon walked out of the palace and into the glaring light of day, his eyes stinging with barely-suppressed emotion. There was no chance he could save his faltering marriage now, and even less that he could save his immortal soul.

# 5

# Into the Vortex

Dayn stormed across the room, the force of his anger threatening to pull everything not tied down into it.

"How could you have said that to him?" he shouted. "How could you have been so stupid!"

Alicine took a startled step back. "I—I'm sorry," she stammered. "I didn't mean it like that."

"No? Then what did you mean by it exactly? Didn't you see the look on Reiv's face when you came in? Didn't you see how happy he was? You would have had to be blind not to."

"I wasn't prepared to see him, that's all!"

"Don't hand me that excuse, Alicine. You knew full well he would be here to see us today. He told you himself he would be back for Market."

"But I didn't expect to see him looking like that. I…it caught me off guard. I didn't know what I was saying."

"You knew exactly what you were saying. And you should have taken back those words right then and there, the moment you saw how hurt he was by them. But no, you spewed on and on."

"I said I'm sorry. Please, Dayn, don't be mad at me."

Alicine placed a hand on his arm and looked up at him with pleading eyes. Dayn set his face hard against her. "Don't bother using your tears on me. Maybe it worked in the past, but not any more. I'm smarter about things now, including your girlish manipulations."

Alicine gasped, taken aback by his reproach. "It's just this *place!*" she cried.

"No, it's not this place. It's you! I'm tired of your threats to leave. Every time something goes the least bit wrong it's 'this place', or 'you're homesick', or 'you don't belong here', or some other excuse. Well, we're here and we're staying here until I say we go. I'm someone who matters now, someone who's making a difference—"

"At the risk of your life!"

"It's my choice. Mine! Not yours, not our parents', not Brina's, not anyone's but mine. Now, as for Reiv, I want him in my life, even if he wants to pierce and tattoo every part of his body and have a hundred Shell Seeker wives and children. All that matters is that he's happy. But that's your problem with him, isn't it? That he's found happiness without *you*. Well, I won't sit back and see you hurt him."

"I never said I wanted to hurt him!" she shouted.

"Then grow up and stop behaving like a spoiled girl who is too much of a child to know what kisses can lead to!"

Alicine's hand flew to her mouth. "I can't believe you said that."

"I'm not stupid, little sister. You wanted Reiv to kiss you that night, didn't you? I remember how you always looked at him, how ever since the first day we met him you couldn't take your eyes off of him. Did you think I didn't see it, or that he didn't? I'm not saying his touching you was right, but you were just as wrong. What do you expect him to do? Stay away from us forever? Or would you rather he come back and pine for a girl who made it perfectly clear she can't wait to leave this place and him behind forever? Reiv has a life to live, Alicine, and if he finds someone else, then you'll have to accept it and put your petty jealousies aside."

"How *dare* you say those words to me!"

"Well, it was time they were said!"

Alicine straightened her spine, clearly primed to launch the defense working in her mind. A rap at the door stopped her short.

Dayn turned his face toward the portal, then back to her, his eyes flashing. "You'd better hope it's him!" But when he swung open the door, his emotions were a mixture of disappointment and delight. Though it was not Reiv as he had hoped, it proved to be the next best thing.

"Brina...Jensa!" he exclaimed. He would have loved to hug them both right then and there, not only for joy, but also for the need to grab hold of someone.

Brina, however, did not hold back her feelings at all. She wrapped an arm around his shoulders, squeezing him tight. "Son, I have been counting the minutes until this moment." Her eyes gleamed as she stepped back and looked him up and down affectionately.

"Come in, come in," Dayn said. "Alicine and I were just having a, uh...conversation."

"Yes, we could hear it all the way up the path," Jensa said. She scanned the room. "Where's Reiv? I left him at the door not long ago. He came in, didn't he?"

"Yes, he was here," Dayn said, "but he left."

Brina became suddenly alert. "What do you mean, left? Where did he go?"

"I don't know where he went. He was upset and—"

"Upset? Why was he upset? Did you discuss the issue in question?"

"I didn't get a chance to." Dayn glared in Alicine's direction.

Brina turned her attention to Alicine. "There was a fight between you?" she asked. "Alicine...was there a fight?"

"I said some things I shouldn't have and he left, that's all," Alicine said.

Brina's mouth compressed as she removed a long bundle
from beneath her cloak and leaned it hastily in the corner. "I
have to find him," she said as she moved to the door.

"No, Brina, you stay," Jensa said. "I know my way
around better than you, and you don't need to be seen wandering around. Dayn, will you come with me? There are
places a woman shouldn't go alone."

Dayn moved toward her, then looked at Brina and
nodded. "We'll find him. Don't worry."

He shot Alicine a scowl, but said not a word to her, and
walked out with Jensa, slamming the door behind him.

Brina stared at the door momentarily, lost in thought,
then turned and made her way past Alicine to the kitchen table. "Come. Sit with me," she said, motioning Alicine over.

Alicine took her place on the bench across from Brina,
struggling to look anywhere but at the woman's concerned
face. The realization of her own role in Reiv's sudden disappearance left a guilty taste in her mouth. "I'm sorry I
angered Reiv and caused him to storm off like that," she
said. "But I'm sure he'll be fine. He can take care of himself. He's certainly proved *that* on a number of occasions."
She attempted a laugh, but it sounded feeble.

"Yes, let us hope so," Brina said. She lowered her face
and paused as though debating whether or not to continue,
then leaned in and raised her eyes to drive her point home.
"Alicine, Reiv is in danger. He should not be out alone."

Alicine jerked her head, surprised by Brina's perilous
tone. "But, he's a Shell Seeker now," she said. "Nannaven
said few Jecta would dare challenge a Shell Seeker."

"It is not the Jecta I am concerned with. It is the Tearians."

"The Tearians? But they banished him. Why would they...?"

"Much has happened in Tearia these past several weeks,"
Brina said. "And it concerns Reiv. I meant to tell you all together, but..." She looked toward the door, then rose and
poured two mugs of tea. She offered one to Alicine. "There is
much to tell. We might as well make ourselves comfortable."

Alicine took the mug, but found it trembling in her grasp. She set it on the table, and clasped her hands in front of her. "What's happened, Brina? What's wrong?"

Brina took a deep breath and paused to collect her thoughts. "As you probably know, Reiv was once destined to be the King of Tearia. When he lost his right to the throne, some people were most unhappy that he had been taken from them. Those were the ones who believed with all their hearts that he was to be the Red King. All Tearians expected him to be a King who would make Tearia greater, although everybody's idea of 'greater' was not necessarily the same. You see, not everyone believes in the ways of the Priestess, but the belief system is firmly entrenched. To speak against her would only serve to bring down the wrath of those in power, namely the Throne and the Temple. The Throne is tightly bound to the Priestess. She is powerful and very dangerous. Those who oppose her have always kept their views to themselves. For a while the quiet ones turned their hopes to the future Red King, but those hopes were dashed when Reiv was disowned."

"Didn't anyone speak up for Reiv, Brina? Anyone at all?" Alicine asked.

"That is not the way of things in Tearia. It is the will of the Priestess, and no one questions her. But then a most unexpected thing happened, for when Reiv became disowned he became unnamed. As you know, he was once called Ruairi, but that name was stripped from him and he was forced to take the name of Reiv. Although the quiet ones at first feared they had lost the leader they believed in, they soon came to realize that hope itself was not lost. It seems there is an ancient prophecy that speaks of one who will come and change Tearia forever, one who will reveal new truths as well as old lies. And that person is called the Unnamed One.

"Most people have forgotten the Prophecy. It is ancient and long of word, and all written records of it have been destroyed. Of those who do remember, most do not believe in it. The Prophecy did not come from any priestess, but

from an outsider, a Jecta sorceress it is said. Because of
that, it has not been taken seriously.

"But there are some who do believe, and although most
of the words of the Prophecy have vanished from memory,
bits of it remain alive in people's minds. After the un-
naming of their Prince, talk of it sprouted and began to
grow. Needless to say, there has been much uneasiness on
the part of the Priestess and the royal family, but they have
put on a great show of indifference. They believe that to
acknowledge the Prophecy will only serve to give it power."

"I remember when we were arrested," Alicine said, "people in the streets laughed at Reiv. But there were some who
seemed angry that Crymm was treating him like that."

"Yes. When Reiv was marched through the streets with
you and Dayn, the quiet ones became a little less quiet.
They were most unhappy to see their Prince mistreated like
that, and began to talk more and more of the Prophecy and
the part they believe he plays in it. Since then, many have
taken it into their hearts that Reiv is indeed the Unnamed
One. Of course, the Prophecy has not for a moment been
forgotten by the royal family or the Priestess. During the
hearing that was to decide what was to be done with the
three of you, a great deal of consideration was made of it.
Reiv's life was on the line that day."

"His life? You mean he could have been—?" Alicine shook
her head as though saying the word would make it true. "But
he didn't do anything, Brina. He didn't steal those things."

Brina placed her hand over Alicine's. "I know, but it
would not have mattered. It was Crymm's word against his."

"What made the Priestess spare him?"

"From what I understand, the Priestess communed with the
Goddess who told her that to execute the Unnamed One would
give him power through martyrdom, and to imprison him would
give his supporters cause to fight for him. Instead, it was felt his
influence would be weakened by simply having him fade away.
And so it was decided the best place for him to fade was Pobu.

The Priestess undoubtedly expected a disgruntled Jecta to solve the problem for her. As you know, there are many Jecta who bear a grudge against the royal family and would be happy to see him dead. If that happened, talk of the Prophecy would be put to rest. But now a month has gone by, and by the grace of the gods Reiv is still with us. I fear the Priestess has grown tired of waiting for chance to do her dirty work. It is only a matter of time before she orders someone to do it."

"So this Prophecy...do you believe in it, Brina? Do you think Reiv is the Unnamed One?"

"I do not believe anyone can predict the future, Alicine, but I do believe in the power of prophecy. I say this not as a contradiction. While I do not believe a prophecy is the truth in its initial telling, I do believe it contains the possibility of the truth. If enough people believe in a prophecy, then chances are it will become true. It is the belief in it that makes it so. Reiv may not be the one this prophecy speaks of, but it will not matter. If enough people believe him to be so, then he will be. The power of the Unnamed One will be his only because the people give it to him, not because the gods will it, or because he chooses to have it. He will have no say in it at all, really. Once again, Reiv will be what people expect him to be, not what he wants to be."

Tears stung Alicine's eyes. "It's all my fault he's out there now. I'll never forgive myself if something happens to him."

"Tell me, child. What happened between you and Reiv? Surely it is not so terrible as that."

Alicine bit her lip. For a long moment she remained silent. Then she said, "One night, before Reiv went to Meirla, I was helping him treat his hands and...things got out of control."

"Out of control?"

"We kissed and..." Alicine tensed as she awaited Brina's condemnation, but Brina seemed neither surprised nor disappointed.

"Go on..."

"Well, I let him kiss me, and I kissed him back, I don't deny it. But I wasn't ready for it, Brina. I was scared, but I

didn't know how to stop it. Then Reiv said 'sin' and I realized
what we were doing *was* a sin. So I pushed him away and—"

"He said what?"

"Sin…he said 'sin.' He said he was sorry, that he was thinking of someone else and knew it wasn't right. I'm sure he was
thinking of Jensa."

"No, I do not think it was Jensa. Do you not know of
Cinnia?"

"Who?"

"I feel fairly certain that when Reiv said 'Cin', he meant
Cinnia. That was what he called her. This is something Reiv
should have told you himself, but it is a very difficult subject
for him. Considering what happened between you, it is
probably best that I tell you.

"Reiv was once very much in love with a girl named
Cinnia. He had known her his entire life and they were in-
separable. When he was fifteen and she fourteen they were
engaged to be married, but the marriage was not to take
place for a year yet, after she came of age. This was to have
been that year. In fact, the very day he met you was the day
of the wedding."

"Whose wedding? His and *Cinnia's*?" Alicine asked.

"No, Cinnia's and his brother's."

"His brother? But why—" Alicine's confusion morphed
to sudden understanding. "You mean because he was disowned he could not marry Cinnia, and his own brother
married her in his place? I can't believe it."

"It is difficult, but yes, it is true."

"No wonder Reiv hates his brother so much."

"Whyn had little say in any of it. He and Reiv were always close, and Whyn has tried to make amends. But Reiv
rebukes him. It was Whyn who intervened on your and
Dayn's behalf. He told me so himself. He knew Reiv was
friends with you, and he could not bear to see anything else
taken from his brother. I think if it were not for Whyn,
you and Dayn might not be here today. The Priestess has

little patience for Jecta. To her you are nothing. But Whyn talked her out of harming you that day. She seems to have taken a liking to him. For that we should be grateful."

"If only Reiv had told me."

Brina placed her hand on Alicine's arm. "Reiv is very proud and has lost a great deal in his short life. Please, be patient with him. I know he cares about you very much. If he made you feel uncomfortable with his attentions...well, I am sure the emotion of Cinnia is what moved him to it. I know that does not give you comfort, but please know he has the utmost respect for you. But the days surrounding the wedding were particularly difficult for him. With that, and everything that happened with the arrest, the banishment, and you...well, surely you can see the state he was in. I do not mean to justify inappropriate behavior on his part, but please try to understand."

Alicine nodded. "Thank you for telling me. He deserves an apology; more than that really."

"Just do not make Reiv think you pity him. That would make things far worse," Brina warned.

# 6

# Game of Chance

Dayn and Jensa made their way along the streets and alley-
ways of Pobu, but saw no sign of Reiv. The sun had long
since disappeared behind the hills, and the city was draped in
the shadowy hues of night. The only light to guide them was
that which seeped through the tiny windows of the mud
houses they passed. Muffled voices mixed with laughter
wafted through the night air. Dayn and Jensa frequently
paused to listen for Reiv's voice, but they always moved on,
disappointed. The streets had become more and more deserted, and Dayn began to fear they might never find him.

As they turned yet another corner, they heard the dron-
ing talk of men punctuated by spurts of rowdy laughter.
Jensa grabbed Dayn's arm.

"The tavern," she said. "Maybe he went to the tavern." From
the look on her face, Dayn knew this was not a good thing.

The tavern was another mud-brick structure, set apart from
the others by the smoky glow that beamed through its open
door and the noisy energy that radiated from within. From
where they stood, Dayn could see that the drinking establishment was packed with patrons. And from the sounds of the
voices inside, the men were well on their way to drunkenness.

"I can't go in there," Jensa said. "Women aren't allowed. You'll have to go in alone."

Dayn nodded, but considered the task with dread. He had never been in a tavern before and couldn't imagine what awaited him inside. He walked slowly toward the entrance; then after a brief, nerve-tingling pause, took himself inside.

The place was smoky and hot, and the smell of sour wine and rank sweat permeated the air. Dayn put his hand up to cover his nose, then wisely decided against it; no need looking like an inexperienced boy unaccustomed to the stench of a tavern. He scanned the room, seeking the red head that would surely stand out against the rest. There were battered tables surrounded by men playing games of dice and runes and cards. Mugs of ale and wine passed from server hands to patron mouths in a never-ending flow. Pipes of unknown weed also made the rounds, filling minds with more artificial contentedness. But there was no sign of Reiv.

Dayn edged between a wall of men, apologizing politely as he weaved his way through. His apologies only served to irritate some of the men, so he scowled back at them and did his best to blend in. A large group of patrons encircled a table in the far corner, and Dayn turned his attention to it. He saw no sign of Reiv, but then he heard, "You can do better than that, Prince! Have you no mettle at all?"

Dayn headed in that direction, terrified at the thought of what they might be doing to his cousin. But when he reached them, he was relieved to see Reiv laughing and arm-wrestling with a man nearly twice his size. Reiv lost the arm battle, though he didn't seem to care, and ordered himself and the victor a round of drinks.

Dayn planted his feet next to the table and folded his arms. "Reiv, we've been looking for you everywhere," he said crossly.

Reiv turned his eyes up to him and a great smile stretched across his face. "Why, it is my little cousin Dayn!" He stood and swayed a bit, then draped an arm around Dayn's shoulders, leaning into him and grinning like a fool. "Look everyone! It is little Dayn. My little, little cousin." Reiv laughed and all the men laughed with him.

"Here, little cousin," one of the men said, thrusting a mug at Dayn, "have yourself a drink. You've some catching up to do!"

"No, thank you," Dayn replied coolly. "Reiv, you need to be coming home with me now."

"Home? Nooooo...I cannot go home. I have not yet finished the contest!" He leaned into Dayn and whispered, "You see, I have challenged everyone here and have promised each and every man who beats me a drink. But if I win, they must buy *me* a drink. Thing is, it does not much matter to me if they win, for even when they do, I buy myself a drink anyway!" He laughed boisterously, losing his balance.

Dayn caught him in his arms and lifted him upright.

"Oh dear," Reiv said. "The room seems to be moving. Did you feel that Dayn? You usually are so sensitive to those things." He did not wait for a reply, however, and plopped back onto the bench, pulling Dayn down beside him. He then called the next man to the challenge.

Reiv lost again and ordered another round of drinks, paying for them with strands of shell beads from around his neck. He had long since run out of coin and had begun trading his shells for drink instead. His hair now hung loose around his shoulders, the cockle band that had once bound it long since gone. Most of the beads that had covered his chest were also missing.

Dayn watched as his cousin threw his head back in merriment. In that instant he caught sight of Reiv's ear. His jaw dropped at the sight of it. "God, Reiv, what have you *done*?"

At first Reiv looked puzzled, but then seemed to realize where his cousin's attention was focused. Reiv laughed and pulled his hair away from his ear. "Pierced. Do you like it? I won it in one of the matches when the loser had no coin to buy me a drink. But he did have this earring and offered it instead."

Reiv's earlobe was caked with dried blood and the earring that dangled from it was made of crudely fashioned metal inlaid with oily stones. It looked old and none-too-clean.

"How did you pierce it?" Dayn asked, concerned by the look of it.

"Oh, uh..." Reiv paused for a moment, his expression blank. He turned his eyes toward the crowd of men gathered across the table from him. "My friends, how did we pierce my ear exactly? I do not seem to recall."

The men glanced at each other as though struggling to remember the details of the piercing incident.

"I think it was a fork or something," one said.

"No, no...it was a cork-knife...from behind the bar. Wasn't it?" another added.

"Don't be a fool," a third chimed in. "We just shoved the earring in. Remember?"

Reiv then turned his attention back to his unhappy cousin and shrugged a shoulder as though resolved to the fact that neither he, nor anyone else, was in any condition to recall at the moment.

"You know, if I win a few more rounds," Reiv said, his speech beginning to slur, "I will leave looking like a true Shell Seeker... well, except for the tattoos." His face lit up. "Friends, can anyone here do tattoos?"

"That's it. We're leaving," Dayn said, rising from the bench.

The crowd of men groaned and jeered at Dayn, and many muttered that they had not yet had the opportunity to challenge the Prince. It was obvious Reiv had little power in his hands and had, thus far, proved to be an easy match for the much older and stronger patrons. There were still a few beads left to be won, and the men obviously wanted their chance at them.

A hand from behind shoved Dayn back onto the bench. The next challenger took his place across from Reiv whose elbow was firmly planted.

But Dayn persisted. "Reiv, enough of this. Under no circumstance are you to test your body further. You'll be lucky not to lose your lobe to infection as it is. Come on. You're in no shape to contest anyone."

Reiv did not respond, his concentration fully upon the battle of the arms. He lost quickly and pulled another strand from around his neck.

"Beads or drink?" he asked the victor.

"Drink!" the man replied.

Reiv motioned the waiter over and held up two fingers. The waiter was standing by, and gladly traded two full mugs of wine for two strands of bead. Reiv chugged his down and slammed the mug on the table, then wiped his mouth with the back of his hand. "Who's mext...I mean next......yes, I nean next," he hollered.

Suddenly a voice boomed from behind the crowd, "The Prince has had enough. He leaves now."

Dayn and Reiv swiveled their heads in the direction of the voice as a sea of glazed, blood-shot eyes turned toward it. Complexions momentarily paled, and a few went almost green. Mutterings fell to hushed whispers and low grumbles.

Reiv rose and swayed by the bench. "Well, if it is not Torin," he practically shouted. "My friends...this is Torin." He waved an arm toward the Shell Seeker now standing at his back.

Torin stared at him in silence, his muscular arms folded across his chest.

Reiv leaned across the table toward the crowd of onlookers and whispered loudly, "He does not like me very much, and I cannot stand the sight of his ugly face either!"

The crowd muttered their sympathies and agreements. Reiv stepped past the bench and wheeled around to face Torin. "What is your business here?" he demanded.

"My business is with you. But I'm not here to argue our affection for one another. I'm here to fetch you from this place and take you home."

"Home? Home?" Reiv guffawed. "Let me see, where might that be exactly? No, I think *this* will be my home from now on. I rather like it here." Swaying a bit, he braced himself against the table, then ordered, "No, *you* go home and leave me be. I have no use for you or the charity of your sister."

Dayn slid from the bench and took his place alongside Torin, facing the increasingly agitated Reiv with a frown. "You are full of drink, cousin, and you're going to say something you'll regret—if, indeed, you remember anything after this night."

"Well, Dayn, since you have nothing nice to say to me either, how about you take yourself out of here with Torin. I have need for neither of you at the moment."

Torin's tolerance was clearly lacking. He stepped toward Reiv and grabbed him by the arm. Reiv glared at the hand upon his person and attempted to pull free, but Torin's grip was much too strong. Reiv was quickly spun round and pinned with both arms at his back. Some of the patrons moved to his defense, but Torin shot them a warning that backed them down immediately.

Torin turned Reiv toward the door, but his attention came to rest on a man standing nearby. "What do you have there?" Torin demanded.

The man followed Torin's gaze down to the shell bracelet he had stretched around his own thick wrist. "I won it from the Prince," he said defensively.

Torin let loose his grip on Reiv and took a step in the man's direction. Reiv staggered as the room began to spin. Dayn grabbed his elbow in an attempt to steady him.

"Well you did not win it fairly, then," Torin said to the man. "Hand it over."

The man bristled. He glanced at the other patrons who were wearing their own shell winnings, all necklaces or shell strands draped around their necks. But none had anything as fine as the bracelet, and the man was clearly not keen on parting with it.

Torin leaned in threateningly. "I said hand it over. It belongs to the Prince."

"He seemed eager enough to wager it," the man said with a scoff. "Obviously there wasn't much value in it for him."

"The boy's in no condition to determine what's of value and what's not."

"Well, he was in good enough condition when he offered it. It was the first thing won from him tonight."

Torin turned to Reiv. "Is that true, Reiv?"

"I do not see that it is any of your business," Reiv snarled.

"Well it is my business. I watched Kerrik work for hours to help you craft it, hours he could have spent looking for shells to help put food on our table."

"Sorry, I did not know I needed to pay you for his services."

"Regardless, would you rather it adorn the arm of a comfort woman than that of the girl it was intended for?"

"Why should I care!"

Torin's lips compressed into a thin line. He pulled a coin from his money pouch and tossed it to the man. "This should keep you in drink and women for a while," he said. "Now hand it over."

The man caught the coin in his large fist, all the while glowering at Torin. Risking a look at the coin in his now-opened palm, the man's expression brightened. He yanked the bracelet off and pitched it to Torin.

Torin stuffed the trinket in his money pouch and turned his attention back to Reiv. He steered him toward the door. "You are going to sorely regret this in the morning," he said.

"I will regret nothing!" Reiv barked. But as soon as they exited the place and the fresh air hit him full in the face, he buckled at the queasiness in his stomach and the pounding in his head. His legs went out from under him, and he quickly found himself suspended by Torin on one side and Dayn on the other.

Jensa approached from the shadows and gasped at the bloody ear that was barely visible in the light from the tavern.

"What happened to your ear?" she exclaimed.

"I pierced it," Reiv replied, grinning. "Do you like it?"

"No," she snapped.

"What is it about me that always makes girls so cross?" Reiv lamented. "Jensa, please say you are not angry with me. I could not bear for you to be angry, too. You like me, do you not?" He looked at her like a boy seeking his mother's forgiveness.

"Yes, Reiv, I like you, but not when you are drunk and stupid! As for my being angry, I think I have good reason to be. I've been looking all over Pobu for you and have been standing there in the shadows waiting for Dayn to fetch you. Thank the gods Torin showed up or I'd be waiting there still."

"He wouldn't listen," Dayn protested. "What was I supposed to do? Throw him over my back?"

Jensa rolled her eyes at Dayn, then flashed them back to Reiv. "Who do you think is going to treat that ear of yours when the infection sets in? Me, of course. So yes, I'm angry and will probably stay that way for quite some time."

Reiv groaned as he struggled to put one foot in front of the other. Torin and Dayn were walking far too quickly for him to keep up, and soon his feet were mostly dragging along. The jerking movement as they half-dragged, half-walked him back to Nannaven's did nothing to settle his stomach. Before long he was leaned against a wall, spilling the contents of his belly into the dirt.

When they reached Nannaven's house, he was in a poor state, and Torin had to practically carry him inside. By then the Spirit Keeper had returned. As soon as she caught sight of them she turned to her shelf of herbs and mixed up a brew. They dragged Reiv over to the table, propped him on the bench, and thrust a mug of Nannaven's concoction under his nose.

"Drink up," Torin ordered. "It will make you feel better."

"I will feel better when you are out of my sight!" Reiv said, shoving the mug away.

Brina crossed over to her nephew and leaned down to him, her hands on her hips. "Reiv, enough of your foolishness. Now, drink."

Reiv looked up and squinted in an effort to make her out. A pitiful smile replaced his sour expression.

"Brina...my Brina...where have you been? I thought you did not want me anymore, but you came back..."

"Yes...yes...now drink this up and let us see if we can get some sense into you," she said.

He drank it down, then doubled over and threw it right back up. But Nannaven had placed a bucket in front of him, fully prepared for what was to come. Jensa knelt beside him with a wet cloth and wiped his face, while Brina refilled the mug and told him to drink it down again. He complied, for he hadn't the strength to argue about it.

After a few more mugs, Reiv began to feel better, though his eyes were still glazed and his words somewhat slow in coming. He pushed up from the bench and swayed for a moment. "I need to lie down," he said, and attempted to walk to the corner near the hearth.

Brina hooked her arm through his and led him to a mat that Nannaven had hastily spread out for him. "Reiv, we need to talk and I cannot stay much longer. There are new dangers in Pobu. That is one of the things I came to discuss with you."

Reiv lowered himself down and curled onto his side. "Not now, Brina," he said, closing his eyes. But the spinning in his head forced them back open immediately.

Brina knelt beside him and stroked his hair. "Reiv, I must tell you something, even though you may be too muddled to comprehend it. Please try to listen. You are in danger here."

"What else is new?" he muttered.

"Reiv, hear me. Much has happened in Tearia this past month. Do you remember the old prophecy about the Unnamed One?"

"A children's story."

"Perhaps. But ever since you were unnamed a year ago, quiet talk has been making the rounds about it."

"What does that have to do with me?" he said.

"Some think you are the Unnamed One the Prophecy speaks of. Even the Priestess has her suspicions."

Reiv grimaced. "Ridiculous."

"Perhaps, but you are at risk here. You cannot go wandering about like you did tonight."

"If she thinks I am this...this person...then why did she not do something about it before?"

"Whyn came to your defense."

"I doubt it," Reiv mumbled. His eyes drifted closed.

"Why do you say such things? You know Whyn loves you. He has tried to make amends, to do what he can for you. Why do you continue to rebuke him?"

"Because of what he said."

"What do you mean? What did he say?"

Reiv forced his eyes open and turned them up to her. "He said what happened to me was for the best...that he should have been King-heir all along. Then he..." Reiv swallowed thickly. "He said Cinnia was happy to be rid of me."

Brina was clearly taken aback. "When did he say that? No, Whyn would never..."

"He said it, Brina. I heard him." Reiv spoke the words with effort through his stupor, but he knew what he was saying and had every intention of saying it. "The night of the fire...you stepped out to speak with the healer. Whyn stayed in the room. A priest came and...they talked. They thought I could not hear them. But I could."

"What did you hear, Reiv? What did they say?"

Reiv drew some saliva into his pasty mouth. "Whyn said he was glad to take my place. That it could not have worked out better if he had planned it...that he had no intention of letting it slip back into my grasp. I know he has always been more suited, but when I heard him say how glad he was for...for what happened, and when he said what he did about Cinnia..." Reiv eyes drifted closed once more. "I really need to sleep." Then as quickly as the last word had escaped, he was asleep.

Brina rose and crossed back to the others who stood silently to the side. They looked at her with sympathetic eyes, but no one dared speak. Finally Brina broke the silence. "If what Reiv says is true, then I have placed too much confidence in Whyn. But two can play this game."

"What do you mean to do?" Dayn asked.

"Whyn thinks I believe him to be on Reiv's side, and I did until this moment. With that in mind, I will need to listen to Whyn's words more carefully. If I provide him with false information, it may buy us more time, and keep Reiv safe a while longer. Meanwhile, a meeting must be called. Torin, can you arrange it? Since everyone is here for Market, tomorrow night would be the perfect time."

"Of course, Brina. I'm sure rumor will be rampant by then."

"Speaking of which, how can we assure Reiv's safety?" Nannaven asked. "Word is sure to have spread about his presence at the tavern."

"I'll send men to watch your house," Torin offered. "If we were to take him back to Meirla now it would look suspicious, and there are few men in the village to defend him if it came to that. But the minute Market is over we'll hustle him back."

"Very well," Brina said. "It is unfortunate Reiv has revealed himself as a Shell Seeker, but he will be safer in Meirla than here."

She turned to Dayn and Alicine. "Children, you will need to keep Reiv occupied tomorrow, though I doubt from the state he is in tonight he will feel like doing much. And Alicine, as much as he deserves it, you had best not do any shouting in his vicinity tomorrow."

Alicine nodded while Dayn suppressed a laugh.

"Dayn," Brina added, "you must tell Reiv about your part in all this. I see no way to avoid it."

"I had intended to tell him, and I will," he said.

Brina crossed over and hugged them both. "I must go. Please be safe."

She waited for Jensa and Torin to say their goodbyes and the three of them departed the house, leaving Nannaven to tidy up while Dayn and Alicine checked on the still-sleeping Reiv.

"What is this whole thing about a prophecy?" Dayn asked Alicine who was covering the curled-up figure on the floor with a blanket.

"It's a long story," she replied. "Brina told me about it while you and Jensa were out looking for Reiv. She wanted to tell us all together, but didn't get a chance." She glanced up at her brother's exhausted face. "You're tired. Why don't you take yourself up to bed. I'll be there in a minute."

Dayn looked at her, then at Reiv. He nodded and turned to make his way up the ladder. "Don't be too long," he called back. "I want to know what's going on and don't know how much longer I can keep my eyes open."

"Only a minute," Alicine said.

She knelt beside Reiv and watched his sleeping face, then placed his hand in hers.

"Reiv," she whispered. "I know you can't hear me, but I need to say something and I won't get a moment's sleep until I do. It's cowardly, I know, to tell you while you're like this, but I'm sorry for what I said. I didn't mean it, honestly I didn't. I was jealous and spiteful, and if you hate me forever, I'll deserve it. I miss you, but I know you're happy now. I'll try to be a better person for you. I promise."

Reiv's hand squeezed hers tight and she caught her breath. But he made no other indication that he was awake or that he had heard her words.

"Reiv?" she asked cautiously.

Reiv's grip weakened and his hand went limp.

Alicine watched his still lashes, then leaned down and kissed his cheek.

"I love you," she whispered. "You'll be in my heart forever."

# 7

# The Catalyst

Mahon sat in the darkness of Brina's private bedchamber, waiting. He had exhausted every avenue he knew
of to find her, but had met only dead ends. All of her
friends had been contacted. None claimed to have seen her.
Mahon wondered if there was some sort of conspiracy
amongst them, but it was probably his own paranoia. Whyn
had certainly given him reason enough for it.

He kept his eyes on the crack beneath the door, staring
trance-like at the sliver of light that stretched across it. As
he watched, he willed a shadow to darken it, willed Brina
to open the door and sweep into the room. But there was
no shadow and no movement, only a motionless string of
light. Mahon shifted in his chair, trying to ease his aching
back. How long had he been sitting there? he wondered.
The moon had been high for hours now. What if Brina
wasn't coming back at all? Mahon shook the thought from
his head. Of course she was coming back. No matter how
proud she was, no matter how noble, he knew she would
never give up the comfortable life she led. If Reiv hadn't

tempted her away from Tearia by now, nobody would. Except perhaps Dayn.

Mahon rehearsed yet another speech in his mind, but it turned out like the dozen or so he had already practiced. With each version, the subject of Dayn always seemed to take precedence over that of Reiv. Now here he was, thinking of Dayn again, fighting back the fear that the boy was his son, clinging to the belief that Brina had killed Keefe with her own hands as she'd claimed. Surely she would not have lied to him about something as important as that. That would have been the coldest, cruelest blow she could have dealt. But now, knowing what he did about the planned Purge, Mahon had to get the truth from her once and for all.

The door latch rattled and Mahon jerked with a start. The door opened and a swath of light swept the floor as the silhouette of Brina entered the room. Then the door closed and there was darkness again.

"Where have you been?" Mahon asked from the shadows.

"Mahon!" Brina cried. "What—"

Mahon did not rise, but lit the lantern on the table next to him. He turned his face to hers and watched as her expression changed from surprise to annoyance. Raising a hand to quiet the words he knew were coming, he said, "Save your temper, wife. I have not come seeking comforts from you."

"What have you come seeking then?" she asked.

"Information. Now...I will ask you again. Where have you been?"

Brina stepped over to her dressing table and pulled the clips from her hair, tossing them onto a silver tray. "I do not have to explain my whereabouts to you."

Mahon rose. He watched her pale blonde hair cascade down her shoulders, stirring the longings he still felt for her. For a moment he imagined taking her into his arms, but he brushed the fantasy aside. He had to stay focused on what was real, not on dreams that would never be.

"I am not here to argue," he said, "but I need to know where you have been."

Brina laughed. "Why do you need to know?"

"Because the King ordered it."

Brina spun to face him, her expression hopeful. "The King?" she asked. "Sedric ordered you to find me? He is better then?"

"No, not Sedric. Whyn."

Brina studied his face, the realization of his words taking form. "You mean...Sedric has passed? Oh gods." She raised her hand to cover her mouth, but it did not stop the sob that escaped it.

"Hours ago; and you, the Queen's own sister, nowhere to be found. I am accustomed to being the last to know when it comes to family matters. Imagine my discomfort when I was called to the new King's receiving room and informed of my wife's disappearance."

"I—I am sorry, Mahon. I did not mean to put you in that position."

"You have put me in a position much worse than that, Brina. Whyn has given me some directives, and one of those was to find out if you have been in contact with Reiv."

Brina turned her back to him. "Of course not. Reiv is in Pobu. How could I possibly be in contact with him?"

"That is exactly what I would like to know."

She wheeled to face him. "I told you...I have not seen him."

"Then where were you?"

Brina did not answer.

Mahon walked toward her. She backed away, but her legs rammed against the dressing table, stopping her short.

"Listen to me," Mahon said firmly. "Do not form lies in your mind as I speak. Do not plan your words rather than listen to mine. I cannot tell you as much as I would like, but I will tell you this. You cannot see Reiv any more. Nor can you leave Tearia for any reason."

"What are you saying?"

"Whyn issued more orders than my merely finding you."

"What sort of orders?"

"I cannot tell you. But there is something you must answer me, and you must answer me true." Mahon watched her face carefully, prepared not to miss a single glimmer of expression that might betray her words. He realized in that instant that what he learned from her now would be the catalyst for his decision. Either he would risk all for his King, or he would risk all for his son.

"Is Dayn our son?" he asked.

Brina's eyes widened, then narrowed. "Do not be ridiculous," she scoffed.

"How do I know this is not another one of your lies, Brina? And if it is, why? If he is my son, I have a right to know."

"You gave up your rights a long time ago in that regard. But even if Dayn were your child, what would you do? Bring him home to live with you? Proclaim him your heir for all to see? You would sooner have him murdered in his sleep and tossed into an unmarked grave."

Mahon leaned toward her threateningly. "How dare you tell me what I would or would not do? You do not know my heart, Brina. You have not acquainted yourself with it for sixteen years!"

"I know all of it I wish to know."

Mahon thought to shake her, or maybe even to throttle her, but he felt incapable of exerting the energy required to do either. "Very well," he said, and turned and walked to the door.

"Mahon," Brina called after him. "Why does Whyn ask of Reiv?"

Mahon paused. Should he offer her a chance to give her precious nephew warning? He lifted his head and straightened his shoulders, then continued out the door without a word.

# 8

# Burden of Truth

It was late when Reiv opened an eye to the stab of morning light. The moment he did, he regretted it. He moaned and squeezed it shut. His head was throbbing and he felt as though he had been batted against a wall. Something about drink and an earring stirred his memory. He reached a hand to his ear, but felt nothing there other than a tender spot covered by a blob of ointment. Footsteps could be heard padding across the floor in his direction. He yanked the blanket over his head, praying whoever it was would leave him be. He was not ready to face the world just yet.

"Reiv? Are you awake?" Dayn asked softly.

There was no response.

"Reiv?"

"Must you shout?" Reiv mumbled beneath the covers. "I am right here."

"I'm not shouting," Dayn said in an exaggerated whisper. "Can I get you anything?"

"A coffin," Reiv said.

"Some breakfast in your empty belly might be better."

Reiv groaned, his head still buried beneath the blanket. "I do not think I will ever eat again."

"Some tea, then?"

"And I will definitely never drink again." Reiv eased the blanket from his face and squinted up at his cousin. "I feel as if I have been beaten by ruffians. Was I?"

"Nothing as exciting as that. The only ruffian that beat you up last night was yourself. Do you remember anything?"

Reiv rotated his head in an effort to release the pain radiating from the top of his skull to the base of his neck. "Um…a tavern…something about arm wrestling for drinks I think…an earring…you and Torin…that is about it."

"Do you remember Brina?"

"Brina? She was here…um, yes…I think she was here." Reiv's mouth was thick and his words slow. "Could you fetch me some water?" he asked.

"I'll get it," Alicine chirped from across the room.

"Oh, gods." Reiv moaned and pulled the covers back over his head. "I do not think I can take any more pain at the moment."

Alicine's footsteps headed in his direction. He could see her shape looming over him through the weave of the blanket.

"I promise, no more pain," Alicine said. "At least not from me. Here." She leaned down and held out the drink.

For a moment Reiv did not move, but then he pulled the blanket off and sat up. He reached for the mug with a trembling hand.

"I'm sorry about yesterday," she said. "I didn't mean it."

Reiv nodded, but remained silent. He lifted the mug to his lips. The first gulp hit his stomach like a stone, but his mouth ached for it, so he forced it down, though in much slower sips.

"I need to get up," Reiv said, struggling to push himself from the floor. He swayed for a moment, then frowned at his tunic. It was spotted with wine and crusted with puke.

"And I need to clean myself up." He glanced up to see Alicine eyeing his untidy state. "Would you mind giving me some privacy?"

"Oh, of course," she said. "I'll fetch more water and leave you to it." With that she gathered up a bucket from the corner and headed out the door.

After Reiv had relieved his bladder, stripped off his filthy tunic, and pulled on one of Dayn's clean ones, he dragged himself to the bench by the table and sat. "I seem to recall sitting in this spot last night." He winced at the dull memory.

"I need to talk to you about something," Dayn said. "But if you're not up to talking right now..." He watched Reiv's face, obviously hoping he would ask him to go ahead and tell it. But Reiv just stared across the room with unfocused eyes.

"Well...later then," Dayn said. He sliced up a pear and put it on a plate with a bit of cheese and a piece of crusty bread. Then he set the plate on the table next to Reiv and eyed him with crossed arms and a motherly expression. "You really should eat something."

Reiv stared at the food and felt certain that his face had gone gray. He reached for the bread and brought it slowly to his lips, then forced it into his mouth.

"Where is Nannaven?" he asked between stiff chews.

"At Market. She told us to stay here with you."

"You asked if I remembered Brina last night. I recall some of it, but I think I will need reminding. My head is a bit muddled at the moment."

Dayn took his place on the bench across from him. "What do you remember?"

Before Reiv had a chance to organize his thoughts, Alicine poked her head through the door. "May I come in now?" she asked.

"If you insist," Reiv said. He saw her face fall. "I mean...I am in a foul mood this morning, Alicine. You might find the company of wasps preferable."

Alicine smiled. "Well, I deserve a dose of your foul mood considering the dose of my temper you received yesterday."

"As I recall, that was the catalyst for my stupidity last night," Reiv said.

"I'm sorry," Alicine said.

Reiv dismissed her apology with a wave of his hand. "No more apologies between us...agreed? Market is only two days. We had best enjoy what time we have together. Maybe later, when I am feeling better, we can get out of the house."

Alicine and Dayn exchanged looks of apprehension. This did not go unnoticed by Reiv. "What is going on?" he asked suspiciously.

"You have to stay in...Nannaven gave us orders," Dayn said.

"Stay in? Why? Is it not a beautiful day?" Reiv rose from the bench, walked to the window, and pushed the shutter open a crack, squinting his eyes against the sunlight. He turned to face them. "You said I have to stay in...what about you?" he asked, realizing Dayn's words.

"We need to talk," Dayn said. "Sit, Reiv. Your legs are still wobbly, and after you hear what I have to say you might find them even more so."

Reiv did as Dayn suggested, then stared his cousin full in the face, working to prepare his aching head for some obviously unwelcome news.

Dayn took a steadying breath. "Brina came last night, but only stayed a short time. A strange series of events has been taking place in Tearia and it involves you. Do you remember her telling you about the Unnamed One?"

Reiv frowned and tilted his head. "Yes, but I thought I must have dreamed it. She said something about people thinking I am the person spoken of in some old prophecy. But that prophecy is nothing more than a child's tale told at bedtime. It is ridiculous. Nothing to be taken seriously."

"Well, the Priestess is taking it seriously. It seems she expected you to simply fade away in Pobu, but you've done quite the opposite in the hearts and minds of your followers."

"Followers?" Reiv laughed. "I have no followers. Is this some sort of joke?"

"It's no joke," Dayn said, his eyes growing wider. "Last night when you went to the tavern, you could have been in terrible danger. Fortunately you weren't harmed, but that doesn't mean one of the Temple's spies didn't see you there. You can't risk being seen again. You have to stay hidden."

"So I am to hide from the world for fear of some ridiculous superstition? And what happens when I return to Meirla? Am I to crouch in Jensa's hut like a coward? Or am I to be flanked night and day by bodyguards, never to have a moment's privacy? Listen, Dayn, I am finally beginning to get my life together and I will not have it ruined by this nonsense. I do not believe in prophecies. They are for desperate people who have no hope left in their sorry lives, people who will grasp at anything, even lies and children's stories. You tell whoever needs to be told that I am not the person they seek in their so-called prophecy. They need to forget this foolishness once and for all and leave me in peace."

"It's not so simple. You can't ignore it, and denying it will not change minds so easily. Besides, there's more." Dayn folded his hands on the tabletop and stared down at them for a moment. "There's a movement here in Pobu. It's been going on quietly for a long time, but interest is gaining, especially now that there are some in Tearia who will lend their support."

Reiv narrowed his eyes. "What sort of movement?"

"A movement of Jecta who are tired of Tearian oppression. They've been meeting secretly for years, but during the past several months their energy has been renewed. What happened to you was unprecedented, Reiv. Though the rulers of Tearia may deny it, it shook their powers to the core. For the Jecta, it was seen as a weakening of the royal line. For the Tearians who support you, it's taken on the embodiment of a prophecy. You've given them hope."

"I give them nothing!" Reiv said. "How can you sit there and tell me this like it is good news? They are traitors—all of them."

"Then I'm a traitor too," Dayn said.

"What are you saying?"

"I'm saying I'm going to help them. Ever since I started working with Gair at the smithy, we've been—"

Reiv threw himself up from the bench. "You come here from someplace else, totally unaware of our existence, much less our ways, and within a month's time you've banded with a gang of radicals whose sole aim is to challenge Tearian authority? What right do you have to involve yourself in such a thing?"

"I have every right!" Dayn said, rising to meet him. "Have you forgotten that I was born Tearian? Have you forgotten that because of your long line of priestesses my own mother was forced to either kill me or abandon me? I've spent the past sixteen years of my life in a world where I didn't belong, with parents who lied to me and people who hated me. I was bullied and beaten up and made to feel worthless. Are you saying I deserved it? Are you saying that children like me—or like Kerrik—don't deserve to know their own parents and be loved by them? Are you saying that because your hands are scarred you don't deserve *your* family? God, Reiv, what loyalty do you owe Tearia?"

"Obviously more than you owe Kirador."

"You're wrong. I'm not Kiradyn, I know this. They treated me as badly as the Tearians treat the Jecta here. But it was my home for sixteen years, and there are people there that I love. Kirador has its own problems. They are bound by superstition and beliefs based on half-truths. The moral leaders have too much power, just as some of the landowners do. There are disputes over water rights and hunting territories. The judicial system is unbalanced, based on who owns the most. I could go on and on. If someday I can make a change for the better in Kirador, I'll do it. But I'm not in Kirador right now; I'm here. And here is where I can make a difference at the moment."

"You know nothing about how things work here. You know only what the Jecta have told you."

"What I do know is that the Jecta have no rights. They are not allowed to own property and must work the land for the Tearians in order to gather scraps from the harvest." Dayn took a step toward Reiv and fixed his gaze upon him. "But you know all this, don't you? You were a foreman, and worked your crew from sunrise to sunset. Were they ever paid for their services? Or even thanked? How much of the harvest were they allowed to keep?"

"They were given enough," Reiv said defensively. "They welcomed it."

"Do you honestly believe that? They can barely feed their families, Reiv. They aren't allowed to hunt the forests. The best they can hope for is a carcass left behind by the Tearians. How many mouths does that feed? They can't carry weapons. Even their tools are eyed with suspicion. Surely you don't condone this."

Reiv said nothing and held his expression in check. As much as he knew Dayn's words were true, a part of him was unable to turn his back on his own heritage.

"Whether you approve of my decision or not," Dayn said, "I intend to join them in their fight to make things better."

"And just how do you plan to do that?" Reiv asked.

"I spent many an hour hiding in a blacksmith's shop in Kirador, and learned a lot about metal work. There I learned how to fashion spear tips and knives for hunting. Here I'm making daggers and swords so the Jecta can defend themselves."

"You are breaking the law and it will not go unnoticed! By the gods I shall have Gair's head for involving you in this." Reiv aimed his finger at Dayn threateningly. "Mark my words, Dayn, you will soon find yourself back behind bars. But next time your sentence will be far worse."

"Then I have to risk it. Listen, Reiv, I know this is hard for you to understand, but I had hoped that in telling you I would have your trust and support."

"Well, you have neither. You are not the cousin I thought you were, and now I see you are not the friend."

Alicine, who had remained silent, rose and stood to face him.

"You're wrong, Reiv," she said. "I don't like Dayn's involvement in this either. Not because I think he's wrong, but because I'm afraid for him. You know I would have him out of here in a heartbeat, but he's determined to see this through. He doesn't do this to betray Tearia. Don't forget he is Tearian. He does this to make it better. You, of all people, should understand the need for change. Will you turn your back on Tearia when so many are turning to you now? What about your friends in Pobu and Meirla? Think what *they've* had to endure. Remember who it is that turns to you, Reiv, and who it is that turns against you. Then you can judge who's friend and who's foe."

Reiv lifted his head defiantly and moved toward the door. "I need to be alone to think."

But Dayn stepped in front of him, folding his arms across his chest. "Then you will think here."

"Out of my way," Reiv barked. "I will not be locked up like a thief!"

"Then you will be locked up like someone too stupid for his own good," Dayn said.

The door burst open and Jensa and Torin blew in, neither waiting for an invitation.

"Good, you are up," Jensa said. "Gather your things, Reiv. We are leaving."

"What? Now? But I thought—"

"Something's happened and we don't know what the repercussions will be," Torin said. "We need to get you out of here, now."

"What's happened?" Dayn asked. "What about Market?"

"Cancelled." Jensa said.

"Cancelled? But why?" Reiv asked.

"Dayn," Jensa said, "will you retrieve the bundle Brina brought for Reiv last night."

Dayn nodded and headed for a cupboard against the wall where he pulled out the parcel. He handed it to Reiv. "Here, Reiv. Brina brought us our things last night and she brought this for you."

"Our things?"

"Yes, you know, Alicine's dress and my 'bottoms'." Dayn forced a laugh. "And your sword."

"My sword? The Lion Sword?" Reiv's jaw dropped. "How did she get it?"

"While we were in jail she slipped back to your apartment and retrieved it along with our clothing," Dayn said. "She was afraid Crymm would remember you had the sword and go back for it. She also didn't want to risk our clothes being seized and somehow used against us."

Reiv did not bother to unwrap the sword. He knew it by touch, even beneath the cloth. He looked at Jensa and Torin, both watching him with solemn expressions. "Why was Market cancelled?" he asked. "Market is never cancelled."

Jensa approached him and placed a hand on his shoulder. "I don't know how to tell you, but there's no way around it. The King has passed. Your father is dead."

Reiv stood as though frozen, a sudden current of painful emotion coursing through his veins. He could not make sense of her words, though he knew exactly what she had said, nor could he make his lips, his eyes, or any part of his body move in response to them. The sword slipped from his hand and fell to the floor with a dull *chunk*.

For a long moment no one spoke and no one breathed. "Reiv, we have to go," Torin finally said. "Whyn is King now and we don't know what this means for you. We must get you out of here."

"I—I cannot go," Reiv said, "I have to stay for my father's funeral. I am his son. He would expect me to be there. He would—"

"You know you can't go."

"But I must. I have a duty to him."

"Reiv, please," Jensa said.

"He is my father!" Reiv screamed. "He is my father!" He made a sudden dash for the door, fully intent on running all the way to the palace to throw himself across his father's body and beg forgiveness.

Torin grabbed him and held him tight. "You're going nowhere but back to Meirla with us," he said.

Reiv flew into a rage, swinging his fists with all his might, writhing and kicking and shoving against the man who would keep him from his father's deathbed. He screamed, the sound of it so loud he felt certain the Guard in Tearia would hear him and come to his rescue. But no one came, and he soon found himself flat on his back beneath Torin, who could barely contain him, and Dayn, who had come to Torin's aid.

"Let me up!" Reiv shouted, tears of fury streaming down his face. "You have no right to keep me here!"

"Reiv, stop! Stop it now, do you hear me?" Dayn yelled. "You're not welcome in Tearia. You're not welcome at your father's funeral. Your family doesn't acknowledge you. Have you forgotten? They'll seize you the minute you step foot there. Now, calm down and do what Torin tells you. You'll do no one any good dead and buried in a Jecta grave."

Reiv squeezed his eyes shut as sobs wracked his body. Anger drained out of him, only to be replaced by despair. He covered his eyes with his fists, intent on hiding his shame for the way he had treated his father, intent on hiding the sorrow he felt for the loss of him. At that moment the thought of a Jecta grave seemed preferable to the overwhelming anguish he felt. How much more did the gods expect him to take? He went weak with the realization that he had no power whatsoever. No hope for happiness at all.

He was helped from the floor and guided out the door, no longer able to resist them, no longer caring enough to try. He did not recall saying goodbye to Alicine or Dayn, nor was he aware of anything during the silent walk through the back streets with Torin and Jensa. Although he managed to put one foot in front of the other, that was all he was able to do.

When they reached the outskirts of the city, the Shell Seekers had packed and were already making their way down the road leading from Pobu. Kerrik ran up to Reiv, but even he said nothing. Kerrik took Reiv's hand in his, and held it tight, but Reiv did not pull away as he usually did. There was no feeling left inside of him now, just the overwhelming weight of weariness. He could only stare with indifference at the tiny hand now holding his.

# 9

# The Crooked Child

Tenzy wrapped her shawl around her thin shoulders, but it did little to stave off the cold of her cell. Cold: For years now, it had been her only waking companion, wrapping her like a cruel lover, owning her body and soul. She no longer knew what it meant to be warm, just as she no longer knew what it meant to be loved. She had never felt the embrace of a man, nor the feel of a child growing in her belly, something she had longed for, but steadfastly refused to bear. There could be no flowering of a child without a seed, and the thought of a man pressed against her had always been abhorrent. Her mother had died at the hands of men, many men, swarming over her like flies. And Tenzy and her younger sister had been forced to watch. The cold that wrapped Tenzy's body had been her only mate for nigh on sixty years now.

She shuffled over to the table that dominated the center of her dismal cell. It was stacked high with parchments and

ancient tomes, their leather covers tooled with the markings
of many races, some familiar, some not. Her eyes swept over
them. They should have brought her comfort, should have
been her companion in the lonely hours of her life. But they
were only the shackles of her miserable existence.

Her gaze rested on the tome that had recently been
slammed onto her table. *"You will interpret it,"* the Priestess
had ordered, *"and you have three days time in which to do
it."* Tenzy had yet to open the book. She knew what it contained, just as she knew by whose hand the pages had been
written. It was not the tome, however, that had her insides
twisted into a knot. It was something else the Priestess had
said: *Perhaps a crooked child would sway you.*

"You'll not have him," Tenzy said with determination.
But how to protect him? She surveyed the book, her hand
hovering over it. The crooked child was within those pages,
as were the players in so many other prophecies, some true,
others false, but all very powerful. It was the prophecy of
the child, however, that held the greatest power of all.

The crooked child had visited Tenzy's dreams many times,
so many that she had come to think of him as her own. But he
was not. He belonged to everyone, though she had become self-
ish in her attempts to claim him. He came to her when she slept,
and so she slept often, but he did not come with the purpose of
bringing her joy; he came to remind her that he was waiting.

She lifted the cover and slowly turned back the pages, her
emotions fluctuating from fear to comfort and back again. So
many beautiful words were contained within, words of hope and
optimism, but also words of foreboding. The pages fell open to the
stanzas of a song. *The Song of Hope.* She smiled in spite of herself. She no longer felt hope, that had long since been drained
from her, but she remembered her mother writing the words of
this song onto the page now opened before her, and realized it was
probably the last time she had felt the very emotion it celebrated.

Tenzy paused and gazed at the piles of books that surrounded
her. In all likelihood they were the last remaining documents

of her people. The stacks also included writings by Tearians and other societies, some extinct, others assimilated into the masses. The writings she found most fascinating were from a race of people to the north, a region burnt into the sea during the event that became the catalyst for the Purge. They were the ones who had told the story of the child. It had been such a favorite of hers during childhood that she had asked to be its transcriber. As she flipped through the pages now, she became determined to find it. If she could lay her eyes on the story of the child one last time, perhaps she could find the courage to do what needed to be done.

She sat on the bench at the table and searched the pages until at last she found what she was looking for. There it was, tucked between a tale of a sinner's redemption, and the musings of a long dead philosopher. The story of the child revealed no author, nor did it indicate a title, just some lines that at first glance seemed inconsequential. But from the moment she had first lain eyes on it in the dim light of a cave all those long years ago, until the moment when she would read it one last time, she knew it would bring salvation to this world and a golden path that would take her into the next. Perhaps she had not lost hope after all.

Tenzy ran her fingers lovingly over the lines, her eyes glinting as they traced the familiar words.

*He breathed his breath and cried with Joy,*
*but Love was stolen from him.*
*Into the Darkness he was cast,*
*O crooked child of Blindness.*
*Hunger, Terror, Pain, and Sorrow;*
*all wrapped him with abandon.*
*'Til secret hands did raise him up,*
*and bathed his heart with Gladness.*

*His spirit was as pure as Light;*
*and Fire dared not harm him.*
*Vast Water drew him to its arms,*
*to place its kiss upon him.*
*The Earth saw not child's winged path,*
*and sought to keep him planted.*
*But Starlight showed his destiny,*
*and paved his footsteps God's way.*

*Child's Goodness gave forth sustenance,*
*and creatures gathered round him.*
*Upon their shoulders he was raised,*
*all Evil banished from him.*
*The World was lifted into Day.*
*The Night its calm companion.*
*For Child laid claim to Purity,*
*and blessed the World around him.*

Tenzy wept as she realized her love for this child, this crooked, beautiful, unnamed child. He was more than words on parchment; he was a part of her deepest self. They were entwined, he and she, like a mother and unborn child, their blood mingling as one, the breath of their souls in perfect unity. For too many years she had abandoned life, allowing herself to be made a prisoner. And in so doing, she had kept the child a prisoner, too.

She bent and kissed the page. "Child of my heart," she whispered. "I will free you from this place." Rising from the bench, she gazed one last time at the knowledge and history that surrounded her. The writings contained power, and she could not risk the Priestess learning it. Even more importantly, she could not risk the child. Were the Priestess to touch him, she would thrust him into a darkness from which no hand could ever raise him.

Tenzy shivered, for she realized there was only one way to save him, and in so doing she risked the world ever knowing of him. There was but one other record of the child that she knew of. Had it, too, been confiscated? Or was it still buried in the mountainside, never to be found? Tenzy hesitated, realizing the selfishness of her plan, but she vowed to protect him, no matter the consequences. She set her jaw, then lifted a candle from the table and gazed into its flame. With shaking hands she tilted it toward the tome. Wax plopped onto the cover, obscuring the pale symbols tooled into the leather.

"Forgive me, dearest," she said. "But if the world perishes for the want of you, so be it."

She touched the flame to the book, watching as the fire consumed her crooked child. Clutching him to her breast, she allowed his pain to become hers. Then she burst into ethereal light, and her spirit rose to mingle with his in the air.

# 10
# All That Slithers

Whyn stood at his bedroom window, staring out at the morning landscape. But his attention was not on the scenery; it was on the mental image of his brother and the plans the Priestess had for him. Whyn clutched the windowsill, his knuckles white. The Priestess had made it clear there were to be no more delays. She was ready for a young, healthy monarch to rule Tearia by her side, and there could be no more doubt as to who that monarch was.

"Whyn?" Brina asked as she peeked through the barely opened door to his bedchamber.

Whyn spun to face her. "Brina! What are you doing here?"

"I came to see how you were holding up. Not very well, I see." She stepped in, closing the door quietly behind her.

Whyn nodded. "I am grateful that Father no longer suffers, but I was not prepared for his passing."

She crossed over to him and laid a hand on his arm. "Of course not, dear. One can never be prepared for such things."

"Where were you last night, Brina? When you could not be located during the family gathering, I grew concerned. Mahon went looking for you."

Brina sighed. "Well, he found me, or rather I found him. He was waiting for me when I arrived in my room."

"And?"

"We had our usual sparring of words." Brina frowned at the memory. "I am sorry I was absent during the announcement regarding your father, Whyn. It grieves me that I was not there, but I have not been sleeping well and went to the springs to toss in a coin. I thought perhaps an offering to the gods would bring me respite. The gods answered me, perhaps too well. As I reclined on the grass for a moment, I was lulled quite to sleep. Strange how the gods answer prayers, is it not?"

"Yes...strange."

"You look tired. Have you had any rest?"

Whyn turned to the dressing table next to the bed. He leaned in and stared into the mirror. A strange memory flickered through his mind: a feeling of weightlessness followed by terrible pain. His fingers rose to his cheek. As he gazed at his reflection, he realized his face looked different somehow, as though a stranger had crawled into his skin. *I am still Whyn,* he whispered. *Still Whyn.* He turned his attention to the eyes staring back at him: pale blue, with a hint of red circling the irises. He drew a sharp breath and backed away from the table.

"Whyn?" Brina asked with concern.

Whyn turned to face her. "I—I am sorry. You asked me something?"

"I asked if you had had any rest. I understand that in addition to your other duties, the Priestess summoned you."

"Yes. We spoke earlier. She wants the formal transfer of power to happen as soon as possible."

Brina blinked. "You mean...before the eight days of mourning have passed?"

"She wants it on the sixth day instead of the eighth."

"Did she say why?"

"In a sense. She wants my first order as King to be given without delay."

"What order?"

"I cannot say."

"Cannot, or will not?"

"Do not concern yourself, Brina. I have everything under control."

"Does this involve your brother?" Brina asked.

At first Whyn thought not to answer. Who was she to ask him such questions? But he kept his anger in check and said, "The power of Tearia's new King must be displayed with swiftness and fortitude. Since Father's illness, things have slipped out of control. It has to be stopped, and the sooner the better."

"Of course," Brina replied. "And you will be the King to do it. But if you rush things to the detriment of your father's memory, it might only serve to turn hearts against you. You want the people to love and respect you, dear nephew; not resent you or feel they are being intimidated by you. Surely the Priestess understands that."

"Her wishes take precedence over the desires of any King. She made it clear I am not to question her." He lifted his hand to his cheek without thinking.

"Perhaps she is only testing you." Brina smiled. "My dear boy, you must let the Priestess know you have a will of your own. May I remind you that she may be a priestess, but she is also a woman. Perhaps a little friendly persuasion would help her see that you will be an accommodating prince, but one that—"

"What do you mean by accommodating?" Whyn snapped.

Brina was clearly taken aback. "I—I only meant that that smile of yours can be very persuasive. You managed to convince the Priestess to spare the Jecta thieves that day, did you not? You said so yourself. Surely you worked some of your charm on her then. Perhaps you just did not realize it."

"I accommodate no one. Her will is my will."

"The Throne and the Temple have always been strong allies, Whyn, but there must be a separation between the two if balance is to be maintained. Your father understood that."

"Father is no longer here. Tearia is my responsibility now. The Priestess demands that wrongs be made right. She demands nothing less, so I can give nothing less."

"You poor boy. If only that headstrong brother of yours had mended his ways, then he would be King and bearing these heavy burdens instead of you. All those years of training invested in him...but you know, he never was truly suited for it. He knew it and wished to be rid of the responsibilities, but what choice did he have?" Brina paused and sighed. "I suppose one should always exercise caution when it comes to wishes."

"Yes," Whyn said. "Perhaps one should."

"Now here you are," she continued, "thrown into a role you never wanted, forced to take on so much responsibility in such a short time. I wish there was some way I could ease things for you, Whyn. Tell me, how can I help?"

"It would help me to know how things are with Reiv," Whyn said, displaying concern. "I am worried for him. Have you heard anything?"

"Yes, I have made inquiries. You need not worry about your brother anymore. He has found work in Pobu I hear tell, and has finally accepted his fate. I am sure it was not easy for him. I understand he is working for a weaver. Apparently he does well at a loom." Brina smiled and shook her head. "Who would have thought it? Your brother a weaver? But as long as he is happy, that is all that matters I suppose. I must say, I am very relieved. When he was still living within the city walls I stressed over him so. But now I feel I can finally let him go. It is time I focused my attentions on you, my young King. You are the one who needs me now."

Whyn nodded, then cocked his head. "Reiv has become a weaver you say? I heard tell he was a Shell Seeker."

Brina laughed, her expression that of surprised amusement. "Reiv? A Shell Seeker? Oh Whyn, I do not know the source of your information, but I find it hard to imagine your brother a Shell Seeker. Why, he would have to dive into the murky depths of the sea, and I certainly cannot see him doing that. As a boy he did not particularly care for swimming in a calm pool, but amongst turbulent waves? Perhaps he is a Shell Seeker, but I would surely love to see it if he were."

"Perhaps you are right," Whyn said. "Reiv probably would prefer woman's work at a loom to diving into the unpredictable depths of the waters. Besides, there are snakes in the sea, are there not? Reiv never did care for snakes."

"No, he never cared for anything that slithered or crawled. Poor boy. Well, hopefully the weaver's shop is creature-free, or they may find his work disrupted more often than not."

Whyn crossed over to the bed and sat. "I am tired, Brina. Do you mind? I need a moment to rest."

"Of course, dear. I will leave you now. Do not worry. All will be well." Then she left the room, closing the door behind her.

Whyn lay with his hands behind his head and gazed at the white plaster swirls of the ceiling. A *creak* at the door redirected his attention. A grin spread across his face.

"Good, she is gone," Cinnia said crossly. She moved over to the bed and crawled into it, curling her body next to his. "What was she doing here?"

Whyn wrapped his arms around Cinnia and pulled her close. "She said she came to see how I was getting on."

"And how are you getting on, husband?"

He turned his face to hers and kissed her on the lips. "I am getting on well since my beautiful wife brought herself in here."

Cinnia giggled and snuggled close. "What did the Priestess say?"

The tone of Whyn's voice turned grim. "She has great plans for me, but even greater ones for my brother."

"So, it is to be done then?" Cinnia raised herself onto an elbow and stared into his face.

"Yes, it is to be done. My mind supports it, but I fear my whole heart does not."

Cinnia bolted upright. "*You* are King now! That is all that matters! People are talking, Whyn. Some believe Reiv is still Ruairi, the Red King. That his disinheritance was a travesty. That it is he who should sit upon the throne, not you. You cannot quell this unrest by pretending it will go away. You must quash it now."

"I know, but it will be no easy task."

"Well, it will be much easier if you rid Tearia of the canker that has been allowed to fester this past year! I do not wish to be queen to a King whose legacy is weakness."

Her face was flushed with temper and Whyn looked at her with amusement. Then he pulled her back down beside him and wrapped his arms around her once more. "Is that what you think of me? That I am weak?" He twirled one of her golden curls around his finger.

"No. I only want you to be a great King, that is all."

"I promise you, Cinnia, I will be. It is not like I have not been working to solve this issue by other means. You know I swallowed my pride at the Priestess's command and tried to endear my brother with apologies. *That* was a dismal failure. Then I gave him the sword as she instructed. The Priestess expected him to attack me with it, then the guards could have taken care of the problem then and there. But no; he did not raise a hand to me. The sword almost worked its magic when Reiv flaunted it at the gate the night he brought in the thieves. But that fool Crymm, letting him pass, then making a spectacle of everything during the arrest the next day. Do not worry though; orders are in place. The problem will be solved soon enough."

"I am surprised the Priestess allowed Reiv to live when she had her chance to be rid of him. What was she thinking?"

"There was some discussion at the hearing of putting him to death, but the Goddess did not wish to risk him becoming a martyr. But now…"

"Do not let your emotions get in the way of this, Whyn. Your whole heart must be given to Tearia, nothing else."

"Is that all you give your heart to?"

"You know where it lies, husband."

Whyn laughed. "Yes, it lies here in my bed."

"You know you have always had it," she said, pressing her body close to his. "Where is the sword now? Reiv does not still have it?"

"No, its whereabouts is a mystery. It seems when I sent guards to retrieve it from Reiv's apartment it had vanished. There is no way Reiv could have taken it with him, so I do not know how it could have disappeared. Crymm's bunk area has been searched, he was my first suspect, but witnesses at the time of the arrest claim it was not with him. That is most likely true. If Crymm had taken the sword he would have been waving it about for all to see. I never expected to lose track of it, but do not worry. It will turn up."

"Well, it had better," Cinnia said. "It is rightfully yours."

"Just as you are."

Whyn brushed his lips across her cheek. She rolled herself on top of him and moved her face close to his. "Would you do anything for me, husband?"

"Of course. Name it."

Her face turned deadly serious. "Then do what the Priestess asks of you, whatever it takes to make your legacy one that Tearia will never forget."

"She wants much of me. How much are you willing to share?"

Cinnia traced a finger lightly across his lips. "How much are you willing to give?"

"All that I have," Whyn said. "Do not fear, wife. I will do it...for you...and for Tearia. And the first thing I must do is eliminate a weaver."

Whyn gathered Cinnia into his arms, his breath quickening as his hands slid over her. Their limbs entwined. He stared into her eyes, startled by a circle of red surrounding the pale green of them. For a moment doubt threatened his passion. Was he merely a replacement for the love she could no longer have? Then he recalled what the Priestess had said: *You have her heart as well as her body, but I have the rest of her.* Whyn smiled. Yes, he could be satisfied with that. He covered Cinnia's mouth with his, sending a spasm of desire through his body. But a sudden knock at the door startled them both, causing an unwelcome interruption in their play.

"Be gone!" Whyn barked over Cinnia's shoulder.

The door swung open. "My Lord, forgive me," a young male servant said breathlessly. "The Commander sends word that—"

"It can wait!" Whyn shouted.

"But Sire—there is a fire—in the catacombs. The Commander—"

Whyn pushed Cinnia off and sat up abruptly. "Tell him I will be there momentarily."

"Forgive me, Lord, but I think momentarily will be too late."

# 11

# The Far Reaches

Whyn ran from the palace toward the temple, the shouts of servants and barking of guards growing louder with every step he took. Lines of men passed bucket after bucket through the outside door to the catacombs below. Guards marched up and down the lines, goading servants to the task with the crack of a whip.

Mahon raced toward Whyn, his face red with sweat. "My Lord," he said, bowing quickly as he met him.

"What has happened?" Whyn demanded. He continued toward the catacombs, not breaking his pace. Mahon hustled at his side.

"A fire in one of the cells," Mahon said breathlessly. "It was well underway before we received word."

"Which cell? Where is it located?"

"Deep within—in the farthest reaches. But I do not understand how a fire could have started, my Lord. Prisoners are not allowed light within their cells. The only source would be the torches on the walls, but none are within reach of the prisoners."

Whyn clenched his jaw and quickened his pace. When he reached the entrance, he ordered the workers out of his way and stormed inside.

"My Lord," Mahon said at his back. "It is too dangerous. The fire is not yet contained."

"Then it is your responsibility to see that it is kept from me!" Whyn shoved past the dumbfounded servants who paused to bow in his presence. "Order the men not to break stride," Whyn called back to Mahon who had ducked in behind him. "The fire cannot be allowed to spread beyond the cell."

Mahon nodded and motioned a guard to heed Whyn's command. The guard shouted at the servants, and the buckets continued down the line with increased pace.

Whyn wound his way through the crowded corridor, the stench of sweat and smoke filling his senses with fear and loathing. Men leapt from his path; wide eyes darted in his direction. Prisoners screamed and wailed as desperate hands clawed through cell bars.

"Should we relocate the prisoners?" Mahon asked.

"No," Whyn replied.

A grimy hand shot out of a cell window, grabbing hold of Whyn's arm. Whyn gasped and jerked away, then staggered back and stopped. The uneasy memory of his brother doing the same thing a year ago lurched to mind, and the argument that had resulted because of it. *Nothing happened*, Reiv had insisted. *The foul creature grabbed my tunic, nothing more...*

"You allowed yourself to be touched by a Jecta," Whyn whispered. "And a damaged prince cannot be prince at all." He glanced at his arm, fully expecting to see a mark of contamination where the Jecta had touched him. Strangely he did not.

Mahon shot a glance to a nearby guard, ordering him with a silent jerk of his head to take care of the prisoner. The guard nodded and drew his sword, then unlocked the door and disappeared inside.

"Sire, allow me to lead you," Mahon said, stepping forward to round him.

"No need," Whyn said. He waved Mahon back and continued down the corridor. He knew the cell of destination. Even without the line of men leading the way, Whyn would still have been able to find it. There was only one prisoner with access to light, and that prisoner was surrounded by piles of books and brittle parchments.

Whyn turned off the main corridor and into a narrower one. He was immediately stopped by a thick wall of smoke and a crowd of coughing, retreating men.

"You will see the job done!" Whyn screamed, shoving a servant back down the corridor.

The servant cowered for a moment, then grabbed the nearest bucket of water and disappeared into the smoke. Others were forced in after him, but none returned. More were sent in, until at last a few staggered out with empty buckets, gasping for air and assuring the Prince the fire was dying at last. The smoke thinned, but additional brigades were sent in. After some time, the chaos subsided and Whyn was left standing in the passageway, surrounded by panting, filth-covered slaves, and Mahon, who had remained at his side.

"The fire is contained, Commander," a guard reported.

"We shall see," Mahon said, brushing past the guard toward the cell door beyond.

"No!" Whyn said. "I go in alone."

Mahon stopped short and turned to Whyn with confusion.

"You heard me," Whyn said. "I go in alone. Now, hand me a torch."

"As you wish," Mahon said with a quick bow. He grabbed a torch from a nearby wall and handed it to Whyn. Whyn strode past him and into the mucky corridor, stepping over the tangled bodies of slaves.

The air was thick, and Whyn's lungs burned with every breath he drew. He pulled his tunic over his nose and held it with his free hand. Thrusting the torch through the burned-out portal, he worked to focus his watering eyes on what was left of the cell. Even with light from the torch, all he could make out were mounds of black and the occasional glow of a dying ember. He stepped into the room, treading carefully on the slippery layer of mud and ash that covered the floor. There were piles of charred debris, most of it indiscernible, but there was one with an unmistakable shape. Whyn walked over and nudged it with his foot. Chunks of burned flesh and brittle bone collapsed and smoldered at his feet. The bellows-shaped book lying next to it disintegrated into a clump of residue.

Whyn took in the disarray around him and felt fear mixed with fury. Had the fire been started by accident, caused by Tenzy falling asleep with her precious candles lit? Or had she found something within those pages that caused her to seek a desperate end? He scanned the room once more, but realized there was no hope that anything could be salvaged. If Tenzy had done this intentionally, then her attempt to bury the truth had been a thorough one.

Whyn headed out of the cell and into the corridor. Mahon and his men waited a short distance away, their soot-covered faces illuminated by the flickering torches held in their hands. Whyn handed off his torch and ordered them to follow. He then turned to Mahon. "Have the room sealed."

"The body?" Mahon asked.

"Leave it," Whyn said.

Whyn exited the catacombs, and hustled up the steps leading to the grand portico of the temple. As a child, that porch had terrified him. The tall black cressets had reminded him of leggy spiders, and the pillars that lined the top step had seemed like towering sentinels. As his eyes moved from one column to the next, he felt as though his former enemies had become his friends. It gave him comfort, even though he knew he would soon be facing the Priestess with terrible news.

He shoved open the doors and entered through them, hating the fact that he was entering the sacred place with dirt upon his feet and the stench of smoke in his clothes. But he could risk no delay. The Priestess surely knew something of what had transpired in the catacombs, and with a valuable source of knowledge now lost to her, she would be contemplating further instruction for him.

He headed straight to the Room of Transcension. Although he had not been instructed to go there, he knew that was where the Priestess would be. An event of this magnitude would warrant consultation with the Goddess, and this was the one place where that communion could occur. He pushed open the double doors that led into the room. They were covered with gold and inlayed with depictions of Tearian religious history. The last time his eyes had moved over those images was when he had been summoned to the hearing concerning Reiv and the two Jecta thieves. It was during that time that the Priestess had communed with Agneis, goddess of purity and supreme deity of Tearia. And it was during that time that Reiv and his two friends had been sentenced to fade away in Pobu.

Whyn entered the room, not surprised to see the Priestess sitting on her chair atop a tiered platform. She was lined on either side by rows of towering statues, each a marble replication of a god or goddess. At her back loomed the grandest figure of all, that of Agneis, pale and beautiful. Whyn approached the platform and stopped before the Priestess. He bowed from the waist, keeping his head low. "Priestess, I come with news of the fire."

"Rise. Tell me," she said. Her crystalline eyes were as cold as the tone of her voice.

"Tenzy is dead and all contents of the cell destroyed with her. I inspected it myself. Nothing survived. I ordered it sealed."

Whyn felt the ground rumble beneath his feet as the Priestess rose from her chair. "Destroyed?" she shouted. Her eyes grew dark as a cold wind swept through the room, causing the torches along the walls to flicker.

Whyn clenched his hands at his side. "The witch must have set the fire herself," he said. "Perhaps she discovered something within the pages of the tome. I fear there is no more evidence of it."

The Priestess stood in a whirlwind of fury. Whyn waited, tense and silent, for the sting of her anger to reach him, but it did not. The wind died as suddenly as it had appeared, and the Priestess was left staring at him, smiling. Whyn worked to steady his pounding heart. Perhaps the Priestess had communed with Agneis who had given her comfort. Or perhaps her plan was so grand even Tenzy's despicable act could not thwart it.

The Priestess sat back down on her chair and draped her hands upon its scrolled arms. "Fire can be friend or bitter enemy. Perhaps in this case it was our friend. The tome was confiscated but days ago from a Jecta, a potter found making his way back to Pobu from the hills. He was questioned of course. The wretch claimed to have found it in a cave while searching for clay. Evidence points to the truth of it, but we learned little else from him. Unfortunately, the interrogators were overzealous in their methods."

"How is the tome's destruction a blessing, Priestess?"

"It is unlikely the potter knew its contents, though why he would risk being caught with it is a mystery. However, if it contained any evidence of the Prophecy, that evidence is now gone. I do not care what the Prophecy says, for I know it to be a lie, but had the information fallen into Jecta hands, it could have been used against us. It is unlikely anyone among them could have interpreted it, but even so, it was the gods who willed us to find it. How else could one explain how easily it fell into our hands? With all Jecta documents now destroyed in the fire, and plans for the Purge underway, there will soon be no more threat to Tearia."

"Orders are in place for increasing our spies in Pobu. The Guard is preparing for it as we speak."

"You have spoken with Mahon, then?"

"Yes. He will do his duty."

"He had no qualms regarding the issue of Reiv?"

"His only concern was for me."

The Priestess raised an eyebrow. "What of his wife? I understand Brina has remained loyal to Reiv. What duty does Mahon have toward her?"

"He has agreed to keep a closer watch on her. I do not think we will have much to worry about in her regard. I have spoken to her myself. She swears allegiance to me, though she does not know of the plan to dispose of Reiv."

"Can she be trusted? It would not do well to have a member of your own family working against you."

"I expressed great concern for my brother's well-being. She seemed convinced of my sincerity. When I asked of his whereabouts, she told me she had learned he was working as a weaver. I received word through an informant that Reiv is a Shell Seeker now, but Brina found the idea amusing."

"Amusing?"

"Reiv never cared for water so deep he could not see his feet. In childhood he was doubly fearful of anything that slithered." Whyn laughed. "I doubt he would enter a place crawling with sea snakes. More than likely he is a weaver as Brina said."

"Do you have spies in Meirla to be sure of that?"

"Few. The Shell Seeker village is more remote and tightly grouped. It would be difficult for a new member to blend in this late, but Mahon is attempting infiltration, as well as utilizing any spies in Pobu who may be in touch with the Shell Seekers. I am sure it will not take long to learn of Reiv's whereabouts."

The Priestess's eyes narrowed. "Perhaps. But just in case, I have another way of reaching him if he is in Meirla."

"Another way?"

"I have an ally in the sea. A terrible ally. If Reiv does prove to be a Shell Seeker, she will find him and take care of him. Of course, if this happens, we will be forced to question Brina's allegiance."

"If Brina proves to be a traitor, what would you have me do? Mahon would never allow harm to come to his wife."

"Of course he wouldn't. That is why Crymm would find himself receiving his first directive from his new King." The Priestess smiled cruelly. "Never fear. We will find the Unnamed One. And you are right. It will not take long."

# 12

# Stone Secrets

Dayn lay atop Nannaven's roof, attempting to get some sleep. The moon and stars were annoyingly bright, but that wasn't what had him tossing and turning on his bedroll. He had been sick three times that day, but today wasn't the first time the mysterious illness had visited him. It had happened several times during the past month or so, and he could no longer blame it on something he ate. Each time it felt the same: the earth would waver beneath his feet, sending nausea to his gut and flashes to his brain. He thought back to the first time it had happened. It had been the day of the Summer Fires Festival, and Alicine had commented that his face looked noticeably green. Another time he, Alicine, and Reiv were confined to Guard Headquarters. Dayn usually did a good job of hiding the sickness when it descended upon him, but he had vomited noisily into the straw that day and there had been nowhere to run. As he recalled the retching incident, he smiled at how Reiv had backed away for fear of contamination. But Dayn's amusement subsided when he realized he might in fact be harboring some unknown plague. The spells

91

of sickness were happening more and more frequently and his bodily discomforts were increasing with each occurrence.

He pitched to his side, trying to push the fear of an agonizing death from his mind. There were plenty of other things to worry about, the argument he had had with Reiv that morning for one. Dayn turned his eyes to Alicine's shadowy form across the way. It was a wonder she could sleep at all, especially since her relationship with Reiv had once again taken a turn. Dayn sighed and rolled onto his back, cradling his head in his hands as he gazed at the sky. He wouldn't solve any problems tonight—the issues would still be there in the morning—and at the rate things were going, there would probably be a few new ones, as well. He focused his eyes on the stars. Maybe if he counted them he could bore himself to sleep.

A muffled rap at the front door below alerted him. He sat up straight. The sound of Nannaven's barely audible voice could be heard, then the slow, loud creak of the opening door. Dayn cocked his head, straining to hear whatever conversation might drift his way. For a moment he thought to abandon his attempt at eavesdropping. The last time he had listened in on a private conversation, he had learned more than he really wanted to know. But he eased toward the trap door anyway and bent his ear to listen.

He glanced over at Alicine. She, too, was up and wide awake. Dayn raised a finger to his lips, then motioned her over. She crept in his direction and knelt beside him. Leaning over the hole in the roof, they moved their gaze beyond the ladder to the candlelit room below.

"What's going on?" Alicine whispered.

"Someone's here." Dayn replied.

They paused and listened. The door could be heard closing, then the voice of a young woman wafted up. Dayn leaned in closer. Other than the words "tenzy" and "fire," he could make out little else. He glanced at Alicine. "What's a tenzy, do you know?" Alicine shook her head.

A shadow swept the floor beneath them as Nannaven and a woman whom Dayn had never seen passed into the kitchen area. The woman was leading Nannaven by the arm, no doubt to offer her some comfort. The women talked softly for a short time, little of it decipherable, until at last the stranger departed, leaving Nannaven alone and crying.

"I'm going down," Dayn said, moving to descend the ladder.

"Maybe we should leave her be," Alicine said. "It's her private business."

Dayn paused on the top rung. "What if it's about Reiv?" he said.

Alicine nodded. "I'm coming, too."

Dayn continued his descent with Alicine following. When they reached the bottom, Nannaven was sitting at the table, staring across the room. Her red-rimmed eyes barely registered their sudden appearance. Dayn stepped hesitantly toward her. "Nannaven?"

Her gaze adjusted. "Oh, children…did I wake you?" She forced a smile and rose from the bench. "I was about to make a bit of tea." She hobbled to the nearby counter and fumbled for a crock. Dayn moved beside her.

"Who was that woman that was here just now?" he asked.

Nannaven glanced away. "That was Mya. A friend. She came bearing bad news, I'm afraid."

"It wasn't about Reiv, was it?" Alicine asked.

"No…no. It was about someone else. My sister." Nannaven wiped her eyes with the back of her hand, then proceeded to scoop some tea from the crock and into a kettle, her hands shaking.

Dayn took the kettle from her and set it on the counter, then escorted her back to the table. "I'll make it. You sit," he said.

Nannaven complied and sat as instructed. Alicine settled next to her.

"Do you want to talk about it?" Alicine asked.

Nannaven paused for a moment, then said, "My sister, Tenzy…I recently learned she was imprisoned in the catacombs beneath the temple." She shook her head. "Such a terrible place. Once it was only for the dead. Now it is where prisoners are kept. I had not seen or heard from her in years. Now I know why."

"Do you know why she was there?" Alicine asked.

"Yes, I think I know," Nannaven replied. But she said nothing more.

Dayn hung the kettle over what was left of the fire in the hearth and took his place on the bench by the table. "I heard something about a fire," he said. "Is that how she died?"

"Yes," Nannaven replied. "There was a fire in her cell."

Alicine placed her hand over Nannaven's. "I'm sorry."

"It is only through chance that I learned of her," Nannaven continued. "Mya's husband, Eben, was recently imprisoned there. You may have heard talk of it, though for your safety I tried to spare you the details. It seems he stumbled across something of value. I know this only because there were witnesses to his arrest. I doubt poor Eben knew what he had found. Unfortunately he did not survive the interrogation. I feel somewhat to blame."

"How can you blame yourself for that?" Dayn asked.

Nannaven studied his face as though debating whether or not to tell him. "It was something he was not meant to find, something I should have made better effort to hide."

"What was it?" Dayn asked.

"It is best you don't know, Dayn," Nannaven said. "At any rate, Eben found it and died for it. I suspect it had something to do with Tenzy. If it were not for word filtering back from the slaves who put out the fire, I dare say I would never have learned her fate."

The kettle whistled and Dayn rose to retrieve it. He poured them each a mug, but no one seemed interested in drinking. Nannaven stared into her tea. For a moment Dayn wondered if she was trying to read the leaves, then he asked, "Is my tea that bad?"

Nannaven smiled. "No, dear, it's perfect." She rose. "You two need to get some sleep. Take yourselves on up. I'll be fine."

Dayn and Alicine glanced at each other, then made their way up the ladder. "Holler if you need anything," Dayn called over his shoulder.

"Knowing you're here is enough," Nannaven said.

After Dayn and Alicine had disappeared to the roof, Nannaven eased her eyes toward the arch of stone that bordered the hearth. She could not risk them knowing of the tome Eben had found, nor the book's twin that was now secured behind those stones. She had hidden it there only hours before, and felt overwhelming guilt that she had not checked its hiding place in the cave sooner. Had she done so, she would have realized the rocks had tumbled away from one of the secret compartments she, her sister, and her mother had worked so hard to create all those long years ago. Then Eben would never have found it, and his wife and children would still have him in their lives.

Nannaven had been but a girl when she helped copy the words onto the pages of that book. Her mother had been one of the last of the Memory Keepers, a secret society of people whose life's work had been to document their heritage. It was at great risk, for it was against the law for Jecta to have any written records. Nannaven, her mother, and her sister had lived hidden in that cave for years, copying stories and songs of old onto parchment by candlelight. Their mother wisely insisted there be more than one copy, and so they had made a duplicate. After their mother died at the hands of the King's guards, Nannaven abandoned all hope of carrying on her work. But Tenzy had other ideas and had left to carry on the secret mission of the Memory Keepers.

Too late to save Eben, Nannaven had recently gone back to the cave. Something had stirred in her memory, words that had compelled her to return to that place. *Fire and light*, words of a song she had written onto the pages of the tome. But now she realized they were much more than that. They were words in the Prophecy. Was it true prophecy, she wondered, or merely words that had evolved, blurred by time, to become something more? She replayed the song in her mind, reminding herself that there were too many similarities in recent events to dismiss them. If the words were true, there was more than one person who had a role to play in it. And one of them was sleeping on her roof.

Her thoughts turned to Tenzy. Her sister had been captured, so her books and parchments had probably been confiscated with her. If they had, what had the Priestess done with them? Nannaven did not understand the workings of an evil mind, but she did know this: the Prophecy was causing the Temple and the Throne much grief and, no doubt, the Priestess wanted to gather as much knowledge as she could about the enemy. But the enemy was not merely the Jecta. Now it included the Prophecy.

Nannaven wondered how long her sister had been confined in the catacombs. Had she been allowed to live only so she could interpret texts for the Priestess? But an even more disturbing question was weighing on Nannaven's mind: had Tenzy revealed the secrets of the tome that had been confiscated from Eben? Fear that the Priestess now knew the full text of the Prophecy wrenched Nannaven's insides, but she suppressed the thought. Surely her sister would have died rather than reveal it. Suddenly she realized that that was exactly what Tenzy had done—she had died rather than divulge what she knew.

"You did not die in vain, sister," Nannaven whispered.

She turned from the hearth and hobbled to her bed, but knew there would be little sleep coming. There were too many stanzas of a song to keep her awake.

A pre-dawn knock at Nannaven's door sent her scrambling from her bed. She opened it with caution, surprised to see the old tavern keeper standing at her threshold. He shoved past her without invitation.

Nannaven faced him with a frown. "Good morning to you, too, Borell. I gather there is some sort of emergency. Another liquor-poisoned patron littering your floor?"

"I wish that's all it was," he said in a disgruntled voice. "It seems a man claimin' to be a customer roused me from my sleep. He was askin' questions about one of your guests. Said the Prince owed him money. But I know better. I don't like people snoopin' around my place asking questions. There're too many spies lurkin' about these days. You'd best do something about that Prince you're harborin' or you'll bring the wrath of the palace down on all of us!"

"I'm not harboring any prince," Nannaven said. "I don't need his kind here."

The tavern keeper arched a brow. "Is that so. Well, the Prince was in my establishment the night before this and was seen leavin' with that boy Dayn. Don't bother tellin' me that one's not here. I know full well he is."

"Dayn's here. It's no secret. As for Reiv, he left weeks ago."

"He shoulda stayed gone, then. The guards must be lookin' for him. He's gonna be the death of us all if he ain't found. The man asked if I knew where the Prince was workin', somethin' about him bein' a weaver. When I told him I didn't know about that, he asked if Reiv was a Shell Seeker. Clearly, if the man'd been a customer in my tavern, he'd of known."

"What did you answer him?"

"That the Prince is a Shell Seeker, o'course. What else would I 'ave said?"

Nannaven pulled in a breath to steady her temper. "Well, Reiv's not here, so what do you want me to do about it?"

"I want you to quit bein' his rescuer. I don't care what happens to him, or the other two, but Pobu can't afford to lose its Spirit Keeper. You're the only decent healer we've got."

"If you allow the guards to take him, you'll have no more need for a Spirit Keeper."

"What's that supposed to mean?" he asked.

"It means the Priestess will have all she needs to destroy the Prophecy and every Jecta with it. Watch your
words, Borell, or *you'll* be the death of us all."

The tavern keeper scoffed. "Prophecies! They're the
stuff of dreams, and dreams don't put food in my mouth!"

"I've heard enough from you," Nannaven said. "Now
take yourself out of my house and your foolishness with
you."

The tavern keeper curled his lip, then pointed a finger
in her face. "Mark my words, Nannaven. Trouble's brewin'
and you're the one lettin' it steep." Then he stormed out
the door, slamming it behind him.

Nannaven spun and headed for the ladder. She stopped
in her tracks when she realized that Dayn and Alicine had
already descended it.

"How much did you hear?" Nannaven asked.

"All of it," Dayn replied.

"What are we going to do?" Alicine asked. "When the
guards learn Reiv's a Shell Seeker, they'll head to Meirla!"

Nannaven eased over to the window and peeked out. "It
appears the Palace thinks he is working as a weaver. I suspect Brina planted that seed. She may have convinced them
for a time that Reiv is still in Pobu, but the spy who spoke
to the tavern keeper now knows otherwise, as does everyone who saw Reiv the other night. There will be some all
too eager to divulge Reiv's whereabouts for a bit of coin.
We must get word to Meirla immediately."

"I'll leave now," Dayn said, moving toward the door.
"Just tell me how to get there."

"No. We'll all go," Nannaven said. "Something tells me
we should." She hustled over to the corner and grabbed up a
pottery vessel. "Here, Dayn, take this," she said, thrusting it
into his arms. "Head for the well at the edge of town. It's always a busy place, even this early. Alicine and I will leave together as we always do and head in the other direction. Then
we'll circle around and meet you there." She yanked her shawl

from the hook and picked up the bag of medicinals she kept by the door. "There's a chance we'll be watched, but hopefully the spies will have their attentions elsewhere."

Dayn stood at silent attention, awaiting her next instruction. She pushed him toward the door. "Off with you now! There's no time to dawdle."

# 13

# Seirgotha

R eiv sat cross-legged on the sand, staring at that place
where the sea disappears over the edge of the world. He
hadn't slept a wink all night, his thoughts far too troubling,
and had slipped out of the hut and taken himself to the
beach. He had been sitting there for hours now, and the sun
was just beginning to peek through the gray-pink haze of
morning. He hated to see the brightness of it spoil his dark
mood. Having to unwrap the cloak of depression would not
come easily or willingly.

"Reiv!" Kerrik shouted as he hustled toward him. "What
are you doing here? We've been looking for you."

Reiv turned his head to look at the exasperated boy standing next to him, then returned his gaze to the horizon.

"Didn't you hear me? What are you doing here?" Kerrik
dropped to his knees and searched Reiv's face.

Reiv sighed, but it seemed to take all his strength to do
even that. "Thinking," he said. "Or trying not to."

"I'm sorry you're sad," Kerrik said. "You know, when I'm
sad I try to find something fun to do, to take my mind off it."

"When are you ever sad?" Reiv asked, convinced the boy never was.

"Oh, lots of times. Everybody gets sad sometimes, don't they?"

"I suppose."

"Well, then, let's think of something fun to do! What would be fun?"

"I cannot remember."

"Can't remember? You can't remember how to have *fun*?"

"It has been a long time, Kerrik. You would not understand."

"All right, then. How about we do something I think is fun?"

"And what would that be?"

"In a few days there will be a contest for whoever brings in the biggest shell. We have it every year. It's lots of fun! I've never won and I really want to. If we start hunting now, maybe we can find one and put it in a secret place."

"Would that not be cheating?"

"Well, it's not like we will actually take it out of the water or anything. I mean, I would still have to dive for it during the contest. So it's kind of like cheating, but not really."

Reiv shrugged. "Whatever you wish. I do not care."

Kerrik jumped up. "Let me go tell Jensa where we are so she won't be worried! Wait here!" He dashed across the beach, seemingly unaware of the twisted foot that should have slowed him down, but never did.

"Yes, I will wait here," Reiv muttered. "There is no place else to go."

When Kerrik returned, he had with him Reiv's belt and pouch, and a knife for prying snails from their shells. "Here," he said, "put this on."

"I thought you said we were not going to retrieve the shell from the water," Reiv said.

"Oh, not the *big* one, but there's no sense going in and coming out empty handed."

They headed down the beach, Kerrik running full speed ahead, Reiv trudging behind. They entered the water in the place closest to the deep reef, an underground range of pock-marked rocks and spiky urchins. There the sea appeared still and black beneath a surface of white-capped waves. The deep reef was where they always had the best luck, but Reiv had never cared for the spot. It was an abysmal place and the waters there were always thick with snakes. But Reiv raised none of his usual objections on this day, resolved to the fact that Kerrik was in charge of the mission, as usual.

Kerrik bounded into the waves, then twisted around at the waist and called back, "Don't forget to tell me if you see Seirgotha! Remember, she's mine." He grinned and dove beneath the surface, no doubt hoping to meet the monstrous serpent. Kerrik had told Reiv the story of the legendary creature. It was said that the warrior who slew her would be granted great knowledge, and Reiv knew Kerrik wanted that knowledge more than any prized shell.

Reiv made his way into the water and pushed out, forcing his arms through waves that slapped against his face. He reached the boy's bobbling head and stopped alongside him. "Seen anything yet?" he asked, trying to sound as if he cared.

"Yes!" Kerrik said. "There's one far down there. I didn't spot it until right before I needed a breath. I'm going back for it. Come down and see!" He gathered a gulp of air and dove down, his feet kicking the water high into the air as he pushed his tiny body downward.

Reiv grumbled in acquiescence, and then he, too, filled his lungs and dove beneath the surface.

The water near the rocks at the bottom was brown and swirling, like a dust cloud in an otherwise calm blue sky. Reiv did not see Kerrik amongst the whirl of sand—the boy had disappeared into the blur—and he found himself eerily alone, surrounded by silent blue fogginess and barely-visible fish nipping at his toes. It was most unsettling. Surely the impulsive boy realized he was not yet a good diver. Couldn't he have waited a moment longer? Reiv paddled in a circle as he scanned the murkiness around him. Where had that fool child gone off to?

He forced his body down through the water, his eyes stinging from the salt washing into them, his lungs burning for want of fresh air. It occurred to him to push back up to the surface, to just leave the boy to seek the stupid shell on his own. But as the strange cloud he had spotted earlier drew near, it became all too apparent that it was not churning sand. It was something else.

It took a moment for it to register that that "something" was blood, but when it did, the horror of it sent bile into his throat. He swam downward, kicking with all his might, desperate to find the small boy he had last seen diving toward a prized shell on the reef below. But there was no sign of him.

As Reiv neared the rocks, the water became suddenly turbulent. He was hit hard in the chest, his breath knocked fully out of him. He pushed upward toward the flickering light of day, fighting both panic and the overwhelming urge to inhale into his now empty lungs. Cool air slapped his face as he broke through the surface. He rasped for air, treading clumsily as he spewed salty water from his nose and mouth. Darkness was beginning to cover the surface of the water, and there was still no sign of Kerrik.

Reiv's eyes darted to the shoreline. In the distance he could see Torin and Jensa strolling along the sand. Reiv screamed, sputtering unintelligible words, and waved an arm in distress. But he only sank for his efforts and found himself fighting for air once more. He bobbed back up, coughing and gagging, and looked back toward the shore. They did not see him, that was apparent, but there was no time for delay. Filling his lungs with one last gulp of air, he dove beneath the surface and kicked his way back to the murky depths below.

He saw it first out of the corner of his eye—the great yellow-green tail whipping and slithering amongst the tunneling rocks of the reef, a trail of dark blood streaming behind it.

He followed, contorting his body with each twisting turn, and struggled with all his might to catch up to the serpent that writhed and dove throughout the rocky passageways. The creature was massive, perhaps thirty feet long, its girth greater than that of a man, its hide slick with the mucous of the deep. Surely this was the monster the boy had told him about. Surely this was Seirgotha, the she-devil of the sea.

Reiv pushed forward, every muscle taut with the effort of conserving his breath and willing his limbs to work harder. The serpent was just ahead, its whipping tail almost within his grasp. He fumbled for the knife at his waist. It wasn't much, its small blade designed only to pry sea life from the security of their shells. But it was all he had. The tail brushed roughly against him, but instead of knocking him aside, it sucked him into its current. Seeing his chance, Reiv plunged the knife blade down, and then again, leaving two small but effective wounds in the hide of the great tail.

The creature whirled its huge, arrow-shaped head to face Reiv. Its dead-black eyes stared at him with contempt. Reiv threw himself back against the biting rocks, nearly dropping the knife from his trembling hand. His eyes went wide at the dreadful sight before him. In the jaws of the great beast was Kerrik, limp and pale, long thin trails of life-blood spiraling from his body.

Reiv clenched the knife tightly, determined not to lose his grip on it. Pushing his feet hard against the rocks, he jettisoned toward the monstrous serpent. For a moment the creature seemed confused, as though contemplating whether or not to drop the small prey in its jaws in exchange for the larger one now heading in its direction. But Reiv gave it no time to choose. In an instant he reached the head and plunged the knife into one of its eyes. He pushed and twisted the blade with all his strength. The snake jerked its head back and widened its jaws, then shook its head in startled response. Kerrik drifted from its bloody maw and tumbled in slow motion through the swirling waters.

Reiv kicked forward and stabbed at the wounded orb again and again; he could not risk the serpent regaining its hold. The beast writhed and coiled, lurching its head forward, snapping at the red and brown water that churned around it.

Reiv dove down and grabbed Kerrik by a drifting arm. He yanked the motionless body toward him and wrapped an arm around the boy's waist. He paddled furiously against the water, forcing the two of them upward toward the surface. *Please be alive, please be alive*, he prayed. He dared not look down at the creature—he didn't even know if it was still there. All he knew was that he had to get Kerrik out of the water. That he had to get him breathing. That he had to stop the bleeding.

It seemed an eternity before they reached the surface. Reiv swam urgently, but clumsily, for shore, paddling through relentless waves with one arm, cradling Kerrik with the other. He thought of all Kerrik had taught him during their lessons. How the boy had patiently endured his awkward attempts at buoyancy. How he had never given up on him, even when he wanted to give up on himself.

"I will not let you die, Kerrik," Reiv said through gasping breaths. "I promise. Hold on. Just hold on. We are almost there."

Torin stopped in his tracks and pointed and hollered in their direction. He sprinted across the sand, then plunged into the water and swam with long clean strokes toward the struggling swimmer and the child being pulled behind. He reached them quickly, and grabbed Kerrik from Reiv's weakening grasp, abandoning the exhausted Prince to his own resources.

Reiv felt his feet touch bottom. He dug his toes into the sand and pushed forward. His shaking legs fought to stay upright against the waves that crashed against the back of them. He reached the shore and staggered across the sand toward the crowd that had gathered. He shoved his way between the horrified onlookers and fell to his knees. Kerrik was sprawled before him, the golden sand beneath him now turned to red.

The ghostly white of Kerrik's skin seemed in stark contrast to the dark blue of his lips. Deep lacerations encircled his waist, chest, and back, where jagged serpent teeth had slashed tender flesh. One arm lay bent with a probable fracture, while ribs pressed outward against pale, fragile skin. There was no sign of life in the tiny body and very little sign of hope.

Torin blinked back tears as he rolled Kerrik over gently and worked to expel the water from the boy's stomach and lungs. It was clear the man hated touching the child for fear he might cause further harm to the already brittle body. The boy vomited bloody water onto the sand and coughed weakly. Torin rolled him back over and put his mouth over his, forcing air into the struggling lungs. Kerrik's chest rose and fell in sporadic breaths.

Jensa tore strips of cloth from her skirt and pressed them against the open wounds with shaking hands. Both hands and cloth became soaked with blood. She continued to tear at her skirt, replacing bloodied cloths with fresh ones.

Kerrik convulsed, twitching and kicking uncontrollably.

Jensa burst into sobs. "He's dying. He's lost too much blood!"

"No!" Reiv shouted. He gathered the boy's face into his hands and leaned down to him. "Stay with us, Kerrik. Stay with us. I promised I would not let you die, remember? And a prince never breaks his promise."

The twitching ceased, as though the boy felt calmed by Reiv's impassioned words. But then the breathing slowed, and before long it stopped altogether.

Reiv grabbed Kerrik by the shoulders and shook him. "Breathe, Kerrik! Breathe!"

"Reiv, it's over. We've...lost him," Torin's halting voice said.

"No! Kerrik—please, gods, no." Reiv buried his face in the boy's sand encrusted hair. "I should have found him sooner...I should have found him sooner!"

The sobs that wracked Reiv's body were matched only by those of Jensa who knelt beside him, her blood-covered hands pressed against her mouth.

Torin placed a trembling hand on Reiv's shoulder. "You did all you could." His voice cracked, and he turned his face away.

Reiv felt his own face go hard. "No, not all," he said. He pulled Kerrik into his arms. The boy's head lolled back. Reiv gazed at the freckled face, once never without a smile, and the eyes that used to twinkle, now rolled to white. "You are not going to die. I will not let you."

"Reiv, please. There is nothing you can do," Jensa whimpered.

Reiv looked at her, the sorrow in her eyes insurmountable, then at the boy still cradled in his arms. "Kerrik," he said as though the boy was alert and listening, "I know you are tired, but all you have to do is breathe. That is all. That is not so hard, now is it? You can do this. You are a warrior, the bravest one I have ever known. Remember the story you told me? The one about Seirgotha? Well, she is here. I know you wanted to slay her, but you are not able to right now. But I will do it for you. Would that be all right? I will kill her and then you will live."

The boy did not move.

"Gods, Kerrik, breathe! Do this much and I swear when you are better I will—I will train you with my sword. Would you like that?"

The boy groaned and stirred ever so slightly. Everyone gasped, including Reiv. Kerrik was breathing slow shallow breaths, but breathing nonetheless.

Reiv gathered the boy up and half walked, half ran, toward the hut. Jensa and Torin followed at his heels, struggling to keep pace. Onlookers trailed behind, murmuring words of wonder at the near miraculous event they had just witnessed.

"Send for Nannaven now!" Reiv barked over his shoulder.

Jensa turned to a man walking behind her and motioned for him to do as Reiv ordered. The man took off in a dead run up the path toward Pobu, but it would be nearly two hours before the messenger would reach the Jecta city, and even longer to find the Spirit Keeper and bring her back. It was not likely the boy would last that long. He was barely alive as it was.

When they reached the hut, Reiv laid Kerrik upon his cot and brushed the hair back from his face. Then he stepped aside to make room for Jensa to be at her brother's side. He moved to his own sleeping pallet nearby and drew from beneath it the sword he had placed there the night before.

"Torin, I need you to bind this to my hand." Reiv said.

"Bind it?" Torin asked.

"Yes, bind it," Reiv said impatiently. "I do not think I will have the strength to hold it in the water, so I need you to bind it."

"Reiv, listen to me. Kerrik's breathing. That's all that matters."

"I will do this with or without your help. Now either bind my hand to the sword or I will go without!"

Torin stared hard into Reiv's determined face. "Think what you are saying, Reiv. You cannot wield a sword under water."

"Well, I have no choice, now do I?"

Torin hesitated, then walked over to a carved chest next to his cot and threw open the lid. From within it he pulled out a bundle and unwrapped it. He held up a dirk, shiny bright and new, beautifully crafted and decorated with a star at the handle.

"Here," he said, holding it out. "Take it, it's yours."

"Where did you get this?" Reiv asked, gaping at the weapon.

"Dayn made it for you. It's fashioned of star metal, something very hard to find. He says it's the best material there is. Gair found the metal months ago and had been saving it at the smithy. Dayn intended to give it to you himself when you went to visit, but when you voiced your disapproval of his craft so strongly…well, he sent it along with me in case you changed your mind…or needed defending."

Reiv set the sword down and took hold of the dirk. "I think you will still need to bind it," he said. "I do not know if my hand will be strong enough to hold onto it."

Torin frowned his disapproval. "Very well," he said between clenched teeth. "If you insist on doing this thing." He grabbed some strapping and wrapped it securely around the scarred fingers. "You know this is madness, and it will not help Kerrik. You risk your life for nothing."

"Saving Kerrik's life is not for nothing! I promised him I would slay the creature and I will. It is his only chance. He may be breathing, but for how long?"

"Seirgotha is legend only. The beast that attacked Kerrik was a large sea snake, nothing more."

"We shall see." Reiv brushed past Torin and headed down the path toward the beach, praying the creature was already dead. But if it was not, he would see the job done. He would slay the devil with a heart so cold it would attack a child, and there was nothing that would stop him. Nothing.

# 14

# Life or Death

Word spread quickly throughout Meirla that the former Prince of Tearia was on the hunt for Seirgotha. As the crowd gathered on the shoreline, onlookers chatted up different versions of the story, craning their necks for the slightest sign of the red-haired boy in the waters. Anticipation rose as a festive-like atmosphere developed. Perhaps today would be the day the ancient legend came to life. Perhaps today the Transcendor would walk amongst them. Everyone knew the story, of course—it had been told for generations—but while some saw validity in it, others scoffed, convinced that Reiv would either die in his attempt or come out looking like a fool. Before long, bets were placed, not only on Reiv's chances of survival, but on Kerrik's as well.

The sun arched high overhead, leaving patches of dark blue water shimmering bright white. People raised their hands to shield their eyes against the glare, and shouted and pointed excitedly whenever a bit of dark hair was spotted bobbing in the distance. But then the flash of auburn would disappear back under the water, and murmurs of disappointment would replace the exhilaration.

Most of the crowd waited patiently, determined not to miss one moment of the spectacle. But others surrendered to the cool shade of their huts. The hunt couldn't last much longer, they said. The Prince would give up soon, or die trying.

A wave of excitement rose. "There! Look there...he comes! The boy comes!" a man shouted.

"Where? Does he have the beast?" others asked.

All eyes shot in the direction of the fingers pointing toward Reiv who could be seen dragging himself from the water, barely able to stand.

Reiv walked stiffly toward them, the dirk clutched in one hand, a large shell in the other.

"Look, he has slain a sea snail!" a voice cried out amusedly. The crowd burst into laughter and gathered, teasing and pointing, around the exhausted Prince.

Reiv held the shell up and gazed at it. He smiled. "Yes, I have indeed slain the snail, or so I shall when I dig my knife into it."

Some of the spectators appreciated his sense of humor and slapped him on the back boisterously. "Job well done, Prince," a man said. "Too bad it's not Seirgotha."

"Oh," Reiv replied, "Seirgotha is quite dead, I assure you." He walked on as he said it, never skipping a beat.

"Dead?" Gasps echoed throughout the mob that followed him in mass.

"Of course," Reiv replied. "What did you think I was doing out there all this time? Hunting for shells?" He flipped the shell into the air and caught it back in his hand, a look of smug satisfaction on his face.

"But where is the creature? Where is Seirgotha?" shocked voices asked.

Reiv looked at them as though they were insane. "Did you expect me to carry her in my pocket? If you want her, you had best go get her."

Several men turned and ran toward the water, intent on seeing for themselves whether or not Reiv had indeed slain the beast.

"Oh, and I would take some rope if I were you," Reiv shouted over his shoulder.

Reiv made his way through the crowd and hustled up the path toward the hut. He would have run except he could barely put one shaking foot in front of the other. He glanced back, viewing the efforts of those trying to retrieve the great snake. A line of men stood with rope in hand, ready to pull as soon as they felt the signal in the water at the other end. But Reiv had neither the time nor the desire to watch them drag the loathsome creature to shore. He had seen enough of the vile thing to last a lifetime.

He rushed through the beaded flap of the doorway, smiling in spite of himself. He half expected to see Kerrik up and alert, but he was sorely disappointed.

Reiv's arms dropped to his side. "Has there been no change at all?" His eyes darted back and forth between Jensa and Torin. He could tell from their expressions that Kerrik was little better than when he had left him.

Torin approached, his eyes wide with anticipation. "Did you—did you do it?" he asked.

"It is done." Reiv looked over at the Kerrik. The boy's wounds were cleaned and bandaged, his ribs bound and his fractured arm splinted, but his face was still deathly white. Reiv's voice rose in agitation. "Why is there so little improvement? I thought once the beast was slain the sick would be healed. Is that not what the legend said?"

Torin frowned and took Reiv's limp hand in his, then began to unwind the wet bindings from around the dirk and the fingers that still clutched it. "Yes, but there's more to it than that."

Reiv's face fell. "More? Slaying a she-devil is not enough? By the gods, what more do they want for the life of one small boy?"

Torin remained silent as he continued to unwrap the dirk. But for some reason Reiv's fingers refused to be released. "Tell me. What more must I do?" Reiv said.

"Perhaps we should wait until Nannaven arrives," Jensa said from Kerrik's bedside.

"What does Nannaven have to do with it?" Reiv asked. "If there is more for me to do, then tell me."

Jensa stroked Kerrik's cheek, then rose. "There is a ritual that must be performed in order for you to receive the gift, and even then you will receive it only if the gods allow it."

"Let us get on with it then," Reiv said.

"It's not so simple," Torin said. "Only Nannaven knows the full details of the ritual. It requires a potion. The risk is too dangerous for you even to consider. For one thing, if the creature you slew is not Seirgotha, you will not survive the ritual."

"And if it is?"

"If it is, the gods might still deny you. Then—"

"Then I still might not survive?"

"Yes." Torin took the dirk from Reiv's slackening grasp and laid it on the table nearby. Then he nodded toward the shell still clutched in Reiv's other hand. "The shell?" he asked, obviously curious as to why someone who had battled a she-devil would have taken the time to hunt a shell.

"Oh," Reiv said, recalling it, "a gift for Kerrik. It was the shell he was diving for when he disappeared. I knew how much he wanted it."

"He will be pleased," Jensa said, turning her head to hide new tears.

Reiv walked over to the cot and sat. He placed the back of his hand on Kerrik's clammy cheek, then tucked the blanket beneath the boy's chin. "Kerrik," Reiv said, "Seirgotha is dead. It is true. And it is all because of you. If you had not found her this morning she would be out there still." Reiv paused and looked at the shell still cradled in his hand. "Here...here is the shell...you know, the big one you spotted on the reef. You have such an eye for them. I swear I would never have seen it had you not told me where it was."

He laid the shell at Kerrik's side and placed the boy's unresponsive hand over it. He watched him closely, hoping for the slightest sign the child had heard his encouraging words. But there was none.

"How soon do you think it will be until Nannaven arrives?" Reiv asked over his shoulder.

"It may be a while," Torin said. "Surely you don't intend to—"

"Of course I intend to! What else can I do? I have taken it this far. I have no choice but to finish the task."

"And what task would that be?" a voice asked. Nannaven stood in the doorway, Dayn and Alicine at her back.

Reiv rose from the cot, newfound hope coursing through him.

"What task?" Nannaven repeated.

"Spirit Keeper," Torin said, bowing slightly. "Reiv has slain a great snake and thinks it is Seirgotha."

"Seirgotha?" Nannaven exclaimed. Her eyes darted to the bed where Kerrik lay. She rushed over to the unconscious child. "The beast did this?"

"Yes," Reiv said, stepping from the boy's bedside, "and I have slain it. Now I understand I must undergo some sort of ritual to save him. Is this so?"

"So legend tells," Nannaven said.

"Then let us get on with it," Reiv said.

Nannaven looked at him, then at Kerrik. "There are many issues to be considered."

"Yes, I know," Reiv said impatiently, "but there is no time to worry about them now. If I must undergo the ritual then—"

"Reiv, you don't understand what you are proposing," she said. "There's too much risk involved. To transcend to the gods is a task no mere mortal has ever undertaken successfully. Only the Priestess has been known to do it. You could be sacrificing your very life."

"What do you mean, sacrificing his life?" Dayn cried, taking a step forward.

"According to Shell Seeker legend," Nannaven explained, "the slayer of a devil such as Seirgotha can receive the gift of knowledge if he transcends to the gods. This can only be accomplished through a ritual whereby the slayer drinks a potion that will take him to the Between Realm, that place between this world and the next. There's no guarantee the gods will accept him or that they'll allow him to return. And if they don't—"

"If they don't, what?" Alicine demanded.

"I die," Reiv said. "But if I do not do this, then I might as well be dead, for I would bear Kerrik's death for the rest of my life. This is my chance to save him."

"I thought you didn't believe in prophecies," Alicine said. "You said they were nothing more than superstitions. Don't you see? That's what this is."

"Perhaps," Reiv said, "but do you also recall that I said prophecies were for desperate people with no hope left? Well, I am one of those people."

"Kerrik would not want you to do this," Alicine said. "He would not want you to drink a potion and risk your life for some silly superstition."

"Reiv," Nannaven said, "whether it's silly superstition or true prophecy, are you so certain this is your part to play in it? There are many who believe your role lies elsewhere. That's why we're here now. Guards are seeking you in Pobu as we speak. It's only a matter of time before they learn of your whereabouts. We were coming to warn you when we met Jensa's messenger on the road. That's why we arrived so quickly; not because you sent for us, but because the King is looking for the Unnamed One. He is looking for *you*."

"How can anyone say for certain what role is meant for whom?" Reiv said. "I do not believe I am the Unnamed One. Is it possible that role is meant for another, that I am meant to be Transcendor instead?"

Nannaven stared at him as though looking at him for the first time. She nodded. "Very well. Prophecy or not, what will be will be."

She turned to the others. "Torin...escort Reiv to the Place of Observance, then you will need to gather some men to watch the road. We don't need any unexpected visitors during the ritual, so we must make haste. Jensa…go to the beach and gather some venom from the beast. The potion will require a touch of the creature's magic. Dayn and Alicine…you may stay and help me prepare the potion." She glanced at Kerrik and frowned. "The boy is waning. The ritual must be performed soon if there is any hope for him."

Everyone went about their errands, leaving Nannaven, Alicine, and Dayn in the hut to make preparations.

"Let me see now," Nannaven muttered. "If I remember correctly, I will need some dried ciralum, some milnwon, and leaves of the pyrolagos—but only the red ones."

"If you remember *correctly*?" Dayn exclaimed.

Nannaven scowled. "We have not been allowed to write things down for many years now, so are dependent on our memories. It has been a long time since this ritual has been attempted, but variations of the formula have been used for other purposes. I'm confident of the measurements, but I'll verify them with the elders to be certain."

"But, Spirit Keeper, you said pyrolagos. You know that's—" Alicine began.

"I don't have time to explain every ingredient to you," Nannaven said. She rummaged about in Jensa's cabinet, pulling out a bottle and a tiny cloth bag drawn together with string. "I'll also need some boshini syrup and a bit of myr. I don't see those here." She turned her head to Alicine. "You'll need to make inquiries in the village."

Shock blanketed Alicine's face. "But, some of those are…Nannaven, those ingredients can't be right."

Nannaven walked over and took Alicine's hands in hers. "Listen, child, Reiv wants to do this. He knows the risk. How do you think he'll reach the Between Realm, with honey water? This is the recipe given to us by the gods. If they see fit to send him back, then it will be done. If not…" She shrugged and shook her head. "It is likely Kerrik's only hope. What would you have me do? Deny Reiv a chance to save the boy? Deny Kerrik any chance at all?"

"No," Alicine said, pulling her hands from Nannaven's grasp. "But I don't believe in such things as this. It's nonsense. This potion is not from any god, just as it's not a god that will choose whether or not Reiv lives. There's only one God and He would not approve of this. If Reiv dies, it will be by our will, not that of any god."

"Then you will not fetch the things I've asked?"

"No, I won't do it!" Alicine spun and rushed from the hut.

Jensa entered through the doorway, backing in as she watched Alicine run in the other direction. The tiny vial of venom that was clutched between her fingers shook within her grasp.

"You have it…good," Nannaven said. "This beast. Is it the one, do you think?"

"It can be no other," Jensa said, her voice barely a whisper.

Nannaven nodded, then took the vial. "There are some ingredients we need to seek in the village. Alicine doesn't have the will to do it."

"Can you blame her?" Dayn said, marching toward her. "You'd feed Reiv poison and watch him die while you proclaim it the will of your gods? This is nothing short of murder and I can't believe he's going along with it. We'll not be a part of it, Nannaven. If Reiv dies it will be on your head!" He stormed out in search of his sister.

The ritual was an ancient one that had been tried numerous times over the generations by those seeking the power of knowledge. But none had ever slain a beast so great as the one now lying on the beach, and none had ever survived the ritual. It was simple in its design, for all it required was a mixture of herbs and a bit of venom from the serpent's fang. Once it was drunk, the person would hover in the realm between life and death, awaiting the decision of the gods. If allowed to return, the Transcendor would bring back great knowledge.

Word spread like wildfire throughout the village that the Prince was attempting the ritual, and all of Meirla was now gathered before the Place of Observance. The beast that had been killed was a wonder in itself, but it was the thing Reiv was about to do that had the villagers in awe.

The Place of Observance was a large circular hut of palm fronds and reeds, carefully woven and tended by the elders of the village. It was where the religious leaders meditated, performed rituals, and taught their lessons. And it was the only place sacred enough for one to Transcend.

As Reiv was led by Torin to the sacred place, he glanced sideways at the villagers lining the pathway on either side of him. Their expressions were nothing like those that had greeted him when he first arrived weeks ago. Now most stood with heads bowed in reverence while the rest gaped at him in wide-eyed wonder. A heavy blanket of silence left him feeling just as uncomfortable as when he'd first arrived in Meirla. That day he had been met by taunts and laughter. The only sounds he could hear now were the roar of the sea, the rustle of the fronds overhead, and the hammering of his own heart.

They stopped before the doorway and Reiv surveyed the carved god-like figures towering on either side of it. Fine hairs stood up on the back of his neck; the mysterious deities looked none too friendly. He glanced at Torin, who stared at him with a grim face. Torin motioned him in, and Reiv took a hesitant step through the threshold. He glanced back and saw appreciation reflected in Torin's eyes.

"I will see it done, Torin," Reiv said.

"Then I am your servant," Torin responded.

"No need. Perhaps a truce instead?"

Torin nodded. Reiv pulled in a breath and ducked into the hut.

Three elderly men met him inside and led him to the far side of the room where they ordered him to undress. Preparations needed to be made to his body, for he was required to meet the gods looking his best. He followed their instructions without question and soon found himself being cleansed from head to foot with cloths soaked in a cool liquid that smelled of mint and herb. While one man combed Reiv's hair and braided it with intertwining strands of cockleshells, another re-adorned his eyes with kohl, meticulously drawn. Since he had not yet been tattooed, designs were painted across his forehead and around his arms. He was clothed in a decorative skirt with a braided belt around his waist. Strands of shell beads were placed around his neck. He grew impatient with the formalities, thinking them foolish and unnecessary when a boy lay dying. But he clenched his teeth and endured it silently, fighting to keep his body from fidgeting throughout the ordeal.

The elders finally finished their task and left him there alone. Reiv paced back and forth, until at last Nannaven brushed through the entrance, the three elders trailing behind her. The men stopped and stood quietly to the side while the Spirit Keeper approached Reiv. She held up a clear glass bottle filled with an equally clear liquid. "Are you certain you still wish to do this?" she asked.

Reiv eyed the bottle nervously, then nodded.

Nannaven instructed him to lie down on a mat that had been placed near the fire pit. He complied and she knelt beside him, adjusting his necklaces so they lay upon his chest just so.

"Is there anything else you wish before we begin?" she asked.

"I would like Dayn and Alicine to be here, if that is permitted."

She nodded and rose, then exited through the flap of the doorway.

Reiv lay upon the mat of palms and stared at the fronds layered above him, watching their delicate branches curl from the smoke spiraling around them. The hut was dim and cool, and the scent of smoky incense blanketed the room. Reiv folded his hands across his belly and crossed his legs at the ankles, determined to stop the nervous twitches that betrayed his fear.

The Spirit Keeper entered soon thereafter with Dayn and Alicine.

Reiv smiled. "I am glad you came," he said, but the glum faces staring down at him did not return the sentiment.

"Reiv," Nannaven said, "before you undertake this ritual, you must understand and accept it. You must be not only willing, but eager to take the journey. You'll drink this and then you'll leave your body and slip into that place between this world and the next. Your heart will continue to beat, and your chest will rise and fall with the breath in your lungs, but your spirit will no longer be housed within your body. But reaching the Between Realm will not be enough; you must pass beyond ego, desire, and fear to reach transcension. If the gods accept you, you will be granted the knowledge you seek and will be sent back to rejoin your physical form. If they deny you, you will not be allowed to return to this world. Once you meet the gods, you cannot return by free will alone. If they don't grant you passage back, then the life of your physical body will ebb away. Do you understand?"

"Yes," he said.

Nannaven knelt and held the potion to his lips. He raised his head to it and drank it down. It tasted foul, but he made no indication of it and laid his head back on the pallet.

Dayn and Alicine sat down beside him. "I still don't understand why you're doing this," Dayn said.

"Dayn, listen, I need to tell you—"

"No," Dayn interrupted, "there'll be time for you to tell me when you get back. I'll be waiting right here."

"I know, but in case the gods are not feeling generous today, I wanted to thank you for the dirk. You are a fine craftsman, cousin. It is what I slew Seirgotha with, you know."

Dayn swallowed hard.

Alicine took hold of Reiv's hand. "I know it's too late to talk you out of this," she said, "but since we have to put up with your stubbornness again, I think it only fair that we're allowed to torture you with the words 'we love you'."

"Oh, gods, that must mean you surely expect me to die," Reiv said, smiling. Then his face went serious. "Well, if we are going to torture each other with truths, then I guess it only fair to tell you that I—"

But before he could finish the sentence, his body arched back and his head pounded violently against the ground.

Alicine cried out and found herself shoved to the side. Dayn pressed his hands upon Reiv's shoulders, fighting to hold the contorting body down. A harsh kick in the chest knocked Dayn quickly onto his backside.

Nannaven shouldered her way in and placed her hands upon Reiv's cheeks. She held his face between her palms and spoke desperate words of comfort, but to no avail. She shouted at him then, commanding him to calm. It was as though she thought her authority would somehow have power over him. But her shouts could not be heard over his screams and loud guttural gasps for air.

The Spirit Keeper's face went white. She leaned back, trembling from head to foot. "This is not as it should be," she said. "It shouldn't be so violent. He was only meant to go into a deep sleep."

"Well then *do* something!" Dayn screamed over his shoulder as he continued to fight Reiv's thrashings.

"Is he dying? Is he dying?" Alicine's desperate voice cried over and over.

"Stay with us Reiv," Dayn begged. "Stay with us."

Reiv relaxed beneath Dayn's hands, and his body went still except for the rapid breaths pushing his chest up and down in successive bursts. His body was bathed in sweat and the paintings on his arms were smeared from Dayn's hold on them. The cockle band that wound through Reiv's hair was broken to pieces, scattered amongst the tendrils now trailing across the mat.

Reiv's eyelids shot open and he stared with wide eyes, their violet color sparkling like crystal reflecting starlight. Then his lips grew still and barely parted, and his eyes went dull as though an opaque veil had been draped across them. All went quiet as one long, last breath hissed from his lips.

# 15

# Beyond
# the Veil

The room was white, bright, and familiar, its furnishings elegant and inviting. A great poster-bed rested against the far wall, its coverlets as soft and billowy as a cloud. The floor was of polished white marble and shone like glass, reflecting the candles that dotted the room. Upon the walls, frescoes were painted, the warriors depicted in them lifelike in their replication. A full-length mirror and carved dressing table stood nearby. Upon it lay a fine sword, a golden lion molded at its hilt.

The boy stood before an arched window, surveying the room with bright, violet eyes. He turned and leaned his elbows against the windowsill, gazing out at a landscape that stretched to an eternal horizon. The hills in the distance looked like lavender scarves rippling beneath a golden sky, and the patchwork fields were like ornamental tapestries draped across the land. The boy drew in a deep breath, relishing the sweet scent of honeysuckle drifting up the trellis.

A tap sounded at the door. "May I come in?" a muffled voice asked.

"Enter," the boy said.

The door opened and a woman swept in. She was not in a swirl of yellow as he had expected, but in a gown of purest white. Nor was her hair white-blonde, but silver-gray and loose at her shoulders. She was elderly and her features were lined, not young like... The boy furrowed his brow and watched as the woman flitted about the room lighting candles and fluffing pillows. She smiled and crossed over to him, her hazel eyes twinkling.

"You were not expecting me?" she asked.

"Who are you?"

The woman arched a brow. "A better question might be, who are you?"

"You mean, you do not know?"

"Oh, I know," the woman replied. "Do you?"

"Of course. I am..." The boy paused and looked down at himself. He examined the fine yellow tunic draped down his body, and the silver braided belt that was wrapped around his waist. He twisted his head toward each shoulder, noting the amethyst clasps that gathered the material there. His gaze moved to his hands and his breath caught in his throat. The skin upon them was pale and smooth, and his fingers straight. He curled them into fists, joyful at the newfound strength he felt within them.

"I am Ruairi," he said, grinning.

"Ah, so you are," the woman said. "Why have you come so soon, Ruairi?"

"Why have I come? Because I live here, of course."

"But you did not live here before."

He tilted his head and fixed his eyes upon her. "No, I think for a time I lived someplace else."

"Do you remember where?"

"I think...I think...No...I do not wish to think. Too much unpleasantness." He turned away and gazed around the room, savoring every detail of it, then strolled to the full-length mirror across the way. He smiled as he inspected his reflection with satisfaction. "I am here now. That is all that matters," he said.

"Are you sure that is all that matters, Ruairi?"

"Well...no..." His smile faltered. "I am not certain of anything at the moment." He held up his hands and stared at them.

"You poor boy," the woman said, shaking her head sympathetically. "It is no wonder you are confused. It is not easy for one to accept coming to the After Realm, even when one sought to do so."

"The After Realm? You are mistaken. This is Tearia."

"Only in your mind. In the After Realm one's reality can be anything one wants it to be. This is your reality, though it could be something else altogether if you wished it."

Ruairi caught her image in the mirror and regarded her with suspicion. He knew he was standing in his bed chamber and it made him feel joyful. But murky images of the beforetime, as well as an overwhelming sense of urgency, concerned him.

"How did I get here?" he asked.

"How does anyone?" she replied.

He spun to face her. "You mean I am dead?"

"Your body, yes, but your spirit lives on here."

Ruairi shook his head furiously. "No, I am not supposed to be."

"Not supposed to be?"

"I am not supposed to be dead! I am supposed to be in the Between Realm. I am supposed to meet with the gods and ask for the gift of knowledge. Then I am to go back to...to...somewhere. Someone is waiting for me there. Someone who needs to be healed."

"And who would that someone be?"

"Who? I—I do not remember who, but...someone..." He flashed his eyes impatiently to hers. "Why am I here? Where are the gods? I have no time to answer all these questions! I must get back before—"

"Before what?"

"Before it is too late!"

"What if it is already too late?"

"It cannot be too late. Not yet. I have only just arrived. I am supposed to have more time."

"So many 'supposed to's. Why are you supposed to have more time, Ruairi? To do what? To heal someone whose name you do not even remember in a place that you describe as an unpleasant memory? What sense is there in that?"

"I do not know what sense there is in it, but my heart tells me I am meant to do it." Ruairi stormed over to her. "I am losing my patience, woman. Will you take me to the god who can give me the knowledge I need or must I find him myself?"

"Patience never was one of your virtues, Ruairi. Perhaps you could work on that while you are here. You will have plenty of time." She chuckled at the crimson rushing to his cheeks.

"Forgive me," she said. "You asked me a question. Now, then, who was it again that you needed to heal?"

"I told you—Kerrik!" Ruairi's face brightened. "Yes…Kerrik. I have come to heal Kerrik!"

"Why do you wish to heal this…Kerrik?"

"You say the name as though he were a thing."

"Well, then, what is he?"

"He is a boy."

"What sort of boy?"

"He is just a boy. A boy who wants to be a warrior."

The old woman laughed merrily. "He sounds like any other boy to me. What makes this one worthy of being saved by the gods?"

"Because he is special. He has a great spirit in him. He believes in things that others have given up on. Like the belief that the world can be healed, and that he will be the warrior to do it."

"Children are idealistic," the woman said with a dismissive wave of her hand. "Of course he believes those things."

"But he makes me want to believe those things, too. Kerrik told me everyone gets sad sometimes, yet I have never seen a moment's sadness in him. He is a boy with a twisted foot, tossed aside by his parents because of it. He does not have many of the things he deserves to have, but he is always with a smile, and is annoyingly determined that everyone else should, too. Kerrik asks to save the whole world. I only ask to save Kerrik."

The woman shook her head. "But if you return you will find yourself back in the sorrows of your world. Back to those painful memories of which you do not wish to speak. Take a look around you, Ruairi." She swept her arm toward the magnificent room. "This is everything you have longed for. You created this paradise yourself. Now it can be yours. Here you can learn all things, have all the knowledge you could ever want. Will you return to the confines of your body, or embrace the freedom of illumination?"

Ruairi drank in the opulence of the room and the splendor of his clothes, delighting in the beauty of his hands and the peace within his once tormented soul. For a moment the overwhelming desire for it threatened to turn him from the task he had come to do. He shook his head determinedly. "I wish to save Kerrik."

"So you would give up eternal happiness in the place of your dreams to go back and save this child."

"Yes."

The woman walked slowly to him and cupped his chin in her hand. "None before you has ever chosen to go back, although all have come with every intention of doing so. Their reasons for it were never powerful enough, it seems. But your reason is pure, my boy, and for that you shall receive what you have come for."

Ruairi breathed a great sigh, then eyed her with suspicion. "You still have not told me who you are."

"I am Agneis," the woman said matter-of-factly.

"Agneis? But, you do not...look...like..."

"What you expected?" She laughed softly. "You have been sorely misled, my dear boy. It seems your priestess, as well as all those before her, claims to represent me when, in fact, she represents someone far darker. But her time will come." She studied his face for a moment. "Perhaps you will be the one."

Ruairi threw himself to his knees and bowed his head to the hem of her gown. "Forgive me, Goddess, for my insolence. I am not worthy of your kindness. Please—"

"Rise, boy...rise. I require no groveling. I know your heart well enough. But if it gives you comfort, your insolence is forgiven." She smiled and placed her hand on his head.

He rose and stood before her, a million questions flooding his mind. "Why has it always been that we worship you through the Priestess when she has loyalty to another?"

"You will learn in time."

"In time..." he echoed softly. "Goddess, you said my body is dead, and it seems as if I have been here a very long time. How can I hope to return?"

"Time in your world is a flicker on the sea of eternity. While it may seem to you that you have been here for a long while, it has only been a blink of an eye since the heart of your body stopped." She moved toward the window and motioned him over. "Come, tell me what you see."

Ruairi walked over hesitantly and stood beside her to gaze out at the landscape. No longer did he see pastel hills and patterned fields; now he saw a vast meadow covered in a sea of white flowers and bright green grasses.

"Why, it is a meadow of flowers," he replied, his voice reflecting the happy surprise he felt at the sight of it.

"What else?"

"What else? There...a girl in a long dress...walking through the meadow, gathering flowers." He leaned out the window and focused his eyes on the distant image of her. "Her hair is dark. She is very beautiful."

"Do you know her?"

He swallowed hard and leaned back. "Yes, I know her." He turned his gaze to Agneis. "Why is she here? Why have you brought her to this place? She is not dead...tell me she is not."

"No, she is an illusion," Agneis replied.

"Then you are trying to trick me into staying with the hope of her!"

"No, Ruairi, you have come for knowledge and you shall receive it."

He refocused his attention on the meadow, then realized he was no longer standing at the window, but in the midst of an eternal sea of white petals and pastel grasses. The flowers around him danced to the rhythm of the breeze, and the sweet fragrance of the meadow lit his senses. He closed his eyes and turned his face to the sun, feeling the warmth of it caress his cheek like a mother to a child, a feeling for which he had so often longed. This was truly paradise, not the stuffy confines of a princely room.

He opened his eyes and his heart raced. The dark-haired girl was standing near, smiling at him. Her long black hair was plaited down her back and she wore a dress of gold, the long full skirt of it covered with hundreds of tiny white flowers. She motioned him forward.

"Alicine," he whispered, and stepped toward her.

She lifted the flowers that were in her hand and nodded her head to them. Ruairi studied them with curiosity for a moment, then moved his eyes to hers. He gazed at her, studying her hair, her skin, her lips. His heart filled with a familiar longing, and he moved closer, his arms extended. But a powerful sensation took sudden hold of him, jerking him back.

A roar of voices struck his ears like thunder, and he looked to the sky that had turned dark and ominous. The ground trembled violently, almost sending his legs out from under him. He reached out to Alicine, but she was gone, vanished into a vapor amongst a blurring image of wilting flowers. The once gentle breeze stilled. Petals curled into dark clumps as a blanket of heat settled upon them.

The voices became deafening. Ruairi covered his ears with his palms, but it did little good. People surrounded him, running and screaming, pushing and shoving. Flames licked at their feet from fissures in the earth. Boulders rained from the sky in torrents of crushing weight. He fell to the ground, shaking so fiercely he felt sure his body would break into pieces. Then, through the deafening roar, he heard a single voice, a familiar voice. He sat up and searched the blinding dust and clamoring crowd for a sign of someone he knew. But there was no one.

He pushed to his knees and felt a stickiness beneath him. Lifting a hand, he stared at it with confusion. A dark, wet redness was painted upon it, the white creases of his palm standing out in stark contrast. He wiped it across his tunic and staggered to his feet.

The sky turned from stormy black to hazy yellow. He knew he was standing in a field, but he could see little else through the mysterious fog. A breeze stirred the air, and sunlight spotted the landscape in patches of bright light. Ruairi recoiled at the sight before him. There were people as far as the eye could see, all lying motionless in the dirt.

The pummeling sound of horses' hooves redirected Ruairi's attention. A rider could be seen galloping toward him, its image a black silhouette against the rising sun at its back. The black stallion stopped within feet of him and reared up as the dark figure mounted upon it raised a sword high into the air. It was The Lion!

Ruairi staggered back, then turned and ran. But he had no idea where he was running to. The scenery shifted around him, changing from a field of golden dust to that of blood red carnage. He tripped and sprawled across a body, the wide brown eyes of it staring back at him. He threw himself off and rolled onto his back, shaking. The rider barreled toward him, poised to attack. Ruairi threw out an arm and screamed in terror.

From out of nowhere a shadowy form leapt between them, his blade aimed in the direction of the rider. But Ruairi could not identify his gallant defender, for the man's back was to him. The rider shouted and kicked his heels into the horse's ribs, sweeping The Lion downward. The stranger's weapon met it with a loud clash of metal. The stallion reared and the man on foot jumped to the side, barely escaping the reach of the hooves. The swords met again and again, neither gaining ground, though clearly The Lion had the advantage. The rider suddenly pulled back and steered his horse in a wide circle. The stranger slowly turned his face toward Ruairi, who gasped then called out a warning. But it was too late. The rider was upon him in an instant, and The Lion's gold was turned to red.

A tumultuous but silent wind wrapped Ruairi's body, twisting him in a whirling cloud of confusion. The images of man and horse evaporated, only to be replaced by even more terrifying visions. He fell to the ground, quaking, and squeezed his eyes against the sting of dust and the flashes of knowledge now searing his brain. A sob escaped his throat. This was not what he had asked for. These were not things he wished to know.

"Agneis!" he cried. "Tell me these are illusions only."

"Illusions play on hopes and fears," Agneis whispered into his mind. "These are visions, and come from a far deeper place."

"Are they the future? Can I change them?"

"You can change only yourself, Ruairi. But first you must accept and understand your own heroic path. Only then can you inspire the changes in others that will lead to a brighter future."

All went quiet and still. Ruairi felt his body relax, even as his mind continued to churn. The ground beneath him became soft and cool. He opened his eyes, then sat up and scanned the landscape around him. A great valley stretched as far as he could see. Green and lush, it was surrounded by a circle of purple mountains tipped in sparkling white. It was like no place he had seen before. Bright blue dragonflies darted around him and birds flew overhead, but he could not hear the sound of them, only the rhythm of his heart, his own beating heart.

"Reiv!" he heard a distant voice call. He stood and turned in a slow circle.

"Reiv!" the voice shouted again.

Then all went dark and Ruairi became only aware of the voice, his other senses extinguished. It was as though he were

floating in a place devoid of light and smell and touch and
taste. There was nothing else, only the voice. He felt confused
by it, denying the name it spoke. But then he realized it was
calling his name—Reiv. Yes, Reiv was his true name.

"Reiv! Can you hear me? Come back...please..."

He recognized the voice then. It was Dayn. Dayn was his
cousin. Dayn was his friend. And he was calling him back.

Reiv gasped as he opened his eyes to the fuzzy reality of the
world. A great rush of air filled his lungs. He pushed his chest
out, drinking in the exhilarating feel of it, then grabbed Dayn's
hand and looked hard into his eyes.

"You...are...here," Reiv rasped.

"Of course I'm here." Dayn's eyes glistened, then he burst
into laughter. "Reiv, I swear I would kill you myself if I weren't
so glad to see you alive."

"Alicine's flowers," Reiv whispered, squeezing Dayn's hand,
"for Kerrik."

Then he saw Alicine, her face leaned to his, tears trac-
ing patterns down her cheeks. She threw herself across his
chest and wrapped her arms around him.

He lifted an arm and draped it across her, then held her for
a moment before his eyes drifted closed. His arm fell to his side
as he floated toward a comfortable dream, but his breathing
sounded steady and his heart felt strong within his chest.

"It's truly a miracle!" Nannaven exclaimed, her hands
clasped beneath her chin. She turned to the three elders standing at her back, their mouths agape. "Go out and tell the people he has done it! Tell them the Prince has transcended!"

The men turned and scurried out, shouting the news,
but their words were quickly drowned by a wave of celebration from the crowd.

Nannaven turned her attention to Alicine. "What flowers does he speak of?"

Alicine sat up and turned to face her. "The only flowers
I know he could be speaking of were the ones I was picking
the day he found us."

"What were they called?"

"I don't remember. They were white...very tiny..." Alicine's voice trailed off as she attempted recollection.

"They were like those on your Summer Maiden's dress, remember?" Dayn said.

"Yes, very much like those! You saw the dress, Nannaven. The one Brina brought from Reiv's apartment. In Kirador we call them Daylies, but Reiv called them something else."

"Frusensias?" Nannaven asked.

"Yes! Yes...Frusensias! That was what he called them," Alicine said.

Nannaven looked doubtful. "Frusensias have never held healing powers. The Tearians use them for perfumes and scented oils only. I don't see how those could be the flowers he's referring to."

"If they're anything like Daylies," Alicine said, "they may prove to strengthen the blood. Daylies have that property when mixed with certain herbs. The mixture doesn't cure infection, but it can give a weak body strength to fight it and it can increase the appetite and—"

Nannaven rose quickly. "Come with me now and tell me what we must do to make this medicine you speak of." Alicine jumped up and followed her out the door.

"Reiv. Can you hear me? Are you awake?" Dayn said. He placed a hand on Reiv's rising and falling chest.

"There you go shouting again," Reiv mumbled. His eyes fluttered open, the color of them clouded from the ordeal.

Dayn grinned. "God, we thought you were dead."

"I was," Reiv said.

"You were? No...surely not dead! It must have just seemed like it."

"Is Alicine with Nannaven? Have they gone to find the flowers? How is Kerrik? Has there been any change in him?"

"Calm yourself, cousin. Kerrik's the same as you last saw him, but he's still alive; and yes, Alicine and Nannaven have gone to find the flowers and mix up a medicine. You were referring to the Frusensias, weren't you? That's what we took you to mean."

Reiv released a breath of relief. "Yes, Frusensias. Kerrik will be well now. Agneis told me."

"Agneis? The *goddess* Agneis? Reiv, are you certain? Maybe it was a dream or a hallucination from the drug or—"

"It was no dream."

Dayn paused and examined Reiv's face. It was strained, but his thoughts seemed lucid enough, and his words had been clearly spoken, void of hesitation or doubt. "Well, for someone who didn't believe in prophecies..." Dayn said.

Reiv smiled. "Now if you will quit talking and let me get some rest. I feel as though I have been to the tavern instead of the After Realm." He closed his eyes and was instantly asleep.

# 16

# Confessions

The mixture of Frusensia and herbs did indeed prove to strengthen the blood, and after but a few forced doses, Kerrik's color began to return and his breathing grew steady and strong. Reiv was led from the ceremonial hut within hours, feeling amazingly well for someone who had been poisoned. Many villagers converged upon him, begging him to heal them or a loved one. He turned them away politely and insisted he had not been given a healing gift such as that. Some were disgruntled, thinking him a fraud. But their minds were quickly changed when it was discovered that one of the ingredients he had drunk was a particularly deadly toxin. The dosage would have been lethal to any ordinary person, and so the fact that Reiv had survived at all further proved the miracle of his transcension. The identity of the culprit who had switched the toxin with that intended for the potion remained a mystery; Jensa had gathered herbs from many people that day. But from that moment on it was clear a traitor was in their midst.

Reiv had little time to spend with Kerrik or answer questions before he was whisked to a place of safety. With his fame now spread throughout Meirla, it was only a matter of time before Pobu and Tearia learned of it as well. Talk was that the former Prince played roles in two prophecies. He was now believed to be both the Transcendor and the Unnamed One. This left him, in the minds of most, with more power than even the Priestess possessed. He remained strangely mute about the entire experience and allowed himself to be shuffled along by Nannaven and the elders who in that short time had made it their mission to direct his every move. They insisted he hide, at least for a while, for they knew he was no longer safe in Meirla. And so they took him to a cave tucked within the rocks of the coastline several miles away.

The cave was not deep, more like a yawn in the cliffs than a cavern. Few knew of its existence; it had been used for ancient rituals long since forgotten. Its entrance was well-hidden, thick with an overgrowth of roots and mossy overhangs. Nannaven and the elders set Reiv up as comfortably as they could, and provided him with some basic necessities. The only thing he requested was that Dayn stay with him, though he would not say why.

"I appreciate your concern," Reiv said when Nannaven had settled him into his hideaway, "but I will do no one any good hidden away. I would like you to arrange a meeting of those you know can be trusted, then send for me. There are issues that need to be discussed. It does not matter to me where the meeting takes place, but Pobu would probably be best. It needs to happen soon, though."

Nannaven agreed, then hurried out the cave with the three elders at her back.

As Reiv watched them depart, Dayn settled onto a mat by the fire that had been lit for their comfort. He held his hands over the flames. "It's cold in here," he grumbled. "And I hate caves."

It rained hard that first night, and continued without ease for the next three days. During that time, Dayn paced back and

forth with boredom while Reiv mostly slept. Restless with con-
finement, and increasingly annoyed with his sleeping cousin,
Dayn marched over and nudged Reiv with his foot. But Reiv
did not move. "Why in the world do you require so much *rest*?"
Dayn muttered. "You seem well enough." He folded his arms
and leaned down toward Reiv. "If you wanted me to come to
this stupid cave with you," he said rather loudly, "you could at
least stay awake and keep me company." Seeing that his words
made no impact, Dayn returned to the warmth of the fire and
plopped down in a huff. Glaring in Reiv's direction, Dayn
cleared his throat with exaggerated effort.

Reiv stirred a bit, then yawned and stretched his arms over
his head. "What is there to eat around here?" he asked. "I am
starved."

"There are some dates and palm nut, there in the basket,"
Dayn said with indifference. Reiv rose and tottered his stiff
body over to the food and sat down beside it. He grabbed the
basket and propped it in his lap. Munching on a bit of nut, he
eyed Dayn warily. "Why the face?" he asked.

"Why the face? Well, let me see…it's been raining ever
since we got here. I've been stuck in a cold, damp cave with
no one to talk to and nothing to do. I have a cousin at my
side who could be murdered at any moment—myself included if I happen to get in the way—and a sister who's off
with a Spirit Keeper rounding up rebels for who knows
what. You're right, why should I be unhappy?"

Reiv laughed. "Oh, little cousin, you are only looking at the
dark side of things. Look around you. It is pouring down rain
outside, yet you are sitting next to a nice warm fire. You have a
basket of fruit, plenty of water, a blanket, and your favorite
cousin wide awake now to keep you company."

Dayn attempted to stay angry, but a grin won out. "Fine.
Hand me a date then."

The two of them sat munching and stared into the
flames that flickered in a tumble of ash and wood. Dayn
grabbed a handful of dried moss and tossed it onto the pile.

It cracked and sparked momentarily before turning into a curling blob.

"Tell me about Kirador," Reiv said.

Dayn lifted his eyes from the fire and shifted his weight as though settling in for a long dissertation. "It's beautiful there, I guess." But that was all he said.

"And..." Reiv said, prodding.

Dayn sighed. "It's more mountainous than here. Colder, too."

"Well, thank you for the geography lesson, but what about the people?" The reflection of the fire glowed on Reiv's face, revealing his sincere interest.

"They're all dark-haired like Alicine," Dayn said, "and not as tall as you and me. They're very religious and have lots of festivals. A matter of fact, the day I left we were at the Summer Fires and—" He frowned.

"What about the summer fires? The summer fires what?"

Dayn shrugged. "When I left everyone was at the Summer Fires Festival. That's all."

"Must I drag every word from you? Tell me about it, more than two words at a time if you do not mind."

Dayn filled his lungs then expelled the air into the cheeks of his disgruntled face. "Summer Fires is a big festival, probably the biggest of the year. I was bound and determined not to go—I hate going to those things—but Alicine tricked me into it. She was being crowned Summer Maiden and it meant the world to her." He paused, noting the question forming on Reiv's face. "Summer Maiden is a girl thing...hard to explain. Anyway, she had worked for months on that dress of hers—"

"The dress with the flowers? You mean to say she made that dress herself?" Reiv was clearly impressed.

"Yes. Well anyway, I'd pretty much avoided all the festivals this past year, ever since I found out I was a demon, or rather, ever since I came to believe I was. But even before I'd found out, it was always miserable going to those things. I always

ended up being laughed at or insulted in one way or another.
Well, to make a long story short, I went and ran into Falyn—"

"Falyn? I have heard that name. Alicine said something
about her before, I think. That is the girl you like, is it not?"

"I don't want to talk about it," Dayn said. He stabbed at
the embers with a stick, sending a funnel of sparks rising with
the smoke.

"Why not? You must like her; otherwise you would not
mind speaking of her."

Dayn tossed the stick into the fire and wrapped his
arms around his bent knees. "It doesn't matter whether I
do or not."

"She does not return your feelings?"

"I don't know. It never came up."

"It never came up? You mean she does not know how
you feel? You never told her?"

"No, I never told her," Dayn said crossly. "God, Reiv,
can't you let this go?" Dayn rose abruptly from his spot by
the fire and headed for the mouth of the cave. He stood
facing out, arms crossed, and stared through the raindrops
trailing from the overhang.

Reiv followed him over and stood next to him. "I understand how you feel, cousin. I, too, have been wounded
by love. First Cinnia, then...well, never mind."

"My sister loves you, you know."

"Oh, no. If you refuse to speak of Falyn, then I refuse
to speak of Alicine."

Dayn nodded and continued his mute contemplation
for a long moment, then said, "I love Falyn. I've loved her
for as long as I can remember. She's smart and beautiful,
and she never treated me badly. Not like the others. There's
nothing about her not to my liking, except her brother
Sheireadan. He despises me and would never allow me to
have anything to do with her. I received many a black eye
and bloodied nose for a look in Falyn's direction, but I
didn't care. She was worth every licking I ever took."

"Surely she knows how you feel about her, Dayn. After all, your face does have a tendency to reveal every emotion."

Dayn forced a laugh. "Well, she mostly saw my backside. I was usually running in the opposite direction."

"You said she treated you kindly when others did not. Are you sure she does not return your feelings?"

"It's probably just pity," Dayn said. He lowered his eyes to the ground and kicked a pebble with his toe. "It wouldn't have mattered anyway. The day I left I'd found out all the fathers had made a decision about me. They decided I'd never be allowed to take a wife. They didn't want to risk any offspring from demon-kind like me. I guess I can't really blame them. At the time I thought I was a demon, too. At any rate, that's when I decided to leave."

"So how does Alicine figure into the picture? I doubt you invited her to come along."

"No, she was definitely not invited. She came looking for me and refused to turn back when she found me. By then I was almost to the cave and bound and determined not to go home. You know how stubborn that sister of mine can be. Well, I matched her for it that day. So, we went in together."

They headed back to the warmth of the fire and sat across from each other, talking about things they had never had much time to talk about before. Reiv told Dayn about his former life as a prince, while Dayn told him about his and Alicine's trek to Tearia, beginning with the adventure in the cave. He told him about the winding tunnels and snaking river, the strange markings and mysterious chambers, the bubbling pits and swarms of flying rats. As he spun the tale, he grew more animated, his arms waving wildly when he came to the part about the monstrous demon. His shadow loomed across the wall, the image contorting with his every move. Reiv watched with rapt attention.

"Gods, you really put yourself through an ordeal to escape that girl," Reiv said with amusement.

Dayn chortled. "I suppose I did."

"Will you go back for her?"

"Go back for her? I don't know. I mean, I did promise Alicine I would take her back to Kirador, but I keep hoping she'll change her mind. I keep hoping *you'll* change her mind."

Reiv's face was solemn. "I cannot keep her here. Her heart belongs in Kirador, at least most of it does. No, she must return home and you must be the one to take her."

Dayn picked up a twig and chewed on it absentmindedly for a moment. "You know, if we do go back, I'm going to walk right up to Falyn and tell her how I feel about her. I mean, if I can make my way through a cave, escape a demon of the deep, *and* put up with the likes of you...why, I should be able to do almost anything. Yes...I do believe I'll march right up to her and kiss her on the mouth." He smiled dreamily. "Right on the mouth."

"So you have not kissed her before then?" Reiv asked.

"Of course not! I'm only sixteen. Even if I had been allowed to court, it wouldn't have been until I was seventeen at least."

"Court? What does that mean?"

"You know, when a boy is allowed to visit a girl at her parents' house and get to know her and at first they're only friends, but then if it goes well you can kiss her—but not when the parents are around, of course."

Reiv's surprise surpassed even his reaction to the cave story. "You mean to tell me you are sixteen...and you have never been alone with a girl... *and* you have never kissed one?"

"Of course not! It would not have been allowed."

Reiv burst into hearty laughter. "Gods, cousin, a boy as healthy as you would have been wedded and bedded by now in Tearia." He grabbed his side and rolled back.

Dayn felt his face blush three shades of red. "I can't believe you said that. Just because I don't walk around half naked, staring and touching and kissing like the people here do."

"We do not stare and touch and...well...we do stare and touch and kiss, but it is a natural thing. Nothing to be ashamed of. You do not know what you are missing."

"Yes, I do. I mean, when I picture Falyn, I get all goosy."

"Goosy?"

"Yes, you know. *Goosy.*" Dayn demonstrated with a display of quivering happiness.

"I never heard it called 'goosy'. How did you come by that expression exactly? Does it have something to do with a goose's neck or something?" Reiv looked completely serious.

"A goose's neck? No. Goosy. Like a bump. You know."

"A bump? I should think it would be more than a bump."

Dayn stared at his cousin like he was talking to a two-year-old. Then Reiv's meaning became clear. "Oh, you think—God, Reiv, I'm not talking about *that*! I mean bumps like on your arms, not—" Dayn threw up his hands in exasperation, then his eyes grew mischievous. "But as for the other, I swear it can be so annoying, can't it? I mean, I see Falyn walking my way and evil thoughts seem to take me over, body and mind." He grinned and found himself squirming. "I think we'd better change the subject. I'm picturing her as we speak."

"Well, you had best get your mind off of your bump in a hurry because someone has come to call," Reiv said.

"What—who?" Dayn turned his head to follow Reiv's gaze. Jensa was making her way toward them, her clothes drenched through and clinging to every part of her body.

Dayn groaned and lowered his forehead into his hand. "Oh, god, please not her. Not now," he whispered, shaking his head.

Reiv looked at Jensa, then Dayn, and his laughter returned. "Go on, cousin, where are your manners? Are you not going to rise to greet her?"

Dayn shot him a glare. "Not funny, Reiv."

"What's going on with you two?" Jensa said. She walked over to the fire and sat down next to Dayn, her knee touching his, and held her hands out over the flames. She leaned across him and reached for a blanket, pulling it across his lap to hers.

Dayn looked past her, struggling to keep his eyes averted from her barely clad body. "I need some air," he said, and jumped up and headed out into the rain.

"What in the world is he doing?" Jensa said. "Doesn't he realize how hard it's raining? Didn't he see how soaked through I am?"

Reiv roared with laughter and threw his head back, attempting to answer between gasping breaths. "I think he is well aware," he finally managed.

Jensa was not amused. "Well, if you wouldn't mind turning off your stupidity for a moment, I came to tell you a meeting has been called."

Reiv composed himself and wiped the tears from his eyes. His merriment faded. "When and where is it to be?" he asked.

"In Pobu, tonight after dark. I'm to escort you both, but with this weather..." Jensa gazed out momentarily toward the rain that had begun to come down in torrents. "Oh, the Guard came to Meirla looking for you, by the way."

"Did they now?"

"Yes, but no one made any indication they had seen you or knew of your whereabouts."

"The Guard did not harm anyone, did they?"

"No, everyone put on a very convincing show. I don't think our people wish to lose their Transcendor so soon. Guards searched every hut, but found nothing." She glanced toward the mouth of the cave and frowned. "Where is Dayn, anyway? He's going to be soaked to the bone."

"Perhaps you had better fetch him," Reiv said with a hint of humor. "After all, you *are* already wet." Jensa narrowed her eyes in response, but she rose anyway and headed out to look for Dayn.

She found him standing beneath an outcrop of rock, but it provided a poor shelter and he had become as soaked through as she was. He stood there, arms wrapped around himself, shivering and staring at the horizon.

"What are you doing out here?" Jensa asked. She went to pull the blanket from her shoulders to wrap around his, but he ordered her to stop with a wave of his hand.

"I'm f-f-f-fine," he said through chattering teeth. "I couldn't breathe in there."

"Well, you're going to drown out here. You're ridiculous." She pulled the blanket off and wrapped it around him. As she pulled it beneath his chin, he reached for it, but grabbed her hand instead. He let go quickly and turned his face away.

"Now you're the one who'll be c-c-cold," he said. His words were directed to her, but his eyes were focused in the opposite direction.

Jensa moved next to him and pulled part of the blanket around her shoulders. "Here, we can share it," she said.

Dayn felt the warmth of her skin next to his, but instead of his shivering subsiding, it only seemed to increase. He thought to pull away, to distance himself as far from her as possible. But where would he go, and did he really want to?

"You're shaking," Jensa said. "Come on, let's go back in."

Dayn nodded, but found his legs would not work. It was as though his feet had become rooted to the mud oozing between his toes.

The rain trickled off the strands of hair hanging down his forehead and flicked at his lashes. Jensa reached a hand up and brushed it from his eyes, gazing into them. "What is it, Dayn? Tell me."

"Nothing. Reiv and I were just talking, that's all."

"About what? I could tell you were not pleased to see me. Did I offend you in some way?"

"Oh, no! It's just that...well we were talking about things I wouldn't have you overhear."

"What sort of things?"

Dayn remained silent for a moment, his knees rocking. "Girls, that's all."

"I see. And were you talking about any girl in particular?"

"Well...yes. There's a girl where I'm from that I sort of care about. But I don't know if I'll ever see her again and—"

Jensa moved her face close to his. "Do you love this girl?"

"Yes, but...like...I...said..." Dayn found himself staring into Jensa's pale blue eyes, eyes nothing like Falyn's, then down to her lips, lips he realized could be his for the taking. But he found his mouth as frozen in place as his feet were.

Jensa reached her hand to his face. She traced her thumb along his lower lip, then moved her mouth to his. The blanket fell from their shoulders and dropped into the mud. The air rushed around them like a blast of cold north wind. Dayn wrapped his arms around her and pulled her close, savoring her scent and the soft feminine curves pressed against him. He kissed her in return, relishing the sweetness of his first kiss, wondering if he was doing it right, wondering if she felt as wonderful as he did at the moment. His questions were soon answered by the enthusiasm of her hands upon him and the passion of her mouth on his. Suddenly he realized what his sister had been so afraid of. He pulled away.

"I—I'm sorry," he said. "I shouldn't have done that."

Jensa looked puzzled, and her mouth parted with lips still red from the kisses Dayn had recently planted on them. "Didn't you like it?" she asked.

"Of course I liked it. You're beautiful and..." Dayn looked down ashamedly. "It was wrong. Forgive me."

Jensa stared hard at him, then set her jaw and nodded. "Very well," she said. "Let's go back in to the warmth of the fire. It's getting colder out here by the minute."

Dayn nodded silently in response, her meaning clear. He reached down and retrieved the blanket from the mud and followed her back into the cave.

# 17

# Birth
# of the Clans

Reiv, Dayn, and Jensa set out in a drizzle of rain that wrapped them like a cold, gray shroud. There was little point in waiting for the weather to clear, it obviously had no intention of doing so, and so they left the shelter in hopes of reaching Pobu by nightfall.

The main road was a series of washed-out ruts, but even had it not been, they had already decided to take an alternate route. Though it was doubtful anyone else would be traveling in such unpleasant weather, they did not wish to be seen, not by friend or by foe. Conversation waned as they plodded through the thick, scruffy grasses of the meadowlands. Dayn and Jensa managed to keep courteous distances from one another, while Reiv trudged behind, lost in thought and seemingly oblivious to the misery of the other two.

The trek took longer than it should have. By the time they were within sight of the city, the sun had long since set and turned the sky from charcoal gray to inky black. Only the occasional twinkle of lights in the distance gave them any guidance. They made their way in gloomy silence, the dreariness of the landscape and the chill of the air matching the aches in their bones and the frostiness of their moods.

Once within the city, Jensa led them through a series of muck-filled back streets until they stopped before a dilapidated two-story building. It was dark and quiet and seemed abandoned. They approached quietly, Jensa leading the way, Dayn hesitating as they reached the doorway. Reiv marched around him and followed Jensa inside, unmindful of the heavy stillness that surrounded them.

A single candle could be seen flickering in a nearby corner of the room. It reflected on Torin's face, his eyes looking like shiny beads against a pallet of distorted patterns.

"Are we to meet in the dark?" Reiv asked.

Jensa went to stand next to her brother. He tilted another candle to the one already lit, then handed it to her. Candles brightened one by one as others in the room followed suit. Before long the entire place was alight with halos of gleaming flames and curious faces.

Reiv took his place next to Torin and leaned into him, inquiring quietly as to Kerrik's condition. Reiv nodded, relieved by the man's smile and optimistic response.

The interior of the place was larger than it had first appeared, and many people were packed within it. Most sat shoulder to shoulder on benches or makeshift chairs, while others lined the walls. Men, women, young and old, Jecta and Shell Seeker, even a few Tearians could be seen scattered throughout. Reiv stepped forward and eyed the crowd, capturing the attention of each and every one of them.

"I know you have all come at great risk," he said.

"Yes, Prince, we have," a disgruntled Jecta man said. "Pray we haven't found ourselves in a Tearian trap!" Voices muttered in agreement.

Torin stepped forward. "You will hold your tongues until the Prince has said his piece."

Reiv placed his hand on Torin's shoulder. "I may not have their trust, but do not worry, I will soon have their ears."

Torin nodded and stepped aside, his arms crossed and features hard.

"The first order of business is this," Reiv said, "I am no longer Tearian, nor am I Prince. I am only Reiv."

"You are more than that," a Tearian woman called from the back. "You are the one the Prophecy speaks of."

"I am not here to discuss prophecies," Reiv said.

The crowd mumbled with confused and conflicted opinions. Reiv raised his hand to quiet them.

"But you're a Transcendor," a young Shell Seeker man said from his shadowy place against the wall.

"I will not dispute that I have undergone the ritual. I am here only to offer what I have learned from it."

"What would that be?" a man said, raising his fist into the air. "Can you offer us freedom from the oppression of the Throne and the Temple? Can you offer us food on our tables and medicine for our sick? Can you offer our children hope for the future, or give us back the pride we've lost? What is it you can offer us?"

"Knowledge. The rest is up to you."

"That's easy enough to say," a woman said. "But what good is it?"

"You will have to be the judge," Reiv replied.

Voices in the crowd began to swell, and Reiv's eyes flashed a command for silence. The room became quiet. Restless bodies stilled as they watched and waited.

"The world of Aredyrah was once a larger place," Reiv began, "but it is larger today than you have been led to believe. There are others in our world, those who live on the other side of the mountains. They have shared Aredyrah from the beginning. The people of the north are different from us in many ways, yet they are more like us than not."

A few gasps were heard, and voices mumbled as heads leaned to listen to their neighbors. Words of doubt made the rounds.

"What proof do we have that what you say is true?" someone in the crowd asked. "How do we know there's this other place beyond the mountains? Who's ever seen it?"

"Dayn has seen it," Reiv said, motioning his arm in Dayn's direction. "Dayn is from the other place. It is called Kirador."

Dayn had remained in the shadows, staring at his feet in quiet contemplation. But his head shot up when his name was mentioned. Reiv's eyes, as well as every other eye in the room, were focused upon him.

Reiv motioned him forward. "Come, Dayn. Tell them."

Dayn stepped forward and gazed at the sea of doubting faces. "I...I am from Kirador. It's true," he said.

"But he looks Tearian!" an elderly man on the front row cried. "How do we know this isn't some sort of deception?"

"It is no deception," a woman's voice boomed from the doorway. All eyes turned in the direction of the shadowy form behind the voice. New mutterings began as Brina stepped into the room with Alicine and Nannaven at her back.

"Dayn is my son," Brina said as she marched across the room and took her place at his side.

Shocked voices echoed around her, but Brina gave the crowd no time for further comment as she ordered silence with a brusque display of her palm. "He was born with a mark," she said, gesturing to the birthmark on his neck, "and for that I was not allowed by Temple law to keep him. I took him to the mountain—"

Words of astonishment resonated throughout the room. "To the mountains? The forbidden place? The home of the gods?"

"Yes," Brina shouted over the voices. "I took him to the mountains to beg the gods to cure him. I did not care if it was forbidden. I would have given my very soul to save him. It was there that I met someone I believed to be a god. He took my child with the promise that he would heal him and return him to me in a year's time. But he never came back. I went there year after year seeking to have my son returned to me, but never again did I see the god beneath the mountain. Then, several weeks ago, I went to visit my nephew, Reiv, and found him with two strangers, a boy and a girl. Reiv believed them to be Jecta thieves, but a miracle happened. I recognized the mark on the boy's neck. When I questioned him I learned he had been taken from the mountains as a babe and raised by a family on the other side of it—a family from Kirador. It is there my son has been these past sixteen years, until fate gave him cause to leave that place and seek the truth."

"Maybe it's just a tale he told," someone accused. "Maybe he lied about his whereabouts."

"My brother doesn't lie!" Alicine stepped to the forefront. "Dayn's my brother, not by blood, but by the life we've shared. I'm also from Kirador and before we came here we didn't believe in you any more than you believe in us."

"Before I lay my life on the line, I want more proof!" a man said. "All we've been given is the word of a former enemy and that of a Tearian woman and two children."

Reiv threw a glare over the crowd. "You demand proof of what you know to be true! I am here to give you the knowledge I was instructed to reveal, so listen well. Truth is a power long kept from you, and it will be the power that frees you."

The room grew silent and eyes turned to him with fearful longing. Even those who had expressed doubt stilled in their seats.

Then Reiv began.

"Long ago our people were not divided by mountains, or fear, or religious superstition. Though our cultures were different, our natures were not, for we were all made in the image of the Creator. While those of the north believed in one god only, and those of the south in many, we all shared the belief in the same Creator.

"Generations ago, long before the mountains exploded and the seas churned, our cultures gathered together beneath the mountain to join in celebration. But there was an evil power at work. One day the earth sent up its fires, and the

mountains burned and the earth shook. Much of Tearia
plunged into the sea. Tens of thousands died. It seemed as if
the world was ending.

"Those who survived cried to the gods, but their prayers were
not answered. The world became filled with famine and plague,
and the Tearians felt betrayed and abandoned. An evil power
whispered in their ears and told them lies. It told them the gods
were punishing them for their sin—the sin of fraternization with
those not of their kind, those of the north, the dark ones.

"The Tearians turned their hearts against their neighbors
to the north, and it was toward them, and those Kiradyns who
had come to live amongst us, or had united with our kind in
marriage, that a terrible purge took place."

Reiv paused. No one said a word or moved a muscle.

"I was once said to be the future Red King, the second
coming of a king of old who brought Tearia back to greatness
after the dark times. It was because of my coloring that I was
identified as such, nothing more than that. But I tell you I
have been given a glimpse of that king, and he was as fair-
haired and pale-skinned as any Tearian. Time and propa-
ganda have twisted the truth of him, for it is easier to identify
him by the color of his hair than by the nature of his deeds.
In truth the red in his title stemmed from the bloody purge
carried out at his command. He led a slaughter against those
he believed inferior, proclaiming it all in the name of Agneis.

"The killing stopped through the intervention of the
gods, but the Purge continued. Those not worthy, those
marked, or of the wrong color, or with any deformity were
cast out, forced to live in the outskirts of our society. Once
the inferiors had been beaten down by the terror of the
sword and the threat of starvation, they were enslaved. And
that is what you all are today—slaves to Tearian masters!"

Mixed emotions rumbled through the room, then a
timid voice up front asked: "But what of those from the
north? Why did we never hear from them again?" Others
demanded similar answers.

Reiv raised a silencing hand.

"After the eruption of the mountain, the old passageways between us became too difficult to travel. To make certain no Tearian ever went there again, the Temple told the great lie that the gods had chosen to reside in the mountains. Anyone who dared trespass was threatened with death. To make certain of it, the Red King sent guards to stop anyone bold enough to try. Some from the north attempted to cross the mountains and contact Tearia, but they met their deaths at the hands of the Guard. After a while no one went there from either side. It is said the mountains are still guarded, but I have been there, as have Brina and Dayn and Alicine, and I tell you this: There are no guards there, just as there are no gods."

"What of those from the north? What fear keeps them on their side?" a woman asked.

Dayn cleared his throat and took a step forward. "We have been taught that demons live in the mountains," he said, "minions of the Dark One who destroyed all the world but us. The demons have always been described as white-haired and pale-skinned. There are many stories of people who went to the mountains and never returned. I was believed to be demon-kind because of my coloring. Maybe what the Kiradyns think are demons are in fact the Tearian guards from long ago that killed anyone who crossed the borders. Our leaders have spread myths about the eruption of the mountain just like yours have, and we have been kept just as isolated."

"Reiv," the same woman said, "you say the gods don't reside in the mountains. So where are they? Why have they deserted us?"

"I have spoken to only one god," Reiv replied, "and that was Agneis. She resides in the After Realm, not the mountains, and she has not deserted us."

"But Agneis speaks through the Priestess!" a voice cried.

"No!" Reiv said. "Agneis is the Goddess of Purity. The Priestess represents another. The Priestess knows the truth of things, but speaks only lies. The power must be taken from her and the evil she represents."

"But if we move to take the power from the Priestess, won't evil's wrath descend upon us?" a frightened voice asked. "What's to stop our total destruction this time?"

The crowd grew loud with protest, and people rose in agitation. Reiv stepped forward and once again raised his hands to silence the crowd.

"I went through the ritual of transcension to ask for the knowledge to heal a child. But Agneis in her wisdom granted me more. I did not come back as one who can lay a hand on the sick and make them well. I did not come back with the power to make wrongs right with the sweep of a hand. I came back with the knowledge of many things I did not know before, and one of those things is that the gods will never forsake us. We, and the gods, and everything of this world are entwined with the Creator. The gods cannot desert us; they are a part of us."

"But we don't have the strength to fight the Priestess!" someone cried.

"There is bad in us, just as there is good," Reiv said. "The Priestess's power feeds on the evil nature of things, but that does not mean she is stronger. Will we simply hand a victory over to her because we are afraid? Will we let her tell us we cannot embrace the gods who represent that part of us which we cherish? Our people did not perish when much of Aredyrah was burned into the sea. We survived, and our world retained its beauty even through its scars. It is only through fear that evil maintains its power. The gods will be with us, but they do not promise the battle will be an easy one. We must prove to them we believe it is worth fighting for and we must trust them to guide us."

A cluster of men in the back raised their fists into the air. "You must lead us!" one of them shouted.

Two Shell Seekers who had been leaning against the wall behind the men took a determined step forward. "You are the Transcendor!" they said simultaneously.

"You have the power of the gods on your side!" a woman on the front row cried. She twisted her body around, eyeing the audience for assurances. "You can speak with them, Reiv!"

A confusion of voices shouted a jumble of commands at Reiv. "You must be the one to lead us! You must be the one to take up the battle cry!" The entire crowd was on its feet then, urging him to consider.

Reiv raised his hand, then his voice. "That is not my purpose here. My role was to tell you, not to lead you."

A Tearian woman rushed forward. "But you are the Unnamed One. Do you deny your destiny?" Others behind her pressed forward also, shouting in agreement.

Reiv took a nervous step back. Torin rushed to his side and barked an order for the crowd to retreat, but emotions were high and the mass of individuals had quickly become a single entity of determination and purpose.

"Silence!" Reiv shouted. "Silence I said!" The crowd quieted. "Think what you are doing! You risked arrest tonight by coming here, and now you fill the air with loud words and reckless actions. Calm yourselves or any hope for reform will be stopped before it is begun. I have come to tell you truths and here is yet another—I am not who you think I am. I will offer what I can, but I will not lead you."

Reiv suddenly pushed forward and shouldered his way through the startled mob. Dayn shouted after him, but Reiv continued on and disappeared through the door. Dayn shoved past the crowd and dashed into the street. He paused, glancing back and forth, then spotted Reiv rounding the nearest corner. He sprinted after him, catching up quickly, and grabbed Reiv by the arm, spinning him around.

"What are you doing, walking out like that?" Dayn demanded. "All those people back there are counting on you. Why is it every time the going gets a little rough you run away?"

Reiv pulled his arm from Dayn's grasp. "I am not running away, but if I stay they will not do what needs to be done. They will continue to look to me for something I am not meant to give. I do not think any more time needs to be wasted arguing the issue."

"What are you thinking? Of *course* the issue needs to be argued. How are they to trust what you've told them if you walk out like a coward?"

"I am not a coward, but I am also not what I used to be. All my life I wanted to be a slayer; first of lions, then of my own brother."

Dayn's eyes widened.

"It is true, Dayn. The morning of the wedding, I was so desperate to have Cinnia back I would have slit Whyn's throat if need be. I swear if guards had not been posted at my door..." Reiv heaved a sigh. "It no longer matters. All that matters is that I no longer wish it. I am different now."

"How are you different?"

"I do not know how to explain it. When I transcended, I went to a place of perfection. It was not easy coming back. It was the hardest thing I ever had to do. I felt at peace in that place, like I belonged. I came back because I had to, and in so doing I waged the greatest battle of all—the battle within myself. I am tired of fighting. I came here to do what I set out to do, to tell the people what they needed to know. It is their fight now."

"You mean to tell me you will just walk away and lay it all on me and bunch of frightened, helpless people?"

"That is exactly what I am telling you."

"I swear, if I had the guts I'd knock you flat on the ground!"

"Then do it," Reiv said.

"Oh, and you think I won't?"

Reiv shrugged, but in an instant he was on his backside, reaching a hand to his bloodied lip. He smiled at his fingertips. "Not bad for a first attempt," he said.

Dayn reached down, grabbed Reiv's hand, and yanked him up. "You're coming back with me!"

"No. I am going home."

"And where would that be? Back to Tearia? Or would you prefer to live with Agneis in her realm of eternal happiness?"

"I am going home to Meirla," Reiv said. "I made a promise to Kerrik and I intend to keep it. Go back inside, Dayn. Do what you have to do." Then Reiv turned and headed down the street.

Dayn stared until Reiv had disappeared around the corner. For a moment he thought to chase him down and drag him back, but he knew he would only be met with increased resistance.

He walked back to the meeting place with a quickened pace. What in the world was he going to do now? Other than send Torin to accompany Reiv back to Meirla, he couldn't think of a single thing.

# 18

# Coronation of Evil

The coronation of the King was to take place in the sprawling space south of the temple.

The lawn there sloped away from the portico and stretched in a semi-circular pattern, turning the grounds into a vast open-air auditorium. It was devoid of seats, except for a row of chairs up front where the yellow-clad royal family sat. The crowd meandered in and arranged themselves in groups according to the color of their clothing, some in pastel green, others in blue or dusty rose. Patrons visited amongst themselves or reclined on the grasses of the lawn as they awaited the commencements. But what would have normally been a festive event was dampened by a line of Guard encircling the area with swords at their hips, their steely eyes watching the thousands of spectators. Voices in the crowd expressed confusion at the unexpected show of arms. Their uneasiness increased as the last of the guests arrived and the circle of Guard closed in at their backs.

161

Whyn stood off to the side of the portico, watching, but hidden from view. As he scanned the sea of talking heads beyond the steps, he could not help but feel jubilant. After his coronation in but a few moments time, they would all be bowed before him. He was eager for the title that would soon officially be his.

The crowd grew quiet as all rose and turned their attentions in the direction of the temple. A row of priests took their place at the back of the portico and stood draped in flowing white togas, their heads lowered and hands folded in front of them. Before them sat an altar of pink and gray marble. On either side were two great thrones, the one at the right for the Priestess, the other at the left where Whyn would soon be seated. One of the priests stepped forward and began to chant, pausing periodically for the crowd to respond in a well-rehearsed chorus. Then all grew quiet as the Priestess made her grand entrance.

She floated across the portico as though walking on air. A headdress of white plumes towered over her head, and she was draped in a gown of iridescent material that cascaded down her body like shimmering stars. She stopped behind the altar and faced the crowd with an expression of supremacy. A priest walked toward her and presented her with a white dove. She took it and held it up for all to see. The quivering bird struggled to work its wings from her grasp, but she held it tight, then plunged a slender golden knife into its breast. She closed her eyes and raised her face upward, then muttered sacred words before laying the limp, blood-spattered body upon the cold altar. Lifting her arms she, too, began to chant. The crowd fell to their knees and lowered their heads to the ground. When she had finished, the crowd rose at her command and waited silently.

At the Priestess's cue, Whyn entered the portico and strolled across it. He was clothed in a fine tunic of yellow silk. A long, velvet cape of the same bright color was draped down his back. His head was bare of any adornment, his white-blonde hair neatly parted and hanging loose at his shoulders. Cinnia entered several paces behind him, as was her role, and stood quietly to the side of him, watching with an expression of prideful admiration. His mother stood there also, her painted lips compressed into a thin line. She was no longer Queen of Tearia. Now she was only the mother of the King.

Whyn took his place behind the altar and stood next to the Priestess. She gathered his hand in hers and placed it on the breast of the dove, leaving a smear of blood upon his fingers. His hand moved to his chest and he laid it across his heart. A stain of red darkened the pale fabric of his tunic. Words of honor, commitment, and loyalty were spoken between them, and when the ritual was finally complete, the Priestess placed a jeweled circlet of silver upon his brow. He bowed to her and she smiled, then raised her hands to the crowd, pronouncing Whyn King of Tearia. The crowd applauded with loud acclaim.

The Priestess seated herself as Whyn walked around the altar to the edge of the portico to address the crowd. His eyes swept over them, resting his gaze on as many individual faces as time would allow.

"Citizens of Tearia," he said in a booming voice, "the era of my father has passed. I stand before you now as your King, a King whose only duty is to lead Tearia to a new age of greatness."

The crowd cheered, raising their eyes and arms up to him in adoration.

"But there is much work to be done, for as of late there have been voices raised against us. As your King I hereby set forth the following proclamations to ward off any insurgency and to ensure Tearia's continued prosperity!"

The crowd shouted words of support and encouragement. Whyn's breast swelled with appreciation, even as he suppressed his resentment toward the traitors he knew to be amongst them.

"A great lie has been circulating," he continued. "A lie that goes against the gods as well as our great city-state. And that lie is the Prophecy! It speaks of our downfall, of one who would see to our destruction. But I say to you now, there is no truth in it. It was a lie perpetrated by a sorceress of old—a Jecta witch who sought to rally our enemies and do us harm."

He lifted a finger and pointed it outward, moving it slowly from one end of the crowd to the other. "Any amongst you who speak of this so-called prophecy and spread its lies and give power to it where none is due is hereby declared a traitor. From this day forward any person—man, woman, or child—making reference to it will be permanently silenced."

Gasps could be heard as the meaning of his words sank in. The people of Tearia had always had the power of free speech, though rarely had anyone raised words against the city-state. But now their King was telling them there were limitations as to what they could say, and death was the consequence for anyone who disobeyed. The audience grew agitated and increasingly restless. The guards fingered their swords. People responded with startled screams. Women pulled children close to their sides.

Whyn raised his hands to silence the crowd.

"Why do you cry out?" he said. "Are you not loyal citizens of Tearia? If you are, you have nothing to fear. For if you are in-deed loyal, you will have no need to speak lies against her. Rest assured, I hold no grudge against any of you who have spoken of the Prophecy before this day. You did not understand what you were doing. No doubt you were lured by a misunderstanding of its purpose. But I tell you this: its purpose is to bring Tearia down, and for that reason, it is treason to speak of it from this day forward."

The crowd quieted for a moment, no doubt grateful that past transgressions were forgiven. Many of them had spoken of the Prophecy, whether they believed in it or not.

"The Jecta are the source of the deceptions that have brought us to this," Whyn said, "and for that reason Tearian residents will no longer be allowed to venture into Pobu. Anyone going to that place will be looked upon with suspicion. There is no busi-ness any of you should have there. There is talk of rebellion within the Jecta population. But fear not, the insurgents will be quashed before they can draw another breath against us. Too long have we been complacent. Too long have we turned a blind eye while plots are made against us."

The people encouraged their King with loud declarations against the Jecta. Whyn waited patiently, allowing the wave of support to rise and fall throughout the crowd. He raised a hand to silence them.

"Now I must speak to you of the most difficult thing of all, for it involves he who was once my brother. But Ruairi is my brother no longer. He chose to disobey the King's command and disregarded Temple law. For that he was unnamed. Now he is called Reiv and lives amongst the others of his kind. Some among you call him the "Unnamed One." Some even dare proclaim him a Transcendor, further fueling the lies. Only a traitor would call him such! I am here to tell you, he is no one. He was arrested for stealing not long ago. Many of you saw him with two others as they were taken. The Priestess in her mercy recognized him for what he once was and took pity upon him. He was released to Pobu, forever to remain outside our walls. But he repays her with lies and claims of a role in the Prophecy. I sought council with him, only to ask that he proclaim the truth about himself for the sake of Tearia. But he hides like a coward. Now I am forced to make this dictate. From this day forward the words 'Unnamed One' and 'Transcendor' are banned in his regard, as are any words related to prophecy or foretelling. I further proclaim that never again are the names 'Ruairi' or 'Reiv' to be uttered in Tearia. If any among you, or your children, have those names, or any part of them sounded within your name, they are to be changed. He no longer exists, nor do his names."

The crowd bowed their heads in submission, though varying degrees of opinion and sentiment could be heard throughout. The Priestess rose and smiled as her eyes scanned her subjects with satisfaction. But Whyn looked at only one person, a member of the royal family seated on the front row.

Brina sat with stiff grace, her expression rigid. Whyn nodded as their eyes met, but she clenched her jaw and turned her face away. Whyn was certain his aunt's heart was breaking, but he felt no pity for her. He knew she was a traitor and she knew it, too. Her time would come, but not yet.

# 19

# Promise Broken

Reiv sat next to Kerrik's cot, waiting. It was nearly High Sun, yet the boy still had not awoken. His breathing was steady, but his face was ashen, and the circles under his eyes left Reiv worried that recovery was not assured.

He placed a hand on the boy's forehead. "Kerrik," he said softly. But there was no response.

"He sleeps most of the time," Torin said as he entered the hut.

Reiv rose, gazing at Kerrik a moment more before joining Torin on the mats by the fire pit. Torin handed him a mug of coconut juice and a bit of dried meat. Reiv looked down at it with curiosity. They didn't have dark meat very often, but he knew better than to ask the Shell Seeker where he had gotten it.

"Don't worry," Torin said, "he'll awaken soon enough and then you'll wish he was still sleeping. His mouth is the one thing that hasn't slowed down." Torin laughed.

"I miss his incessant chattering," Reiv said. Then he frowned. "He still does not look well."

"It will take time, but he's much better than he was. He'll have you diving for shells with him in no time."

"I do not like the idea of him going back into the waters," Reiv said. "It is too dangerous, and he is too little."

"He is a Shell Seeker. That's what Shell Seekers do; they dive. He can't be afraid of the waters. If he is, he'll be forced into them. How else will he earn his living? No, if he shows any fear of it…well, just don't add to it."

"I have never seen him afraid of anything. Hopefully, that has not changed in him."

"I think you'll find he's still the same Kerrik, except for the physical scars and temporary lack of mobility. Look at it this way, now our little warrior has a great new battle to tell tale of. How many people can say they met Seirgotha?"

"Only me," Reiv said.

"But if it wasn't for *me*, you wouldn't have gotten to!" a tiny voice said from the cot.

Reiv grinned and made his way over. "That is right. What a lucky Prince I was."

Kerrik grinned back at him, his eyes sparkling in spite of the gloomy circles underneath them. "Tell me how you killed her, Reiv. Tell me how you killed Seirgotha!"

"Have we not already told you a hundred times?" Torin said from across the room.

"Well Reiv hasn't told me, and he was there, not you Torin."

Torin shook his head with resolution. "You're right, what do I know?"

Reiv told Kerrik the story, elaborating every detail with a peppering of exaggerated hand gestures and facial expressions. The boy watched in rapt attention, strangely quiet during the entire telling. At times Kerrik's eyes would grow wide and his jaw would go slack. With each new piece of gory information he would sit up a little straighter until finally he was upright and clutching at the covers.

"There, now you know it all," Reiv said.

"Not about the ritual; you haven't told me about that!"
Reiv's face grew solemn. "I do not wish to speak about it."
"Oh, please. Besides, I think you *have* to tell me," Kerrik said.
"Oh, and why is that?"

Kerrik twisted his mouth and rolled his eyes as though searching for a quick answer. "Because legend says that if the healer does not tell the sick person everything, then the sick person can't get well."

"You made that up, Kerrik," Torin said.

Kerrik looked offended, but guilty.

Reiv raised his eyebrows suspiciously. "Is that true? Are you making up stories?"

"Well...I'm not making it up. I mean, it popped into my head just now, so maybe the gods told it to me. You know, like the gods told you things."

"I see. Well, if I had known messages from the gods came so easily, I would not have gone through the ritual."

Kerrik put on his most disappointed face. No doubt his injuries had not weakened his power of manipulation. Reiv found his ability to fight that pitiful look far more challenging than battling sea snakes or facing gods. And so he told Kerrik about the ritual, although he did not tell him everything. When he finished, he paused, then asked, "Kerrik, do you remember the promise I made you?"

"What promise?"

"When we thought we had lost you, out there on the beach, I made you a promise."

"I don't remember. What was it?"

"I hesitate to tell you because now I must break it."

"I thought you said princes never broke their promises."

Reiv could not help but laugh. "Ah, so you do remember that much. Well, it seems I must break this one. I promised you I would teach you to fight with The Lion—"

Kerrik jerked with excitement. "You *will*? You—"

Reiv laid a hand on the boy's shoulder. "Calm yourself. What I have to tell you is that I cannot do it. I have found out something about the sword that I did not know before. I will never use it again, nor will you be allowed to."

Kerrik again looked disappointed, but Reiv quickly added, "I have something much better though."

He rose and walked over to his sleeping pallet and pulled the dirk from beneath it. Then he held it up and proclaimed, "This is what I used to slay Seirgotha. Dayn made it for me. It is not as long as the sword, but it is much stronger. It is made of star metal. This is what I will teach you with."

Kerrik's face lit up and he instantly reached for it. Reiv crossed over and placed the dirk into his unsplinted hand. It was heavy and at first the boy had difficulty holding it up. But he fixed his eyes upon it with determination and held the weapon out before him, the muscles in his skinny arm taut with effort.

"You must get stronger if you are to wield it," Reiv said. "It is a man's weapon, but I think you will soon be ready for it. You had best do what Jensa and Torin tell you if you are to get out of this bed. I will train no weakling."

Kerrik nodded, but remained silent. The excitement in his eyes said all that needed to be said.

That afternoon Reiv took Kerrik outside to sit in the warmth of the sun, but he would not allow the boy to take the dirk with him. Though everyone in the village knew Reiv had the weapon in his possession, there was too much risk to be seen with it again. The spy who had attempted to kill him during the ritual had not yet been found, although an old man who lived in the outskirts of the village had mysteriously disappeared in the days following Reiv's transcension.

Reiv's attention turned up the path where he could see Jensa making her way toward them. She had stayed the night in Pobu, and he was anxious to hear what had transpired during the rest of the meeting. She arrived smiling and gave Kerrik a hug and a kiss. "I think you've been out here long enough, Kerrik," she said. "Your face is flushed." She nodded at Reiv, her eyes conveying a silent message.

"Up you go," Reiv said as he lifted the boy into his arms. "Time for sleep. No arguments."

Kerrik mumbled a complaint as Reiv took him inside and lowered him onto the cot. But he closed his eyes as instructed. He had become unusually obedient since learning of the dirk.

Reiv exited the hut and walked over to Jensa who had moved to a cluster of palms nearby. Torin was at her side. "What news do you have?" Reiv asked.

"There's much to tell. Before I left Pobu I received word that your brother was crowned this morning. It seems he made some very interesting proclamations."

"But it has not yet been eight—"

"Regardless, the coronation took place this morning and the King has proclaimed that anyone speaking words of the Prophecy—or you—is a traitor. He has also banned all Tearian travel to Pobu and the outlying areas."

Reiv frowned but did not respond.

"This will make things more difficult for us to receive information from the Tearian clan," Jensa continued, "but..."

"What do you mean, Tearian clan?" Reiv asked.

Jensa smiled. "It seems Dayn had a way with words last night. He managed to organize those at the meeting into groups called clans. Apparently that's how people are grouped in Kirador. Not much else was accomplished, but that seemed to be enough for now. Naturally the Tearians and Shell Seekers grouped with their own, but the Jecta organized themselves according to locations within Pobu and the outlying areas. Each clan elected a representative to see that messages are conveyed more efficiently, and all are expected to brainstorm ideas to present at the next meeting. For now, Dayn has agreed to be the one to call the meeting locations and times. Until his wayward cousin decides to take his place, that is."

"Dayn did all that?" Reiv could not help but beam. "I knew he would do better without me there."

"Is that why you left?" Jensa asked. "You meant for Dayn to take over?"

"Something like that."

"Well," Jensa continued, "with news of the King's proclamation, the Tearians may need to give you a new name."

"They can call me whatever they wish, but I will claim no third name. Two in one lifetime is enough."

"The King didn't say anything about your name not being spoken outside of Tearian walls, so maybe he didn't feel it was worth the effort."

"I am sure he did not. He is not afraid of the Jecta. Whatever show of power he makes in Pobu will be for the Tearians' benefit. What of the Guard? Have their numbers increased in Pobu?"

"No. Actually, there were fewer there than usual this morning."

Reiv knitted his brow. "That seems strange," he said.

"Maybe they were all at the coronation," Torin offered.

"Perhaps, but that still does not seem right to me," Reiv said.

"Well, no matter what your brother has planned, he'll soon find the Jecta are a force to be reckoned with," Torin said.

"The will of the Jecta is strong," Reiv said, "but they cannot win by the sword."

"No," Jensa said, "but they still must be able to defend themselves. Dayn and Gair will continue to make weapons, but that won't be enough. The people must learn other means."

"When is our clan to meet?" Reiv asked.

"When do you think it should?"

"When do *I* think it?"

"Reiv, I volunteered Torin as our representative, but we will still expect your input," Jensa said.

"Well, I am sure Torin will agree that as soon as possible would be best. But I think you should first determine who is with us and who is not. You know your people far better than I do, Torin. What do you think?"

"I think you'll find there's more support here than not," Torin said. "You made believers out of most everyone with Seirgotha and your transcension. But you're right; it's time to weed out the doubters. Leave that to me." He grinned a sinister grin and headed for the village.

# 20

# First Kill

The first clan meeting of the Shell Seekers was held that night and attended by the majority of villagers. Those who did not attend sent a representative from their family or a message of support by word of mouth. There were none amongst them who voiced disapproval. It was agreed that the Shell Seekers did not have the skill for arm-to-arm combat against Tearia, and so it was decided the Seekers would hit them where it hurt. No longer would they provide shells, crafts, fish, or any other food from the waters for their upper class masters. Instead the Shell Seekers would hunt the seas only for their own needs. It was against Tearian law, and there could be dire consequences for it, but they determined the seas belonged to no one group of people, so should be available to all. Plans were then made to cease all transport of goods from Meirla to Tearia.

In Pobu similar ideas were drawn up. When the clans gathered at the next meeting a week later, it was decided that the Jecta would also cease providing services to the Tearians. There would be no loud pronouncement of their intentions, no verbal demands, just a peaceful, quiet boycott. It was agreed by all that the boycott would begin at the next Market, and so when the traditional days of trade came, the protest was sounded by the absence of many merchants. The Shell Seekers were particularly missed, for their wares were always popular with the Tearian elite. Many a disgruntled upper-class woman went home without jewelry for her personal adornment or vessels to house her lotions.

The Jecta laborers and craftsmen within the city walls usually left during Market to work a booth or visit their families in Pobu. And so they did, but this time they did not return to Tearia. The following day there was no one within the city to clean the garbage from the streets or debris from the sewers, just as there was no one to slaughter animals for food or tend to the bodies of the dead. The field laborers also did not go to their posts. Bewildered Tearian foremen stared at rows of untended crops, threatening punishment for their tardy charges. But the laborers never came.

One night, shortly thereafter, the Jecta made a great raid into the fields. The Tearians were not watching, they had never had reason to guard the crops, and so the nearest orchards were picked clean and the outlying fields stripped of their bounty. No longer would they settle for scraps, the Jecta determined, no longer would they slave with no pay. By law they were stealing, and they prayed hard to their gods for forgiveness, but most justified the act as compensation for the years of labor they had provided. It helped ease their consciences somewhat, although not the fear of reprisal from the Guard.

The Guard had been strangely absent in Pobu since the coronation of the King, but rumor abounded that their activity was increasing behind the walls of Tearia. Whispers claimed the King was plotting something, though no one yet knew what. After the raid on the fields, a host of Guard was dispatched to Pobu. They returned to Tearia with prisoners, even though they had found no evidence of thievery. Unbeknownst to the guards, the Jecta had devised a plan for hiding the food. Dayn had suggested the idea of cellars, almost everyone in Kirador had one, but there was no time for digging cellars, so crates were buried in the ground and hidden under furniture and rugs instead. The compartments were easy to disguise, as every floor in Pobu was dirt, and storage bins were simply covered over with the sweep of a broom. It never occurred to the guards to search beneath their feet.

The Tearian clan still managed to get information to Pobu, regardless of the King's ban of travel there. Brina knew of an abandoned tunnel beneath Tearia's walls that led to a nearby hillside, and was only too happy to share the location with trusted clan members. She had no idea why the passageway had been constructed, but had been using it for quite some time without incident.

The Tearian clan began to refer to Reiv as "Agneis". It was the perfect code name, they reasoned, as there was no law against speaking the goddess's name. The fact that it was a female name rather than a male one seemed the perfect ploy. Although they could not participate directly in the boycott, other than to get information out, there seemed to be more trash than usual tossed into their streets after that, and the sewers became mysteriously clogged. It made the streets of Tearia most unpleasant, but it was the least the Tearian clan could do.

In the days that followed, the Guard became more prevalent in Pobu. Loud proclamations were made that all Jecta were to return to work at once. The spectators nodded with faces of confusion, indifference, or carefully disguised amusement. The clans had gathered many to their cause. Even those who had initially expressed doubt had become ardent supporters. Tearian spies abounded and word quickly reached the palace that the boycott was a well-organized one. New arrests were made, which caused fear and unrest amongst the insurgents. But determination won out and the Jecta found courage in their hearts where it had long been lacking.

A meeting was called on the night of the fifteenth day of boycott. It was time for the Jecta to make known their demands. The meeting was held in a different location from the last. With each meeting, the crowd had grown larger. On this night, a building that had once housed multiple apartments was used. The interior walls had crumbled into mounds of earthen brick, and the roof was pocked with holes revealing the stars above. But the weather was pleasant and the place would accommodate the numbers expected to attend.

Dayn stood at the far end of a large room alongside Reiv and Torin, while Jensa and Alicine whispered off to the side. The crowd shuffled in, lighting candles as they entered, and spoke in hushed voices. The place filled quickly to capacity. Maintaining silence became almost impossible.

Dayn stepped forward and made a call to order. Most eyes were turned in his direction, but others stared at Reiv who was leaned against the wall at Dayn's back. This was the first meeting the former Prince had attended since he had told them the truth of things, and everyone was anxious to hear what he had to say.

"We won't be able to meet in secrecy much longer, if we're even doing so now," Dayn said. "Our numbers have become too great. It's only a matter of time before we're discovered. It's time we drew up some demands and presented them."

"Once they're drawn, who'll take them?" a man in the audience asked.

"That's something else we need to decide," Dayn said.

"Reiv should do it!" a voice shouted.

Dayn glanced back at his cousin and raised a brow. "Well," he said, turning back to the crowd, "that's up to Reiv."

The crowd called out encouraging words to Reiv, but he stood with hands clasped and said nothing.

"For now let's just get our demands sorted out," Dayn said.

Many suggestions were made, some simple, others grandiose, but it was decided to keep them reasonable and few. Once successful with the first demands, the others could

follow in time. Reiv, knowing the Tearians better than anyone, offered ideas and criticisms, but made no firm recom-
mendations. Eventually they decided on three demands.

The first demand was that all labor be compensated for
with coin, or in the case of field laborers, a reasonable per-
centage of the harvest. Second, the seas and forests were to
be declared the property of all, and any fishing or hunting
within them was a gods-given right. Third was the legal
right to assemble. It was unlikely the last demand would be
granted, but at least it was a good bargaining chip. If as-
sembly was denied, the Tearians would feel a sense of victory, especially if they conceded to the first two. But as-
sembly was of no real concern to the Jecta. The fact that it
was illegal hadn't stopped them from doing it anyway.

"Now comes the issue of how to present our demands,"
Dayn said. "If they're to be spoken verbally, we'll need to
decide who does it and when. If in writing, then Reiv will
have to put it to parchment for us. But there's still the
matter of how to deliver them."

Discussion buzzed within the clans, but there was no
consensus as to how to go about it. There was risk every
way they looked at it.

Reiv leaned in to Dayn and whispered in his ear. Voices
in the room grew silent. Reiv then took a step forward as
though to address the crowd, but before a single word could
leave his mouth, the door burst open. Loud cries split the
air as a host of Guard rushed in, their swords swinging.

Shouts and screams filled the room as people scattered,
tripping and shoving their way into corners and against
walls. The guards barked orders, but could barely be heard
over the hysterical screams of the crowd. The floor became
thick with bodies that had stumbled to the dirt. Candles
dropped, their flames extinguished. The room became a
place of shadowy confusion. The only light was that of the
moon streaming through the holes in the ceiling, leaving
spots of silver and gray.

Reiv grabbed Alicine and shoved her to the ground while Dayn threw his weight against the dark form of a guard rushing toward her. The guard stumbled and fell hard onto his back. Dayn grabbed up the sword that had dropped from the man's grasp and held it out with a shaking hand. The guard regained his balance and leapt toward him. Dayn thrust the blade forward, plunging it into the man's chest.

Dayn stared at the blood-covered sword with horrified eyes, then tore them away to search the darkness for a sign of his sister. He saw her huddled on the ground and ran to her. Grabbing her by the arm, he pulled her to his side. He then turned his attention to Reiv, who had been standing next to them. But his cousin was no longer there; he had vanished without a word into the madness that surrounded them.

The sound of sword upon sword could be heard, the clash of metal upon metal. Jecta and Shell Seekers rushed forward with weapons drawn and fought back in a wave of fury. Dark forms backed toward the doorway. The outline of narrow blades rose and fell in ominous silhouettes against the moonlight. The Guard retreated out the door and into the street where the clans followed. Before long, the street was a sea of screams and blood and bodies.

Dayn ordered Alicine to the darkness of a corner, and took to the streets with the others. He swung his sword wildly, not really knowing how to wield it. It was clear the other Jecta didn't have the skill either, yet the power of their determination seemed to be all they needed against the startled guards. Many of the Jecta and Shell Seekers had retrieved Guard weapons, but other clan members held very different armaments. In his confusion, Dayn had not given it much thought, but then in a moment's lucidity he realized they were using *his* weapons, the ones he had made in the secret back room of Gair's shop.

He spotted Gair. The dark profile of the huge man loomed over the rest. His powerful arms beat back guards as his voice boomed with every stroke he took. Dayn worked his way toward the smith, swinging his sword in a circular swath.

His attention was caught by the shadowy form of a Jecta backed against a nearby wall, and a guard with a sword positioned for the kill. Dayn called out and rushed in their direction. But he was too late; the blade had found its mark.

Dayn threw himself against the guard and knocked him forward. The man crashed against the wall, then fell to the ground, sprawled across his victim. Dayn grabbed the guard and rolled him over roughly, kicking the sword from his hand. The guard stared up at him, his pale eyes reflecting the hatred behind them. Dayn gasped and took a startled step back. It was Crymm, and lying next to him was Reiv.

Dayn thrust the tip of his sword to Crymm's throat. "You would kill your own Prince?" he screamed.

Crymm stared up at him with fear in his eyes, but then he looked past Dayn toward a presence at his back.

Dayn risked a glance over his shoulder and was relieved to see it was Torin. He kept his sword pointed at Crymm. "This scoundrel has caused us trouble for the last time," he said. "Watch him for me; Reiv's been hurt!"

Torin planted a knee on Crymm's chest and held the tip of his knife within an inch of the man's terrified eyes.

"Don't move a single lash," Torin said, "or you'll never see the light of day again."

Dayn dropped to his knees and ran his hand along Reiv's chest. It became instantly coated with blood.

"You're going to be all right," Dayn said, glancing around for something to stop the bleeding.

"I am fine," Reiv said, his words no more than a mumble.

Jensa was soon by his side, inspecting the gash beneath Reiv's ribs. Alicine rushed over and threw herself down next to them. She ripped a swath of material from her skirt and handed it to Jensa. Jensa pressed it against the wound.

"We have to get him out of here," Dayn said.

He lifted Reiv into his arms, surprised at how light he was. Reiv muttered a complaint, but his head lolled back and he protested no more.

The Tearian forces retreated into the night, gone to retrieve more Guard, or perhaps to plan an assault for another day. It was quiet now, except for soft sobs and the sounds of the survivors picking through the carnage. There were many dead— Jectas, Shell Seekers, and Tearians—but there was only one guard left in the street alive, and that was Crymm. Torin grabbed him up and shoved him into the shadows, while Dayn and the others made their way in the opposite direction.

They did not take Reiv to Nannaven's. That would be the first place the Guard searched were they to come looking for him. Instead they took him to Mya, a young widow who had been friends with Jensa for many years. When they arrived, she ushered them in quickly and without question. Mya directed Dayn, still carrying Reiv, to a bed covered by a quilt of mismatched patterns. As he laid Reiv down, she ran to a shelf and grabbed some clean cloths and a bowl that she quickly filled with water from a nearby bucket.

Dayn stood next to the bed, watching Mya's face as she ripped Reiv's tunic from his chest. She was an attractive woman, he noticed, but had a menacing scar on her face, a dark red ridge that ran from eye to upper lip. There was no time to contemplate her further, however, for she promptly shooed him away and motioned Jensa to the bed.

As Dayn stepped aside, he realized the room was more a shop than a home. There were pottery wheels and lumps of clay, and tables of urns and vessels along every wall and in every corner. A single lantern hung from the center beam and bathed the area in a golden glow. Cots could be seen along the far wall where three children slept.

A dark-haired boy of about nine rose from beneath his blanket, blinking at the sudden commotion. "Back to sleep, Farris," Mya commanded. The boy opened his mouth to protest, but a flash of his mother's eyes backed him down immediately.

Dayn peered over Jensa's shoulder at the gaping wound that was now revealed. It looked menacing, but did not seem to have caused major damage to Reiv's internal workings. The greatest risk was of infection. Jensa rose and Alicine took her place to help clean out the contaminants. Mya handed her cloth after cloth, while Jensa brought fresh water each time the bowl became red. When the bleeding finally slowed, Mya pulled a few bottles of potion from a nearby cabinet.

Dayn paced back and forth, his attentions vacillating between his injured cousin and other thoughts deep and troubling.

"He's not going to die, Dayn," Jensa said, recognizing his anxiety. "Agneis would not have sent him back only to have him killed so soon. Reiv has a purpose. Perhaps this was meant to happen."

"*Meant* to happen? Why would something like this be *meant* to happen?" Dayn said. "Reiv was meant to lead us. That's what was *meant* to happen, not this!"

Reiv moaned as Alicine dabbed at the wound. He slapped her hand away.

"Good! Stubborn as ever," she said.

Dayn marched to the bed and leaned over Reiv. "What were you thinking, going and getting yourself stabbed again. And by Crymm, of all people. I swear, I can't leave you for a minute!"

"You do not have to shout," Reiv said. He struggled to raise himself on an elbow and frowned at Alicine's probing fingers. "Gods, girl. Do you have to be so vicious?"

"Stop your complaining," she said. "Do you want this to fester?" She pushed him back down and poured a cool liquid into the wound. It fizzed a foamy pink.

"Well, I *mean* to shout," Dayn said, diverting Reiv's attention back to him. "You actually deserve far worse than this, you know. How are you supposed to lead a rebellion if you're confined to a bed?"

"I am not supposed to lead a rebellion, fool. You are."

"Can he be taken with fever so soon?" Dayn asked Alicine. "He's speaking gibberish."

Reiv gathered Dayn's attention with a piercing stare. "I am not speaking gibberish. The Unnamed One is to lead them."

"And that would be you," Dayn said.

"No, Keefe, that would be you."

Dayn jabbed his finger in Reiv's direction. "Don't try to shove your responsibilities off on me, *Ruairi*. I'm no leader, and I'm certainly no warrior. I just killed a man and have no intention of doing it again."

"Dayn," Reiv said, "not all wars are won at the end of a sword, but if it is swords that are needed—"

"I told you. I'm no warrior! You are the one who's supposed to do this, Reiv, not me. *You*! You're the one who was a prince. You're the one trained for battle. You've even spoken with a goddess for goodness sakes. I'm a nobody from Kirador who used to get his tail kicked on a regular basis. What sort of warrior is that?"

"Maybe the sort of warrior we need," Reiv said.

"No! I'm not who you think I am!" Dayn turned and stormed toward the door, then paused and barked over his shoulder, "I hope you have some strong medicine, Alicine, because it looks like he's going to need it." Then he left, slamming the door behind him.

Alicine jumped up and followed Dayn out. She found him around the side of the building, his back braced against the wall, muttering to himself.

"Are you all right?" she asked.

"No, I'm not all right!"

"Look, Dayn, I know you're upset about all that's happened, but—"

"But what? But I only killed a man? One minute I'm standing there and the next thing I know I'm plunging a sword into his chest. I don't even know who he was."

"It was him or you. You were only defending yourself."

"Maybe I could have done something different. What right did I have to kill him?"

"You reacted the way anyone would. Are you saying you would have given your own life to spare that of a stranger coming at you?"

"No, but..."

"What did you think all those weapons you made were going to be used for? Did you expect no blood to be shed?"

"Well, I didn't think I was going to be the one to shed it! And now Reiv's in there, wounded. This is too much."

"You know it isn't over. You wanted to help. Now's your chance."

Dayn shook his head. "I don't know if I have it in me, Alicine. And this nonsense Reiv's saying about me being some sort of leader. He's the brave one, not me."

"You're every bit as brave as he is," Alicine said. "I know you are."

"No. I've had enough. Let's go home...back to Kirador...tomorrow. I'll take you back tomorrow."

"We can't go back tomorrow."

"I thought you didn't want me to have anything to do with this. You've sure changed your tune."

"A female's prerogative," Alicine said. She offered an encouraging smile. "Reiv will be fine, you'll see. But we have to stay and see this through. You know that."

Dayn nodded reluctantly. "Yes, I know it. But I sure wish I didn't."

Reiv stared up from the bed at Mya. She was standing behind Jensa, handing her fresh cloths one at a time, concentrating on his wound. Reiv could not remove his gaze from her, but she had yet to allow her eyes to meet his. He suddenly recognized the unusual color of them—one brown, one blue—and an uneasy memory swept through him.

"We have met before," he said.

Jensa looked between the two of them and rose. "I'm going to go check on Dayn. Mya, will you take over for a moment?" Mya nodded and Jensa slipped quietly out the door.

Mya pulled the blood-spotted cloth from Reiv's wound and pressed a clean one onto it. "I'm surprised you remember."

Reiv remained silent for a moment, then said, "It was a long time ago."

"Yes."

"I am sorry about...that day."

"You have nothing to be sorry for," she said "You did nothing wrong."

"My father seemed to think I did."

"And you were backhanded for it as I recall."

Reiv winced at the memory. "My father had brought my brother and me to Pobu to see the 'enemy' as he called you all. I was only seven. I remember a guard pulling you out of the crowd and marching you over to us. You were probably younger than I am now. I should have protested, but I just sat there on my horse and didn't say a word."

"You were a child. What more could you do?"

"Well, apparently I did more than was expected."

"That you did," Mya said. "I remember standing next to your horse, my arm wrenched behind me by a guard, looking up at the face of a little boy with big responsibilities. But what I remember most was your eyes as you stared down at me. They didn't hold the look of superiority or disgust...not like your father's. It was something else. Then you touched my face." Mya sighed. "I always felt sad about what happened, your father backhanding you like that."

"Well, if it's any comfort to you, my father never struck me again. My face was bruised for a week and he worried grievously for it. The guards did not harm you, did they? I do not recall the scar."

"Do not concern yourself," she said.

Reiv's heart filled with guilt. Mya must have recognized it, for she said, "No matter what your father's guards did, I always felt somewhat fortunate to have been selected that day."

"Whatever for? You were so beautiful...I mean...you still are, but..."

"Oh, don't misunderstand me," she said. "I would prefer not to have a scar across my face, but it never kept me from being loved. I had a fine man for a while. Eben. Do you know of him?"

"He was a friend of Jensa and Torin. A potter wasn't he?"

"Yes. He was there the day you and I met," she said with a smile. "Torin was, too. Did you know that? You were lucky the two of them didn't kill you right then and there. They always blamed you for what happened to me. Those two, great friends, but friends who rarely agreed on anything. But they agreed on one thing that day: had one of them allowed the other to defend me, I would have been left with no one to scold for their stupidity."

"No wonder Torin hated me. I guess I cannot blame him."

"Well," Mya said, "he does not hate you now."

"You said you felt fortunate. Considering what they did to you, I cannot help but wonder why."

"I was terrified, of course. But you know, for some strange reason I have always carried the image of you with me. When I looked into your eyes, I was certain I saw compassion there. It gave me hope that things could get better when you were King."

Reiv turned his face to the wall, his role in her disfigurement weighing heavy on his mind. "I fear I would have let you down, then," he said. "If I had not been damaged, I would be walking the same path as my father."

"No you wouldn't."

Reiv turned his face to hers. "How can you be so sure?"

"Because your path was decided a long time ago. And you are walking it."

# ❦ 21 ❦

# Call to War

Two days had passed since the raid, and there wasn't a single person who had not heard of it. The number of dead was thirty-eight: twenty-eight Jecta, six Shell Seekers, and four Tearians. The guards were not included in the count, their bodies scavenged and tossed into the trash heap outside of town. Talk abounded amongst the Jecta that this was a call to war. Now all they needed was a battle plan and someone to lead them in it.

The weapons that miraculously appeared the night of the meeting had, luckily, been smuggled there in advance by Gair. He was not a man to take any chances. The fifty-one assorted daggers, knives, and swords that he and Dayn had made were now officially initiated by blood and distributed into Jecta hands. Dozens of Tearian swords had also been confiscated during the fight and were now assigned new owners along with the twenty or so Guard horses.

Gair and Dayn moved to a new location to fashion their weapons after that. The smithy, they decided, was too close to the main entrance of the city. They labored to produce

187

additional armaments, but all were crudely made; there was no time for fine craftsmanship. The Jecta, meanwhile, gathered up every tool at their disposal—hoes, sickles, stakes— anything that could be used against the enemy.

Reiv remained at Mya's to heal. Few knew he was there, but it was only a matter of time before word got around. He grew restless and grumpy, anxious to leave the confines of the bed and the stuffy room where Mya's three children never seemed to stop jumping, running, and shrieking around him.

"Gods, Dayn, get me out of here!" he said the afternoon of the third day. Dayn had come to check on him as well as give him an update. But Reiv was in no mood for company or reports, only rescue.

"You have to stay a while longer," Dayn said. "You're not yet healed and—"

"I am healed enough! Look—see? Healed." Reiv pulled down the bandage wrapped around his ribs. The wound had begun to scab, but it still oozed a bit and a puffy patch of red circled it menacingly.

"You're dreaming, cousin. Just be patient."

Reiv tossed his head back against the pillow and clenched his hands, kicking his feet beneath the covers. He sat up and grabbed Dayn's arms.

"I swear I will go mad here, Dayn. I will! You will come in one day and find me drooling and pouring porridge over my head. You have to help me, cousin. I beg you; save me from these—these—ruffians!"

Reiv threw a glare at the children, then toward the partially opened front door. Mya sat outside it, working a wheel. She seemed oblivious to his plight, as well as the assault of nervous energy and high-pitched voices going on in the room behind her.

"What is that woman thinking, leaving me trapped in here with these three? Those girls, squealing at all hours. And that boy...I swear, if he asks me one more question! Has Mya no mercy? Gods!"

Dayn laughed. "I'll see what I can do. Maybe we can get you moved somewhere more to your liking."

"Today, Dayn. Please," Reiv begged. Then his eyes brightened. "What about Torin and Jensa? I could go back to Meirla with them."

"They've already gone...left day before yesterday."

"What? So soon? Why did they not take me with them? I cannot *believe* this." Reiv raised himself on an elbow and threw off the covers. "You would think they would have at least had the decency to come by." He slid his legs to the side and dangled them over the bed, then scooted to the edge and pushed his feet to the floor. "Fine. I will get there on my own."

"Oh, no you don't!" Dayn said, placing a firm hand on his shoulder. "You're staying right where you are."

Reiv fell back onto the bed, his legs still dangling over the side. "Well what is going on then? No one has told me a thing."

Dayn grabbed Reiv's legs by the ankles and deposited them back onto the mattress, then pulled up a stool and sat. His face grew serious. "The Jecta are preparing for battle," he said.

"You must be joking. The Guard is thirty-seven hundred strong. How could the Jecta possibly—"

"They say the raid was a call to war." Dayn waved his hand in response to Reiv's obvious need for argument. "I know, but their resentments have been building for a long time."

"They are making a terrible mistake," Reiv said.

"Maybe, but right now they're only making preparations for defense. If the guards come back, they want to be ready."

"Speaking of guards, how is our friend doing?"

"Crymm is doing well. He sends his regards."

"I have had enough of his regards for one lifetime. So, what do you intend to do with him?"

"We intend to keep him in a state of discomfort until he can be used as leverage. He's not good for much else. That's one of the things I came to talk to you about. The Guard hasn't returned. We expected them back long before now. You know their ways, Reiv. What do you think they're planning?"

Reiv winced and inched himself up stiffly, then leaned against the wall at his back. "It depends on what they know, or think they know. I am surprised they did not return for their dead, at least. That should have been the first thing they did. And for Whyn not to send a great show of force in response; it is odd. Possibly he is trying to build up tension or is honing up the forces. The Guard has strength in numbers, but they have grown somewhat complacent over the years. It is possible they are reorganizing in preparation of a major assault to take care of us in one clean sweep. How many weapons do we have?"

"Not enough."

"Are you armed?" Reiv asked.

"No, and I only will be if absolutely necessary. I have no intention of using a weapon again if I can help it."

"That sounds very noble, cousin, but you have to defend yourself. You had best have one ready."

"I know, but we haven't enough weapons to go around and there's little time. We're going to have to find another way to win the battle with Tearia."

"In the meantime, what is being done?"

"More spies have been posted. At least if the Guard comes, there'll be enough warning to run in the other direction."

"How long do you think people can keep running?"

Dayn threw up his arms with frustration. "I don't know, Reiv! God, you act like I'm some sort of expert. We have few weapons. We have no plan. All we have are some people to watch the perimeter of the city and keep an eye out for a possible assault. Maybe the Guard won't come back. Maybe that was the end of it."

"I would not count on it," Reiv said. "Listen, Dayn, I cannot lie in this bed a moment longer. I have to get out of here."

"Oh? And where do you think you would go?" Brina asked from the doorway.

"Brina!" Reiv exclaimed, "What are you doing here? You know it is forbidden for Tearians to come to Pobu."

"That is true," she said, crossing over to the bed, "but I am no longer Tearian."

Reiv looked her up and down. She was no longer dressed in a silken gown of yellow, but in a simple frock of brown. "What are you saying?" he asked.

"I am saying I have made a choice. For sixteen years I have been secretly working against the customs of Tearia and have been forced to sneak around like a common criminal. Now I have been ordered by my own nephew not to utter your name. I will tolerate it no more, Reiv. I will say your name proudly and with all the love I feel in my heart for you. No one, not even a king, will tell me I cannot. When word reached me that you had been injured, well…that was the catalyst I needed. I am here now, at your side. But I have also come to offer a service. I understand the Jecta demands were drafted the other night, but have yet to be presented. I intend to present them."

"No!" Dayn and Reiv shouted.

"Oh, so now you two are going to tell me what to do?" She smiled and leaned over to inspect Reiv's wound. "I see you still have some mending to do."

"Do not try to change the subject, Brina," Reiv retorted. He brushed her hand away from the bandage. "It is too dangerous. To turn against your own family and then deliver a message of demands from the Jecta? What do you think it will accomplish?"

"I think it will send a very strong message, Reiv. I think it will drive a point home to your brother that his proclamations and continued persecution of the Jecta is reaching a breaking point. After all, if his own aunt would turn against him…"

"I will not allow it," Reiv said.

Brina laughed. "Well, I do not think you can stop it. You are, after all, confined to a bed."

"Well, *I'm* not," Dayn said.

"What will you do, son? Tie me to a chair?"

"If I have to."

Brina smiled. "Thank you for your gallant offer to tie me up, Dayn, but I think you will not do it."

Dayn did not respond, nor did Reiv. Both remained silent, working individual plans in their minds.

"Reiv, is The Lion still in Meirla?" Brina asked.

"Yes, I think so. Why?"

"It seems your brother wants it back. Perhaps it could be used as a means of negotiation...unless you have reason to keep it."

"You mean, give it back to him?"

"Yes, unless it still holds value for you."

"No. I have no more loyalty to it, but Whyn must not have it."

Brina narrowed her eyes suspiciously. "You say that with a purpose. Why must Whyn not have it?"

Reiv glanced at Dayn. "I have my reasons. I would rather destroy it than let it fall into my brother's hands again."

"*Destroy it*? But it has been in your family for generations. Why would you wish such a thing?"

"You must trust me on this, Brina."

"Why did Whyn give it to you in the first place?" Dayn asked. "If it's so valuable, why would he part from it?"

"An interesting question," Reiv said. "I am sure my brother had an ulterior motive."

"That he did," Brina said. "I became an avid listener after you told me your suspicions. I overheard him say the Priestess had expected you to use the sword against him that day, then the guards could have taken care of the problem for her." She shook her head. "I fear Whyn is tightly bound to her now. He is not the brother you once knew, Reiv. He has every intention of retrieving the weapon."

"Well, the mystery is solved," Reiv said. "What a disappointment it must have been for him that I did not try to run him through with it."

"Yes, quite a disappointment."

Dayn shook his head. "I don't think I'll ever understand the workings of the Tearian mind."

"Be thankful for that, dear," Brina said. She rose and walked to the door. "I understand the Shell Seekers are

sending representatives today. Jensa and Torin will be amongst
them. We will discuss the issue of presenting the demands
when they get here."

Dayn and Reiv nodded in half-hearted agreement.

"I am off to see Nannaven," Brina said. "She does not
know there will be a new guest under her roof. Dayn, will
you join me?"

"You are both going to just *leave* me?" Reiv cried.

"Brina, Reiv's going mad here. Do you think we could
find him other accommodations?"

Brina studied Mya's children who had been at quiet
play in the corner since her arrival. A sudden shouting
match arose between the boy and his sisters, and the room
filled with torrents of high-pitched screams.

"We will see what we can do, Reiv," she said. Then she
and Dayn exited the hut, leaving Reiv to burrow beneath
the covers.

When Dayn and Brina arrived at Nannaven's, Jensa
and Torin were there to meet them. Nannaven had not yet
returned from her rounds, but Alicine had been there when
the Shell Seekers arrived and was busy in the kitchen preparing buttered bread for the guests. She was delighted by
Brina's unexpected arrival and ushered everyone to the table for refreshment and conversation.

"Brina, what are you doing in Pobu?" Alicine asked.
"I'm happy you came, but I thought—"

"I have come to stay," Brina said. "It was time I made
my choice."

Everyone around the table smiled, seeming to understand her meaning, and no further discussion was made of
it. There were more pressing issues at hand.

Brina turned her attention to Torin and Jensa. "How
many came with you?"

"Three hundred," Torin replied. "The rest stayed in
Meirla to hold things in check."

"What about weapons?" Dayn asked.

"We brought what we could, but didn't have much. Additional spears were fashioned. There are some knives, the dirk you made, and Reiv's sword."

Brina gasped. "You brought The Lion?"

"Of course. It's the best weapon we could lay our hands on. Why wouldn't we?"

"I had just suggested to Reiv that it could be used as leverage," Brina said, "but he insisted it be destroyed."

"Destroyed?" Jensa said. "But we might have need of it. Reiv must have said that for emotional reasons. Maybe he doesn't like being reminded of what it once meant to him."

"Perhaps," Brina said, but the twist of her mouth and the arch of her brows indicated she had other thoughts on the matter.

They had only visited for a short while when a loud rap sounded at the door. Nervous eyes darted in that direction. Alicine made her way over and pulled the door open cautiously. She breathed a sigh of relief. "Mya, come in," she said.

Mya stood outside the door with an expression of anguish lining her face. Her youngest was clutched to her breast, the girl's chubby arms clasped around her neck in a stranglehold. The other daughter clung to her mother's skirts, while the boy stood solemnly behind her. Mya shooed the children in and glanced over her shoulder before entering.

"What is it, Mya?" Jensa asked, rising from the bench.

Mya lowered the child from her arms and stepped forward. "It's the Prince," she said. "He's gone."

"*Gone?*" a round of rattled voices exclaimed. Benches were pushed back noisily as everyone rose and stepped toward her.

"What do you mean, gone? Where did he go?" Brina asked.

"I don't know. He must have gone out the back."

"Did the children see anything? Did he say anything to them?" Brina asked.

Mya motioned her son over to her, but he lingered back. "It's all right, Farris," his mother coaxed. "Just tell them what you told me."

Farris lowered his eyes, clearly shamed. Mya placed a gentle hand on his head. "Come, now. No one will be cross with you."

The boy eased his eyes from the floor, then said, "The Prince was playing a game with us."

"What sort of game?" Brina asked. "You can tell us."

"A pretend game," Farris said.

"How was it played?"

"He said it was like one he used to play at the palace."

Brina smiled. "Reiv played so many games as a child. Could you tell me more about it?"

"The Prince said he had to pretend to be somebody, so we got him Mum's cloak and he put it on and swished around." Farris risked a smile. "It was funny. He looked like a girl."

"Then what?"

"He said he was going to hide so we could find him."

"And?" Brina nodded her head encouragingly.

"Me and Nely and Gem were to get under the covers so we wouldn't see him hide. That was the rule. Then he told us to count, but I was the only one who knew how. He said he would tell me when to stop, but he never did and it got really hot under there."

"So you got out from under the covers?"

"Yes, and he was gone." Farris looked embarrassed. "I shouldn't have let him trick me."

Brina smiled. "Well, Farris, you have nothing to be sorry for. It sounds to me like you followed the rules perfectly." Brina nodded toward the table. "How about you and your sisters have a seat at the table while the grown-ups talk. Alicine made some berry tea." Brina winked at him. "Perhaps your mum will put a little extra honey in it for you."

Farris grinned and nodded enthusiastically. Mya ushered him and the other children to the table while the rest of the adults moved to the corner. Once the children were settled with tea and buttered bread, Mya joined the group and the discussion began.

"He was in no condition to travel," Dayn said. "He could barely raise himself out of the bed."

"Maybe he's coming here," Alicine suggested.

"I didn't see him," Mya said, "but I came the shortest route."

"I think I know where he is headed," Brina said grimly. "He is going to Tearia."

"What?" Dayn said. "Why would he..." His voice trailed off as he recalled the last conversation they had had. "He didn't want you to go."

"No...he did not want me to go," Brina said.

"We have to stop him," Dayn said, making a dash for the door.

"Dayn...wait!" Brina called out.

Dayn spun to face her. "There's no time, Brina! Once he gets outside Pobu he could take any number of routes through the hills to get there. There'll be guards patrolling and—"

"We cannot make a spectacle of ourselves," Brina said. "Word cannot reach untrustworthy ears that Reiv may be making his way to Tearia."

Dayn took a calming breath. "You're right. Let's fan out and try not to draw attention to ourselves. If we go different directions, maybe one of us will find him and turn his stubborn backside around."

They all left to look, except for Mya who gathered her children and hustled them home. The group followed the impromptu plan as best they could, but none of them saw any sign of Reiv. By the time the sun had settled behind the hills, they knew it was too late. If he had indeed headed for Tearia, he would surely be there by now.

"We have to call a meeting," Dayn said when they had all returned to Nannaven's.

"A meeting?" Brina asked.

"If we're going to fetch Reiv back, we'll need a show of arms. The clans need to be called, weapons gathered—"

"Dayn, think what you're saying," Jensa said.

"I know exactly what I'm saying. Reiv is in Tearia and there's no telling what they'll do to him. Torin, where's his sword?"

"Hidden on the roof," Torin said.

"Good. If it's the sword Whyn wants, then it's the sword he gets. But only in exchange for Reiv!"

# 22
## Facing
## the Demon

It was dark when the Guard accosted Reiv outside the city walls. He had long since discarded Mya's cloak, having only worn it to hide his identity from the Jecta, not the Tearians. The dumbfounded guards dropped their jaws at the sight of the outlaw Prince strolling toward them as if he hadn't a care in the world.

Reiv was arrested and immediately taken to the palace, bypassing Guard Headquarters entirely. When they arrived, the guards marched him into the royal receiving room, the clank of their armor vibrating against the pit of his stomach. With a shove, they deposited him before Whyn, who was settled upon his throne.

"Have you come to beg my forgiveness?" Whyn asked.

Reiv remained silent as he raised his eyes to his brother, surprised by what he saw there. Whyn's once gentle features were now hard and drawn. His eyes were still pale, but Reiv could detect a hint of darkness in them. As Reiv studied his brother's face, he wondered if this was what he himself would have become. Would he have been manipulated by the Priestess just as easily? A part of him wanted to deny the possibility of it. The other part knew the probable answer.

"From the gash on your side it appears you are a part of the rebel movement," Whyn said. "I must honor the guard who put it there."

"Crymm will be most grateful," Reiv said.

"Crymm has ever had his uses. I wonder why he did not finish the job, though."

"When you see him, you may ask him that question."

"Oh? So he was not amongst the dead then," Whyn said.

"No, he is with us now. He has been a good source of information." Reiv raised his brow as though he knew something when, in fact, he did not.

Whyn rose, gathering his stature. "The guards tell me you walked into their midst without so much as a protest. What is it that brings you here? Surely it is no favor to me."

"I have come to present a list of demands from the Jecta."

Whyn stared at Reiv as though he were looking at an idiot. He burst into laughter. "Demands? From the Jecta? You must be joking."

"It is no joke, Whyn."

A shadow crossed Whyn's face. "You will no longer address me by that name. From now on, you will refer to me by the title I am due."

"What title would that be? Surely you do not expect me to call you King. A king would not—"

"I grow tired of your disrespect!" Whyn shouted. He gestured to a guard who marched over and grabbed Reiv by the back of the neck, forcing his knees to the ground and his head to the tile.

Whyn motioned the guard to let loose his hold, and Reiv yanked his head up and stared at his brother with contempt.

But a sudden movement to the right redirected Reiv's attention. His breath stalled momentarily as Cinnia strolled toward the dais. Her flowing nightgown was pinned at her shoulders and draped down her body, her alluring shape evident through the nearly transparent material.

"Husband," she said, "I heard we had a guest." She glanced at Reiv with a warm smile, but her eyes were cold as stone.

"Cinnia," Reiv managed to say. As his gaze followed her, she seemed different somehow, and yet her beauty still had the power to enslave him. That much, he realized, had not changed.

Whyn's eyes darted between them. His face went stiff, an old uneasiness resurfacing. "You should not be here, wife," he said. "This is official business, not a social event."

Cinnia's lips formed into a pout. "Oh, please, it has been so long since we have seen your brother. Surely you would not deny me a moment." She did not wait for a response and walked toward Reiv who was still kneeling on the floor. She looked him up and down, then circled him slowly, examining him as if he were a horse at auction.

Humiliation swept through him as her critical stares scraped over his body. But his feeling of degradation quickly flared to anger. "Would you care to inspect my teeth?" he snapped. "Or would you prefer I perform a trick for your entertainment."

Cinnia seemed taken aback for an instant, then her temper rose to match his. She glared at his hands and said, "No, I can see you are of inferior stock."

"Oh, and you are welcome, by the way," Reiv said. He hoped his comment would remind her that his hands were as they were because of his love for her. But she did not seem to notice, nor did she seem to care.

She tossed her head and marched back up the dais. "I am going to bed, husband. You will join me there soon, will you not?" She threw a knowing glance at Reiv, then raised herself on tiptoes and kissed Whyn on the lips. As she strolled from the room, she displayed exaggerated grace, no doubt done at Reiv's expense.

Whyn stared after her as she left. He sighed loudly. "You know, I really am tired...and the bed sounds particularly good right now. We will continue this discussion in the morning."

He motioned the guard with a nod of his head, and Reiv was yanked up and pushed toward the corridor leading out.

"Yes, there is still much to discuss, I can assure you!" Reiv called over his shoulder. But a swift punch to the wound under his ribs stopped any further comment on his part.

As Reiv was shoved against the wall of the holding cell, he felt anger well within him. It was not at his brother who had betrayed him, nor at Cinnia who no longer loved him. It was not even for the once faithful guard who had just shoved him into the cell. No, this anger was at himself. He had mishandled the whole thing; he knew that. Once again he had allowed his emotions to get in the way. He should have kissed Whyn's feet, whatever it took. But he had not. Now here he was, back in a cell, and he had accomplished nothing.

As his eyes adjusted to the dimness, he realized he was not alone in the holding area. He had been ushered into a private cell, recently vacated by the stench of it, but the cell across the way was filled with at least a dozen prisoners. Some he recognized, others he did not; but they all seemed to know him. They stared at him in depressing silence.

A man pushed his face between two bars, his eyes slanted in Reiv's direction. "How'd ye end up in this place, Prince?" he asked.

Reiv walked to the bars of his own cell and surveyed the grim faces across the way. "I came to present your demands," he said.

The faces seemed to cheer for a moment, then fell with realization. "Must've gone bad if you're stuck here with the likes of us," someone said.

"Be encouraged, friends," Reiv said. "I am to meet with the King again in the morning to discuss the issue further." He forced a confident expression, but his insides felt decidedly less assured.

Reiv moved away from the bars and curled up on the straw. *You will have to grovel,* he told himself. *Just do it.*

The next morning Reiv was awakened by the rattle of keys and a loud voice barking orders for him to get up. When he didn't do it quickly enough, he was forced to his feet by a swift kick. He was immediately marched from his cell and led in the direction of the temple, a detour he hadn't expected. As he nervously surveyed his surroundings, he realized the sun was up, but the sky was a blanket of grayish yellow haze that had settled upon the landscape. Pulling in a deep breath, he noticed the air was strangely thick. It was as though he had to concentrate to breathe.

When they reached the last step of the temple, the guard ordered Reiv to halt. He waited in silence until eventually he was led through the double doors and down the corridor to the Room of Transcension. There the Priestess sat on her throne directly in front of the statue of Agneis. Reiv stood before her, moving his eyes up the towering marble deity at her back. The icon looked nothing like the Agneis he knew.

The Priestess held Reiv in her icy stare, while Whyn, who stood beside her, watched him with an expression of mockery. Reiv's mind raced for a plan of escape. As though anticipating his move, the guards pressed closer to his side, then forced him to his knees.

"I understand you have come bearing demands from the Jecta," the Priestess said. "Brave, but foolish." She rose and glided down the steps of the platform, then stopped and stood before him. "You have angered the Goddess with your traitorous ways. She is not pleased."

"You do not speak for Agneis," Reiv said, surprised at his own boldness.

The Priestess's fair features grew hard and for an instant her eyes glowed. "Blasphemous words. You will suffer greatly for them."

"Perhaps, but not by the will of Agneis."

The Priestess laughed. "You have no knowledge of what the Goddess wills. Only I have the power to determine that."

"You determine nothing in her regard."

"And how would someone like you know this?"

"The Goddess told me."

An unreadable expression crossed the Priestess's face and for an instant her features seemed to morph into those of another. But her likeness resumed its pale beauty as her golden lips stretched into a cutting smile. "Only one who travels to the After Realm can speak with a goddess. Perhaps I will send you there."

"Thank you, but I have already been. That is where Agneis told me the truth about you. I know who you really are."

Reiv struggled to his feet. The guards moved to shove him back down, but the Priestess waved them away. "I heard rumors of your transcension," she said, "but I took them for nothing more than that. I will not make that mistake again."

"That is only one of the many mistakes you have made," Reiv said. "But I will keep that information to myself, I think."

"It will be easy enough to learn your thoughts," she hissed.

The Priestess splayed her fingers before Reiv's face, sending a host of terrors scurrying through his mind. Cold flooded through his veins, freezing his heart, trapping his breath. She slithered through his thoughts, exploring even the most private corners. Reiv attempted a retreat, but his brain could not seem to get the message to his feet. His limbs, his voice, his will, all were frozen in place.

The torches that lined the walls flickered as a rush of cold air swept the room. The Priestess's crystal eyes dimmed, then darkened like parchment charred by flame. Her mental attack suddenly ceased, but then her body began to elongate. Slowly...slowly, she coiled her body around his.

Reiv closed his eyes as he fought to free his mind from her. *Illusion plays on your hopes and fears,* he whispered to himself.

The Priestess tightened her grip; Reiv clenched his fists, then refocused what little strength he had on the advice Agneis had once given him. *You must accept and understand your own heroic path...*

"Foul boy!" the Priestess hissed. "I shall strip the violet from your eyes!"

Reiv's eyes shot open as the evil form breathed her stench upon his face. His eyes became filled with searing pain. He screamed and tried to raise his fists to them, but was unable to move at all.

The pain diminished as a wave of comfort rolled through him. The oppressive weight that encircled his body retracted with a hiss, releasing him momentarily. The Priestess moved to regain her hold, but a voice not his own escaped Reiv's lips and said, "Serpent of Evil, you will not harm this boy!"

Reiv felt strength return to his body, and he stepped around the Priestess in a wide circle. She followed suit, the two of them facing each other poised for battle. Reiv's fear mounted; he knew he was not under his own command. As though reading his thoughts, the voice that had left his lips whispered into his mind: *Do not be afraid, Reiv. I am here.* Then he knew; Agneis was with him. He searched deep within himself for what was left of his courage.

The earth trembled and a great rumbling noise filled the room. Lanterns swung wildly; statues teetered on their bases. One by one the lights flickered and extinguished. The room went black as the blackest night.

Reiv's feet lifted from the floor, his body twisting in a helix of mystical power. He threw up his arms, convinced he would soon be dashed against the ceiling. His breath quickened and his eyes grew wide. He worked to focus on his surroundings, but he could make out nothing at all. His ascension ceased, and he hovered mid-air, his arms and legs extended. With eyes clinched tight, he awaited the inevitable drop to his doom.

"Leave this boy, foul demon," Agneis said through him, "or my wrath will put an end to you forever."

"You have no power over me, Agneis," a deep voice said as it swirled around Reiv. "The Unnamed One of your misguided prophecy will bother me no more."

"You know nothing of prophecies," Agneis said.

The evil presence tightened its grip around Reiv's body, then let out a deafening shriek. It whipped with lightning-like speed, sending Reiv careening into a wall. He hit the stone hard and crumpled to the marble surface below. The impact knocked the breath from his lungs and shot new agony into his bones.

"Your cruel treatment of my children will stop with this one!" Agneis screeched.

Reiv raised himself onto all fours, desperately trying to draw air into his deflated lungs. "Reiv," Agneis whispered. "Do not allow her illusions to become yours. She will play upon your fears." Reiv staggered to his feet, trying to expunge the image of serpents from his mind. He had found the strength to slay one for Kerrik, but this one would require much more. It demanded the power of the mind, not that of the sword.

Then it began, the battle between the Demon and the Goddess, Reiv trapped in the middle of it. His eyes could see nothing, but his mind played the events unfolding around him. The room grew small, or perhaps it was he who had grown large. The Demon uncoiled its body to match Reiv's unnatural stature, and reared its head to strike. Simultaneously they lurched toward each other, enmeshed in a fury of wills.

Anguish could only describe what Reiv felt as they battled back and forth. At times Agneis would provide him with a moment's respite, but the serpent would regain its hold on him more cruelly than before. Reiv's limbs went weak as excruciating pain consumed him. It stripped him of his energy, of his very will to live. His spirit ebbed, and he knew he could bear it no more. Only Agneis could save him now.

# 23

# Forewarned

Dayn threw himself against Nannaven's table and held on for support. The room was spinning, and a blinding light was pulsating behind his eyes. He clutched his roiling stomach with one hand and held fast to the table's edge with the other.

Brina rushed over and grabbed him by the arm. "What is it?" she cried as she struggled to keep him on his feet.

"Everyone has to get out!" he said.

"What are you talking about?" Brina asked.

"Spread the word that everyone must get out of Pobu!" Dayn's breath grew labored. He threw himself onto the nearby bench, then raised his eyes to Brina. "Do it!"

Brina looked at him, confused, then raced out the door, shouting an order to the men who were waiting outside.

Alicine moved to Dayn's side and placed a comforting hand on his back. "Is it the same?" she asked.

"Worse. Did you feel it?" Dayn asked her. But he knew in his heart she hadn't.

The earth continued to waver. Dayn's nausea increased, but this time he knew it was not from a bit of undigested

food or the symptoms of an illness. The earth was unsteady,
he was sure of it, and the images were not illusions, but visions from a higher power.

Nannaven rushed to her herb cabinet and threw it open.
"What are you feeling, boy? Tell me," she said, shoving bottles and jars aside.

"Nothing your potions can help," he said. He doubled
over, dry heaving as he stared at the blurry ground.

Nannaven grabbed a small pottery jar from the cabinet,
then a mug and a water jug. She hurried to the table, prepared to mix him up a brew.

Dayn raised his head. "There's nothing you can do for
it. It will have to leave in its own time."

Nannaven looked at him with anxious eyes. She nodded
and set her supplies on the table. "How can I help?"

"You can leave Pobu with the others."

Nannaven headed straight for the hearth and began to
pull at a large stone embedded in it.

Dayn doubled over again, retching into the dirt. He
wiped his mouth with the back of his hand and shot his
attention to Nannaven. "Didn't you hear me?" he said as
he spat the foul taste from his mouth. "You have to get out.
There isn't much time."

The Spirit Keeper continued to work the stone until at
last she was able to ease it from the hearth. She tossed it to
the ground, then reached into the opening and pulled out a
thick tome. Dayn and Alicine watched as she hustled to her
bag of medicinals and shoved the book inside.

"What are you doing with that?" Alicine asked. "You
know it's forbidden. If you're caught..."

"I do not think it matters now," Nannaven said. She
grabbed her shawl and headed for the door.

"You, too. Out of here," Dayn barked at Alicine.

"I'm going with you, Dayn," she said.

"No...you're—"

"You heard me. I'm going with you."

Dayn knew there would be no debating it, but his gut felt like retching again at the thought of his sister facing a battle at his side. He nodded, grim faced, and attempted to rise from the bench, but found himself back down in an instant. He worked to focus his eyes on something stationary, but there was nothing in the room that wasn't spinning. He clenched his eyes until the feeling subsided, then squinted them open to scan the room. He sucked in a breath. The room had calmed at last.

He stood up with shaking legs and wrapped the scabbard that held The Lion around his waist. Then he shoved the dirk into his belt and headed for the door. "It's time," he said.

He and Alicine hustled out and into the street. They made their way quickly into the crowd of men and horses that stood ready and waiting. Many voices could be heard murmuring in uneasy curiosity at the order Brina had shouted but moments before. Dayn and Alicine climbed atop two of the Guard horses that had been confiscated during the raid. They took their places next to Torin, Jensa, and Brina who were also mounted and ready to ride. Dayn was horrified to see so many women amongst the volunteers, and insisted they remain behind. He even made another attempt to dissuade Alicine from coming. But she and the other women would hear nothing of it, and the men did not seem inclined to back Dayn up. They saw no reason why a woman who wanted to fight should stay behind.

The remainder of the twenty or so horses in the group were ridden by the clan leaders who led the procession through the streets. They were followed by hundreds of others, Jecta and Shell Seekers, both men and women, all armed with makeshift weapons. More and more joined them as they advanced down the street. Others hurriedly made their way in the opposite direction, obeying the sudden and disturbing order to evacuate to the hills.

The brigade paused in the courtyard that led out of the city. Gair approached from the smithy with Crymm in his charge. The guard's hands were bound at his back and a rope was tied to his neck like a leash on a dog. Dayn glared down at Crymm as Gair took his place on the largest horse. "Lead on, young Dayn!" Gair bellowed.

The band of Jecta was at least a thousand strong. It had become more than a rescue party; it had become an army. It moved like a shadow through the haze still cloaking the hill-sides. Tearia loomed before them, but all that could be seen was a dark shape where a bright city usually stood. Dayn raised his hand to stop the approach. The troop at his back halted, silent and waiting.

Torin nodded in Dayn's direction and kicked his heels into his horse's side. He took off in a full gallop toward the city, a rolled parchment clutched in his hand. He was not gone long and when he returned, his face bore the look of supreme satisfaction.

"Was it was delivered without incident?" Dayn asked.

"I'll cherish the looks on their ugly faces for the rest of my life," Torin said. "They didn't have a chance to react before I was gone."

"Good," Dayn said. "Now we wait."

The Room of Transcension became warm and instantly bright again. The flames in the torches glowed without so much as a flicker. Reiv lay sprawled upon his belly. Whyn was crouched beside the throne, while his guards cowered against the far wall. The Priestess was nowhere to be seen.

Whyn rose and stormed down the steps, shaking with fury. "Where is she!" he screamed. He fell to his knees be-side Reiv and grabbed him by the hair, jerking his head from the floor. "I said, where is she!" Whyn threw Reiv's head against the tile and rose to stand over him. "Guard! Bring me my sword!"

The guard moved to comply, but just then a messenger ran into the room, a rolled parchment in his hand. "My Lord," the messenger said between gasping breaths, "a message from the Jecta."

Whyn took the parchment and unrolled it. His face spasmed as he read the words.

He glared at Reiv. "Guard, bring him. We have business at the gate."

# 24

# A Vision Fulfilled

Reiv was marched up the steps to the parapet and shoved against the wall, his breath nearly knocked out of him at the impact of rib against stone.

"Now you will see what happens to enemies of Tearia," Whyn said.

Reiv gazed out past the wall and worked to focus his eyes through the haze. A slight breeze stirred the murky landscape, but little could be seen other than a large, dark shadow draped across the hillside. The wind picked up, dissipating the haze here and there. The sun broke through in quick ebbing streams upon the countryside.

Reiv gasped out. "Gods, Whyn, what do you intend to do?"

"I intend to see that Tearia is safe."

"Safe? Safe from what? Safe from those who ask only to live as the gods intended them?" Reiv clenched the cold stone of the wall and leaned out, staring at the ragtag Jecta army massed on the hillside.

Whyn yanked him back by the arm and shoved him to the ground. "What right do you have to dictate what the gods intend?"

Reiv grabbed his wound, now reopened and bleeding. "You would murder innocent people in the name of what, Whyn? In the name of Tearia? Is that the legacy you wish for yourself? Do you wish your name to be forever synonymous with the slaughter of innocents?"

"My name will long be remembered as the King who saved Tearia from the rabble that would seek to bring her down. Those innocents, as you call them, will be remembered only as traitors, nothing more. If blood is required, then that, dear brother, is the price."

Reiv pulled himself up and searched Whyn's face for the brother he once knew. "So you will be the Red King after all," he said.

Whyn appeared startled by the remark, then collected his pride with a toss of his head. "Something you would have never been suited for."

"I thank the gods for that."

Whyn stepped to the wall and gazed toward the hills. "It seems your people wish to negotiate for your return. I will be happy to take you to them. There is no reason why you should not all suffer the same fate."

Whyn barked an order and Reiv was led down the steps to a regiment of mounted guards gathered at the gate. Mahon could be seen seated upon a great chestnut horse. He was dressed in full armament and his face was set in a careful display of Guard fortitude. As Reiv walked past him, he could not help but notice a hint of distress in his uncle's eyes. He attempted to decipher any message of hope that might be there, but Mahon reined his horse and abruptly turned away.

A guard at Reiv's back pushed him forward. "Bring his mount," Whyn ordered.

The guard complied and returned, yanking the reins of a dark brown horse with a blue-black mane. The horse reared, its eyes wild with fright, and stomped around in a circle while the guard shouted and fought to control it. The sudden snap of a whip brought the horse to a halt. The animal's flank twitched where a cruel new mark was etched.

"Gitta," Reiv whispered, recognizing the horse he had once called his own. He stepped toward her, but an arm was thrust in his path. He felt his wrists as they were bound in front of him, but all he could do was stare into the eyes of the frightened horse.

"She will let no one ride her," Whyn said. "You had best hold on tight." Then he laughed and mounted a stallion whose eyes were as cold and black as its sleek muscular body.

Reiv was lifted up by a giant of a guard and thrown onto Gitta's back. He pressed his thighs against her and leaned in, whispering soft words into her ear. She calmed immediately, much to the chagrin of Whyn, who snapped an order for the gates to be parted.

Reiv glanced behind him and felt his heart sink. As far as he could see, the Guard was assembled for battle, the metal of their polished armor glimmering even in the dull morning light. The pace of his horse quickened. He turned his attention forward as he was led up front to join Whyn and Mahon. Thirty or so guards took their places as escorts, while the rest stayed behind the walls and waited with anticipation.

"Why are you going?" Reiv asked Whyn, anxiety creeping into his voice. "You are King. Should you not stay behind?"

"I have nothing to fear. Besides, it might be fun."

"What about the risk of damage to you? Tearia would not tolerate a damaged King, just as it would not tolerate a damaged Prince."

Whyn scoffed. "The Jecta would not dare harm me. Even if they entertained such a notion, the Guard will see to it they do not. I appreciate your concern for my safety, but do not worry about me." Then he grinned and urged his horse forward with a kick of his heels.

The eerie fog began to thin, leaving the landscape bathed in milky light. Twenty Jecta on horseback could be seen advancing slowly toward them. When they were within a reasonable distance, their fair-haired leader raised a hand to stop his line. Both Jecta and Tearians stood face to face, eyeing each other with disdain.

Reiv's belly churned as Dayn advanced his horse a few more paces. What was his cousin thinking, facing Whyn and the Guard like this? Then Reiv realized it was he who had declared Dayn the warrior that the Jecta needed. He felt a sudden wave of regret. Even in the distance he could see that Dayn had taken great pains to present himself as that warrior. A broad leather band held Dayn's hair back, and his face was painted with black designs that lined his forehead and circled his eyes. A glimmer at his ear indicated he wore an earring, something he swore he would never do. The dirk was shoved into his belt, clearly in view, and a barely visible sheath hung at his waist. Reiv held his breath as he watched his cousin stare Whyn down. Dayn's painted face may have exuded bravery, but Reiv knew the expression was as painted on as the designs that outlined it.

Dayn caught Reiv's eye and nodded, but Reiv averted his eyes rather than have Whyn see an acknowledgement between them. Reiv's gaze moved toward the riders at Dayn's back and he felt himself go weak. Torin was there, and Jensa, Alicine, and Brina. He hated that they were there on his account and wished more than anything he could scream them all away. For a moment he thought to do so, to shout for them to run for their lives. But then he felt Mahon move his steed forward a step or two. Reiv glanced over at him. The man was staring with suppressed, but obvious horror at the sight of his wife sitting amongst the others.

"We have come to offer a trade," Dayn said across the distance. "We do not wish to fight. We only wish to negotiate for Reiv's return."

"What could you possibly offer that is worth any sort of trade?" Whyn called back. He grabbed the reins of Reiv's horse and advanced several steps with Mahon at their side. He ordered the rest of the guards to stay back.

Dayn reached out his hand and Gair handed him the rope. Dayn kicked in his heels and advanced slowly. The rope in his hand grew taut. Gair nudged Crymm forward with a kick of his foot. The guard stumbled behind Dayn's horse, a mixture of humiliation and hostility blanketing his features. Dayn stopped within several feet of the Tearian group, then yanked the rope.

"I believe this belongs to you," he said as Crymm lurched forward.

Whyn guffawed. "There is little value in that. No, I think there will be no trade."

"Oh, you misunderstand me. You can have your dog back for nothing. What I've come to trade is this." Dayn pulled the Lion Sword from the scabbard at his waist and held it high. Sunlight burst forth from the evaporating clouds. The blade glistened, its reflection dancing in Whyn's covetous eyes.

"You are a thief!" Whyn hissed.

"Yes, that's true," Dayn said with a sigh. "I did in fact steal it. From Reiv." He looked at Reiv and shook his head. "Sorry, cousin."

Mahon's mouth dropped.

Whyn narrowed his eyes. "*Cousin*? Why do you refer to him as such?'

"Because he is my cousin, just as you are. Brina is my mother. I was once named Keefe, but now I am Dayn." Dayn cocked his head. "We resemble each other, you and I, don't you think? If I hadn't been sent away and unnamed as I was, maybe we would have been friends. Funny how things work out, isn't it."

"Unnamed?" Whyn rasped the word. His horse sensed his agitation, and reared and danced about. Whyn held tight to the reins and twisted his head to keep his focus on Dayn. "Lies!" he shouted as he forced the horse to a halt.

Brina advanced her horse next to Dayn's. "My son does not lie," she said.

"Brina...no," Mahon whispered. His face went ghostly white and his eyes fluttered as though he were about to faint.

"So, Brina, you are in on this conspiracy," Whyn said.

"Yes, nephew, I made my choice," she said. "I side with the people I love. You were once included in that love, you know."

"You never loved me as you love Reiv!" Whyn said.

"Of course I did, until your words became nothing but lies. You are no longer the nephew I loved, Whyn, though I pray he is still in you somewhere."

"What's it going to be, cousin?" Dayn said. "Do we have a trade?" He rotated the sword in his hand and eyed it with interest.

"I will trade nothing for that which already belongs to me!" Whyn shouted.

Then Reiv spoke up. "But you gave it to me, Whyn. Remember? As I recall you said it belonged to me. Were those not your exact words?" Then Reiv fixed Dayn his stare. "And because it is mine I demand that it not be traded. Under no circumstances is it to find its way into my brother's hand, Dayn."

"I have had enough of this game!" Whyn said. He slid his sword from its sheath with a hiss of metal, and raised it above his head as he shouted a command. The gates of Tearia burst open and a host of Guard on horseback swarmed through. Those at Whyn's back lurched forward.

Dayn raised a signal, and the Jecta streamed toward him, their voices lifted in high-pitched battle cries. Those on horseback rushed to Dayn's side, their weapons poised and ready.

The Tearian cavalry was upon the Jecta in an instant. A rain of arrows streamed through the sky, sailing in opposite directions. Warriors from both sides collapsed to the ground. Horses fell, spilling their riders into the dirt. The Guard advanced with spears, crossbows, and swords. The Jecta met them with knives, sickles, and bows of their own design. The battle roared in an ear-splitting explosion of red, silver, and brown.

Reiv struggled to stay on his horse, but Gitta bolted, and he soon found himself tumbling to the ground. Hooves

thundered around him, kicking dirt into his face. He rolled
to his knees and staggered up, his hands still bound. Two
guards galloped toward him, their swords swinging in his
direction. He threw his body to the side and landed hard
onto his belly.

Reiv raised his head and scanned the dusty swirl of horse
and warrior. He saw Jensa and Torin in the distance, still
mounted and fighting side by side. Brina and Alicine were
nowhere to be seen. Reiv rose, panicked for their safety, but
then he spotted Dayn reining his horse in his direction. Dayn
urged the animal forward, but Crymm, whose bonds had been
cut, suddenly rushed forward, yanking Dayn from his mount.

The Lion fell from Dayn's grasp and landed with a *thud*
into the dirt. Crymm dove and retrieved it in a flash. Dayn
pulled the dirk from his waistband and positioned his body
for defense. With a loud shout, the guard lunged at him, but
Dayn leapt aside. Crymm spun to face him, his face contorted
with rage. He lunged again, slamming the force of his weapon
against that of his less experienced opponent.

Reiv screamed out as Dayn was knocked to the ground.
Crymm grinned as he straddled Dayn, now on his back.
Crymm raised The Lion for the strike, but paused as though
savoring the moment. Reiv rushed forward and threw his fists
against him, shoving Crymm into the dirt. The guard rose
and wheeled to face Reiv, then leapt forward, a guttural sound
resonating from his throat. Reiv staggered back, while
Crymm's eyes gleamed with anticipation.

A riderless horse appeared out of nowhere and careened
toward them. It reared on its hind legs, bringing the weight of
its massive body down upon the unsuspecting guard. Crymm
fell to the ground, contorted and unmoving. Blood pooled
around his head, tracked into the dirt where the horse had
stepped away from him.

Gitta made her way to Dayn and lowered her head. Dayn
grabbed hold of her mane and pulled himself to his feet, then
rushed over to cut the bindings from Reiv's wrists. They both

paused to stare at Crymm, neither saying a word. For a moment the man seemed to stare back at them, but his eyes saw nothing at all.

Reiv turned and search the ground. "Where is the sword! Where is the sword!" he cried. Then he froze. Whyn could be seen climbing back onto his mount nearby, the Lion Sword grasped in his hand.

Mahon galloped toward Reiv and Dayn. Reiv tensed, certain his uncle meant to kill them both. But the man sped past and headed for Brina, who could be seen fighting to control her frenzied horse.

"Get to the back of the line!" Mahon shouted at her. "Take the women to the back of the line!"

Brina nodded, pale faced, and steered the horse as best she could. She commanded the animal in Alicine's direction, and the two of them retreated from the chaos.

Whyn thundered toward Dayn and Reiv, a blood-curdling scream tearing from his lungs. Reiv leapt to the side and fell, sprawled across a body. A vision flashed before his eyes—this had happened before! He rolled off quickly, then rose to his hands and knees. A stickiness coated his palms; he jerked them back and wiped them across his chest. A shadow suddenly swept the ground before him. The horse and rider! He twisted around to see his attacker, but in an instant Dayn shouted and planted his body between them. Dayn raised the dirk with a determined hand. The Lion Sword swung down to meet it.

Reiv watched as his cousin and brother fought, their images black shapes against a palette of morning light. The terrifying *clank* of blade upon blade rang in his ears. Whyn clearly had the advantage, but Dayn managed to hold his own. Whyn's horse suddenly circled away, and for a moment appeared to retreat. Dayn risked a glance at Reiv, his face awash with confusion. Whyn reined his mount back toward him and dug in his heels, the sword raised high. Reiv thrust out a warning hand, but before he could shout a word, Mahon rushed between Dayn and Whyn.

Mahon was on foot; his steed had been swept from beneath him by the pierce of an arrow. But the man stood fast, facing Whyn with obvious determination. He motioned Dayn back, and aimed his sword at Whyn, more as a warning than an attack. Whyn halted and stared him down. No words passed between the King and his Commander, but the message in their eyes was clear: Mahon intended to save his son; Whyn intended to slay the Unnamed One.

Whyn kicked in his heels and the horse lunged forward. Blades glinted in the air, then met with a *clash* as the horse swept past. Whyn stopped abruptly and turned his mount around. Mahon clutched his sword with both hands as he readied for the next attack. The horse barreled toward him, brushing against him and knocking him to his knees. The Lion descended, slashing Mahon from shoulder to breastbone.

Blood gushed from the wound and dripped into the dirt. Mahon staggered up and turned to face Whyn, who was reining his stallion to make another pass. The horse reached him in an instant. Mahon swung his weapon with effort, but for all his determination, he had little strength left. He swiped again, his body spinning from the weight of his sword. Whyn plunged The Lion into Mahon's unsuspecting back, screaming a shout of victory.

Mahon threw his head back and crumpled to the ground. Whyn stared down at him in disgust. "Traitor!" he hissed.

Dayn rushed to Mahon's side and pulled him into his arms. Mahon looked into Dayn's face, then grabbed his hand and held it tight. "I am… sorry…son," he said. He kept his gaze on Dayn a moment longer, then his grasp went limp and his eyes grew still.

"Father!" Dayn cried as he shook him hard. "Father, please!"

"Now you may join him," Whyn said, advancing toward him.

Dayn rose quickly, his hands trembling with fury. But in an instant he felt the earth tremble and shift beneath his feet. He stumbled, throwing out a protective arm as he fell to the ground.

The battle stopped as eyes darted around in confusion. A deep rumble was heard as the shaking of the earth grew more violent. Warriors from both sides fell to their knees. Voices cried out in terror as horses reared and bucked. All eyes turned to the mountains where the tallest peak was sending a billow of dark smoke high into the sky. The cloud rose, then imploded and rolled across the mountain range like a great tumbling wave.

The wall surrounding Tearia buckled, then crumbled to ruin. The towering buildings of the great city swayed and jerked. People on the battlefield scattered, the Guard heading toward the city, the Jecta running in the opposite direction. Reiv and Dayn staggered to their feet, then stood, paralyzed by the horrendous sight.

Whyn wheeled his horse to face the city. Buildings broke apart in massive chunks. Clouds of dust rose high into the air as stone and marble plummeted to the ground. Whyn kicked in his heels, screaming a command for his horse to gallop forward, and disappeared into the carnage that was Tearia.

# 24

# Aftermath

The world continued to tremble in the days that followed. Tearia was left as little more than teetering
walls and piles of block. Thousands of people perished and
thousands more were injured as the wall that had been
built to protect them had only served to entrap them. Some
structures were left standing for a time, but one by one
they were leveled in the aftershocks that followed.

Tearian survivors massed outside their city, forced to
abandon rescue attempts until the earth ceased its shudder-
ings. The mountain to the north continued to smoke, but the
billowing clouds had begun to dissipate. People staggered
around in a daze, tending to the injured as best they could,
scavenging for medical supplies, food, and water. Wells were
tainted and the fresh water streams that had previously cascaded down the slopes were now buried. New sources needed
to be found in the hills between the city and the mountains,
but few would risk going there. The gods were still too angry.

The once abundant supplies of food housed in Tearian
storerooms were lost, and the orchards and crops nearest the

city were all but destroyed. Those that survived were quickly raided. Treks were made to the far fields, but the destruction there was equally severe. The wildlife, once abundant in the forests, had scattered, leaving only rodents and lizards to scurry about. The Tearians were soon starving; they did not have the skill to utilize the alternative sources that nature provided.

Meirla suffered a different kind of damage. The palm trees scattered throughout the village had swayed until one by one they thundered to the ground. The seas had roiled and churned, and with each new aftershock the waters grew darker and more turbulent. Great waves crashed upon the shore, sweeping huts away with them. More life was lost from the cruel surge of the waters than from the quake itself. Even though the sea had finally calmed, the Shell Seekers feared to go into it.

Pobu was a pile of mud brick and broken timbers. Much life was lost within the Jecta city, but the casualties were far less than in Tearia, thanks to the mysterious last-minute order for evacuation. Those who had received the warning, and heeded it, found refuge to the south of Pobu. They had watched from the hills as their city crumbled like a sand castle toppled by a giant hand. Remnants of walls were all that remained of their homes, but without the risk of unstable buildings, the Jecta were able to get to work far more quickly than the Tearians.

The Jecta managed to dig up some of the crates of food that had been taken from the fields during the raid weeks before. They found much of it to be relatively unscathed. They scavenged the hillsides, fields, and forests, finding a small, but edible, supply of food. They knew which plants provided nutritious roots, leaves, and berries, and knew many recipes to make them more palatable. But their most dependable source of food in the days that followed proved to be the rats that swarmed the ruins of their city. The Jecta had long ago learned to survive on whatever they could find.

A Jecta encampment was set up to the south, not far from the wreckage of Pobu, but miles from Tearia to its north.

There was no contact between the people of the two cultures at first, but by the end of the first week following the cataclysm, refugees from Tearia, hungry and desperate, began to solicit aid from the ones they had once enslaved. They were met with only disdain.

A gathering of the clans was called, and they met under a patch of barren trees that had once been part of a lush orchard. The ground sloped downward, and Dayn and Reiv positioned themselves at the highest point. The rest of the crowd sat scattered before them. Minds still seemed to gravitate toward the two of them for leadership, especially Dayn, who was now revered for his life-saving premonition. To some it seemed odd that two mere boys had proved to be the real leaders amongst them, but there were no complaints as all eyes turned to them now.

Reiv raised his hands to calm the disgruntled crowd. "Your anger is understandable," he said. "But the Tearians need your help. Will you refuse them?"

A man rose and shook his fist in the air, denouncing any suggestions of charity. Others shouted in agreement.

"Before you deny them, consider this," Reiv said. "You have an opportunity to rebuild your world without Tearian rule. Their power has been stripped away. They depend on you now more than ever. Are you going to stand by and watch them starve? If that is your decision, so be it. History may well show you to be no better than they are."

"History or no, they come seeking our help, but we'll get nothing from them in return," an elderly woman said.

"You do not know that for certain," Reiv said. "Perhaps in time their hearts will turn our way."

"Maybe some of her people will turn our way," a voice in the back shouted, "but the King and the Priestess never will!"

Reiv lowered his eyes for a moment. "I do not know the fate of the King, nor of anyone in his household. But I do know that of the Priestess. She will trouble us no more."

"How can you know?" a young man asked.

Reiv's face stiffened. "Agneis saw to her destruction. I was there."

The crowd gasped almost as one, then mutterings of wonder made the rounds. The young man spoke up again. "Why did Agneis forsake us? Why did she and the gods see to our destruction? You said if we faced our enemy we would not be deserted. We heeded your words and look what happened."

"What happened was not the will of the gods, it was merely the way of things. But were you not all warned?" Reiv gestured his hand toward Dayn who was standing off to the side. "Did Dayn not see what was to come? Did he not call for the evacuation? That, my friends, was the will of the gods."

Eyes turned to Dayn in appreciation and the people calmed momentarily as they considered the wisdom of Reiv's words.

"You're right," a woman said. "We survived because of Dayn and for that we're grateful. No one could have known what was going to happen without the guidance of the gods."

"You must understand," Reiv said. "We live in an unstable world. It has always been so, and will be until the end of all things."

"What are you saying?" someone asked.

"I am saying nothing is eternal except the After Realm, and even that magnificent place goes through transformations. With each ending there is a new beginning. That is the way of the world."

One of the clan representatives rose and turned to face the crowd, looking from one end of it to the other as though seeking support. "I for one am willing to consider aiding the Tearians," he said. "There were some among 'em who sided with us. I'm not a cruel man, but before I lift a finger to help, I want assurances from their King that there'll be no vengeance against us. I want our demands to be addressed, but all of 'em this time, not just a few, and with no compromises on our part. Only with the King's promise to accept and abide by those demands, drawn up and documented before witnesses from both sides, will I ever agree to help."

Support for his idea was swift, and heads nodded as words of agreement were muttered.

"You must be the one to meet with the King, Reiv," a man called out to him. "He's your brother. You should do it."

Reiv felt a momentary pressure in his chest as words of refusal prepared to leave his lips, but then he realized that it was his task to do, not only for the Jecta, but for himself.

"Very well," he said. "I will take your demands to the King. But after that is done, the clans must select someone to lead them in council. I will be going home to Meirla, and Dayn—" Reiv turned to watch his cousin's face as he said, "Dayn will support you as long as he is able, I am sure. But even he has choices to make." Then he looked out across the crowd. "You have divided yourselves into clans with representatives from each. You have started a governing body, different from that of Tearia, but far more powerful. Elect a leader, work together, and all will be well."

Reiv waited for no more comments or questions, but moved swiftly through the audience with Dayn at his back. There was no need for further discussion. The sooner he undertook the task with Whyn, the better. The crowd thinned as people returned to their business, and Dayn and Reiv headed for their makeshift shelter in the encampment.

Their shelter was like the hundreds of others that surrounded it. It was nothing more than several poles stuck in the dirt, topped with a ragged tarp that snapped in the wind and moved its supports in a precarious dance. When Dayn and Reiv arrived, they were surprised to find Alicine and Nannaven there, deep in conversation.

"I thought you two went to see about a sick child," Dayn said as he ducked beneath a drooping portion of the tarp.

Alicine's face looked strained. "We did. The babe is not doing well."

"But you said it only had a slight fever," Reiv said.

"It did, but by this morning..."

Nannaven shuffled to the far corner, then bent down to rummage through a pile of bottles she had scavenged. "The illness came quickly, but the child's not the first. There are others, but this illness..." She shook her head. "It's like nothing I've ever seen before."

Reiv lowered himself to sit cross-legged on a blanket. He leaned his forehead in his hand. "Agneis give me strength," he muttered.

"Could it be the food or the water?" Dayn asked. "I mean, the water smells really foul and I actually saw people eating *rats*!"

"Could be. Can't be certain," Nannaven replied. "But I doubt it's the rats. They have been a part of the Jecta diet off and on for years. As for the water..."

"We'd better get word to the clans just in case," Dayn said. "If it's the water, a new source will need to be found. As for the rats, I'm going to suggest people find something else to eat anyway. Whether the things are causing illness or not, they're still disgusting!" Dayn moved to leave, then paused. He turned to Brina who sat silently to the side. She stared past him with vacant eyes.

"Brina?" he asked.

She blinked and focused her attention on him. "I am fine, son. Do not worry about me. Go on...take care of the business at hand."

Dayn nodded, then left.

"You are not fine, Brina," Reiv said, rising and crossing over to her. "What is it?"

"My burden, Reiv, not yours."

He knelt in front of her. "Tell me."

She turned her eyes away, then said, "I always had Mahon's love, but I threw it away. All these years I blamed him for everything when I should have shared in it equally. Now he is dead and I can never tell him how sorry I am for it."

"Forgiveness is a difficult thing. I am struggling with it myself. But you have to forgive yourself first, Brina."

"I do not know if I can. Mahon gave his life for our son. His love was there for Dayn, just as it was for me."

"And he gave it without hesitation," Reiv said. "You can honor it by accepting that which you cannot change. Mahon would have wanted that."

"When did you become so wise?" she said, admiration glinting through her tears.

Reiv shook his head and smiled. "I would not describe myself as wise, but I guess I have learned a few things these past months."

"That you have. Well, let me offer you one more piece of wisdom. If you truly love someone, latch onto them with all your heart and soul. Do not toss love aside over wounded pride or foolish misunderstandings."

Reiv felt the overwhelming urge to look at Alicine, but refrained from doing so. "Sometimes tragedies force us to realize things about ourselves we never knew," he said. Then he rose and took a step back. "Now I must do some forgiving of my own. I am off to find Whyn."

"What?" Brina cried, raising a hand to stop him.

"The clans refuse to aid the Tearians unless a pact is drawn up with their King. I have offered to seek him out and present the demands."

"Please, Reiv. You do not know how he will react. He tried to kill you before; he might do it again!"

"I do not think that will happen," Reiv said. "Whyn's people are in desperate need. He will have no choice but to listen."

Brina rose and wrapped her arms around him. "Please do not go," she whispered.

"I will be back soon." Reiv took her by the shoulders and leaned her back gently. "Is there anything you wish me to tell him?"

"Yes. Tell him I forgive him...and I love him."

Reiv nodded. "I will."

He had turned to exit the shelter when Alicine called out to him, "Reiv, take the dirk at least."

He nodded, feeling foolish for almost having left without it, and retrieved the weapon from beneath his bedroll and tucked it into his waistband.

"Oh, and Reiv..." Alicine ran up behind him.

He stopped to face her. "What is it?"

"I wanted to tell you something before you left, that's all."

"Can it wait?"

"No, it can't wait. I want to thank you for everything you have done for Dayn and me, and I want to tell you—"

"That you expect I am going to die again," he said with amusement.

A wave of temper crossed her features. "That is certainly not what I wanted to tell you!"

"What then?"

Alicine opened her mouth to speak, but nothing came out.

"Then I will say it," Reiv said. "I love you. There... it is done." He bent down and kissed her startled face. "I will be back shortly. Perhaps by then your lips will be working."

He smiled and walked away, leaving a strangely silent Alicine staring after him.

# 26

# City of Rats

It was early afternoon when Reiv reached the Tearian encampment outside what remained of the walls. Strangely, no hostility greeted him when he arrived. The eyes that followed him as he passed were full of pain and longing. No longer did they taunt him with their stares. No longer did they turn from him in disgust. Once beautiful and arrogant, the Tearians were now filthy and haggard, their misery equally distributed regardless of class or distinction.

Reiv made his way through the crowd, ignoring the uplifted hands and pleas for help. His mission was to find his brother. There was no time for charity. He scanned the host of grimy faces, but saw no sign of his brother. Realizing Whyn would not be huddled amongst the rabble, he set his sights on a group of guards posted at the entrance to the city.

The entrance was nothing more than a place in the wall where the wreckage had been cleared away. No traffic was coming or going through it, no doubt because of the guards. Why they were there was not clear; there did not seem much beyond the wall worth going in for.

Reiv reached the guards and was ordered to halt. "What is your business here?" one of them asked.

"I have come to speak with the King. Do you know where I might find him?"

The guard seemed uneasy for a moment, then he said, "He is at the palace, what is left of it. He refuses to leave."

Reiv nodded and walked past. No one made a move to stop him.

As he inched his way through the wreckage that was once the main street, Reiv kept his attention on the skeletal remains of the buildings on either side of him. He knew the slightest tremble, maybe even the tiniest gust of wind, could send them tumbling in his direction. He clambered atop a mound of debris, pausing to gain his bearings. Street signs and former landmarks were all but obliterated; little about the place seemed familiar to him anymore. He turned his eyes toward the hill where the palace once stood, surveying the twisting maze of stone that lay between him and his destination. He began his descent from the mound, but something scurried across his foot, throwing him off balance. Vermin swarmed from beneath the rubble, screeching and clattering as they skittered away. Reiv shivered. His once beautiful home had become a city of rats.

He made his way through the rocky mess as best he could, keeping his eyes primarily on his feet, but he was soon halted by the pungent smell of death. A body, half- buried, lay just ahead of him. Reiv's stomach roiled. From where he stood, the body was barely recognizable as a person; only the trace of its clothing revealed it as such. Reiv threw his hand over his nose, but the stench would not be erased. For a moment he thought to turn and abandon his mission altogether. He couldn't imagine finding his brother, or mother, or anyone else he knew in that condition. Turning his eyes aside, he directed his path away from the corpse and hurried on.

After what seemed like an eternity he reached the remains of the palace. Surveying what was left of the temple a short distance away, he could not help but feel buoyed by its demise. Once the home of Tearia's religious powers, it was now annihilated, its pillars and sacred statues scattered into a thousand pieces, the influence of the Priestess destroyed along with it. He turned his attention back to the palace. It bore little resemblance to the home of his childhood memories.

The ruined palace was eerily quiet, and the crunch of rocks beneath Reiv's feet shouted his presence with every step he took. Wreckage tumbled in tiny avalanches as he stumbled over it, its echoes resonating against the few remaining walls. As the sun streamed in through holes in sagging chunks of ceiling, it bathed the room in patches of cheery light, such contrast to the dismal aura of the place. The walls leaned in precariously, prompting Reiv to work his way as far from them as possible.

The palace was a huge, jumbled place, and Reiv wasn't sure where to look first. His brother could be anywhere, if he was even there at all. "Whyn," he called softly. He stopped and listened, but heard nothing, then moved forward a few more paces and paused again. "Whyn," he repeated.

He heard a rustle to his left and made his way toward it. Rounding a jagged half-wall, he found himself in the area that was once the receiving room. His eyes gravitated toward that place where the dais would have been. What he saw there stopped him in his tracks.

Whyn sat upon the once elegant throne, the frame of it now lopsided and bent. His chin was slumped against his chest, and his arms were draped across those of the chair. A plate sat on the floor before him, covered by several busy rats. No doubt the guards had attempted to feed their King, but from the look of him, he had not partaken of the offering. His face was drawn and deathly pale, and his hair hung limp and matted. He raised his eyes to Reiv. They were haunted and dull. Even the Lion Sword that lay across his lap bore no glimmer.

Reiv moved slowly toward his brother. "Whyn." But that was all he could say.

A flicker of recognition crossed Whyn's features. His lips parted. Then his eyes shifted to a pile of massive stones nearby and the remains of a tiny hand protruding from it.

"Cinnia," Whyn said, his voice barely a whisper.

Reiv's gaze followed that of his brother. A large knot swelled in his throat. He swallowed, but could not ease the pressure of its grip. "Please, Whyn," he managed. "Let me take you from this place."

"No!" Whyn shouted. "I will not leave her!"

Reiv tensed as his brother's thundering voice bounced off the unstable walls. He nodded as if in agreement, then slowly crossed over to where Cinnia's body lay. He gazed at her for a moment, but that moment seemed like an eternity as visions of happier times worked through his mind. He forced his eyes from her and searched the ground around him. A tapestry lay half-buried beneath a pile of nearby debris. He pulled it out and draped it across her.

"Cinnia would not want you to remember her like this," Reiv said, turning to his brother. "She would want you to remember her as she was."

"She was so beautiful," Whyn whispered.

"The most beautiful girl in all of Tearia," Reiv said gently.

"She loved me, you know."

Reiv hesitated, then replied, "Of course she did."

A flash of crimson rushed to Whyn's face. "It was always me! Never you!"

Reiv felt anger surge in his breast, but then he realized it no longer mattered whether Cinnia had loved him or not. "I know, Whyn. You are right. It was always you." Reiv scanned the room. "Where is Mother?" he asked cautiously.

"Gone...dead," Whyn said with a wave of his hand.

Reiv nodded and fought back the tears stinging his eyes. He walked toward his brother and stood before him.

"Cinnia is dead, Whyn...and Mother...but you are very much alive. You must try to set their deaths aside for a while, if you can. There will be time enough to grieve for them, but right now you have other responsibilities. Your people need you."

"I have failed them all," Whyn said.

"No, but you will if you sit here and wallow in self-pity. You must go to them, Whyn. You are their King."

"King of what?" Whyn said. "There is nothing left."

"Of course, there is. Tearia is its people, not its buildings. Buildings can be rebuilt...and they will be. Right now you need to focus on those who need you."

"What can I possibly do for them?"

"You can show them that you are strong, that you will work to heal their wounds and make Tearia great again. But it can never be as it was before."

"Who are you to tell me what Tearia can or cannot be." Whyn's eyes formed into slits. He fingered the sword in his lap.

"I am here to tell you the Jecta are willing to help if you agree to their concessions."

Whyn moved to protest, but Reiv cut him short. "They only ask for basic human rights. They have been denied them for too long. Put your pride aside, Whyn. You know the truth of things. You know the Priestess did not speak for Agneis. You saw it for yourself."

Whyn shivered and wrapped his arms around himself. "It is as though she took my very soul with her."

"No one can take another's soul unless it is given freely."

Whyn hung his head. "Then I must have done so."

Reiv stepped toward him. "The brother I know would have never done such a thing. You are still Whyn."

Whyn stared at Reiv silently for a moment, his mind sorting through the words. "I fear there is very little of Whyn left in me."

Reiv knelt on one knee and placed a hand atop his brother's. Whyn regarded it with a puzzled expression.

"I know you to be strong," Reiv said. "You will fight this feeling and you will win. In the meantime, let us put the battle between us aside. If we are to move forward, we must find a way to forgive. I do not wish to carry this burden anymore. I want this settled once and for all. After things are set right between the Tearians and the Jecta, I will be leaving and will likely never see you again."

"What do you mean?"

"I am no longer Tearian, Whyn. I am Shell Seeker now and will be going home to Meirla."

"How can you say that?"

"Because it is true. My heart lies there, just as yours lies here. The throne of Tearia is yours. I want no part of it, and have not for quite some time."

Whyn wrapped his fingers around the hilt of the sword. "You wanted *this* not so long ago."

"No more. It is yours now, but the sword's legacy is not one we should be proud of. For a time I thought to destroy it. Now I think it should be kept safe as a reminder of things."

Whyn rose, then stared at the tapestry covering Cinnia. He raised his head and pulled back his shoulders. "What needs to be done?"

Reiv stood and scanned Whyn up and down. "First we must get you looking more presentable. Then we must arrange a meeting between you, your council, and the Jecta representatives. Once the agreement is drawn, the healing can begin. It is the only way."

Whyn nodded. "Then we will do it." His words conveyed hope, but the flat tone of his voice and the emptiness in his eyes somehow failed the mark.

# 27

# Destinations

Whyn emerged from his seclusion with all the dignity befitting a King. No one dared question his mysterious absence in the days preceding. They were so thrilled to see him that there was no room in their hearts for bitterness. Reiv stayed at his brother's side that day, explaining the ways the Jecta could help. Whyn ordered the Guard to reorganize and disperse into groups. They took a careful survey of food and supplies within the Tearian encampment and arranged swift medical treatment for those most in need. Whyn requested that a meeting with the Jecta take place the following morning, and Reiv returned to the Pobu encampment that night to deliver the news.

The sun had long since set when Reiv arrived back at camp, but the moon was bright and cast a pale, silver light. Dark canopies rippled in the breeze, and campfires danced and sparked along the hillside. The smell of smoke and meats cooking on spits mingled with the night air. For a moment Reiv wondered if Dayn's message regarding the rats had been heeded. Voices rose and fell, the hum of chatter mixed with

an occasional burst of laughter. The merriment was music to
Reiv's ears, and he pushed the thought of rats from his mind.

"Reiv...over here!" Dayn shouted.

Reiv smiled and moved toward his cousin who was headed his
way. They grabbed each other in a brief embrace.

"How did it go?" Dayn asked. "Did you find him?"

"Yes, I found him," Reiv said. "He is not as he was when
you last saw him. When I came upon him he was a shell of his
former self. But he has pulled himself together and now works
to make things right. He realizes it cannot be done without the
Jecta. A meeting is called for in the morning. We need to get the
word out to the clan leaders."

"I'll do it," Dayn said. "Get yourself some food. I won't be
long."

"What about the rats?" Reiv asked. "I smelled meat cooking
when I arrived."

"Most have heeded the message," Dayn said. Then he
grinned. "Some hunters returned from the forest today
with three bucks in tow. It appears the wildlife is returning.
That's probably what you smelled."

Reiv licked his lips in response to the thought of venison. Dayn laughed. "Alicine is roasting some on the spit.
You'd better get your share before it's gone."

Dayn headed out to spread the word about the meeting while
Reiv practically raced to the campfire by the shelter. Just as Dayn
had said, Alicine was turning a spit heavy with venison. Reiv walked
up quietly and stood at her back, recalling the words he had said to
her the last time they spoke. Nerves clutched hold of his stomach,
accentuating the hunger that lingered there. He hadn't given her a
chance to react to his unexpected comment before. How in the
world was she going to react now that it had sunk in?

"That smells good," he said, trying to push the other
thought from his mind.

Alicine started at the sound of his voice and spun to
face him. Though bathed in shadow, her face seemed to
blush. She pushed a stray hair from her eyes. "Reiv," she said.

"Did I surprise you?" he asked.

"Always."

He walked toward the fire and eyed the meat, glinting a savage desire to rip it from the spit. Alicine sliced a piece for him, placed in on a chipped pottery plate, and handed it to him. He sat down, tossed the plate to the ground, and held the meat with both hands as he sank his teeth into it.

"Careful, it's hot," Alicine said.

Reiv hadn't really noticed, but dropped the meat back onto the plate and accepted the utensils she thrust into his hands. Based on the condition of his empty stomach, the spoon and knife would be too bothersome, but he used them anyway, more for Alicine's satisfaction than for the protection of his fingers.

When he finished, he wiped the grease from his mouth and glanced around. "Where is everyone?"

"Brina and Nannaven are with Mya. And Dayn..." Alicine craned her neck. "Where did he go anyway?"

"Oh, he went to get a message to the clans. Whyn has called a meeting for in the morning. It looks like the agreement will be drawn up and signed. Hopefully there will be no problems. Tearia is in a poor state. He would be foolish to delay."

"So your brother's well then?"

"He survives. That is all I can say for him at the moment."

"And the rest of your family?"

Reiv stared into the fire, the heat of it adding to the flush he felt in his cheeks. "Mother is dead...an uncle missing...some distant cousins survived...but Cinnia did not."

Alicine followed his gaze to the flames. "I'm sorry," she said.

Reiv rose to face her. "No, it is I who am sorry, sorry for calling you by her name that time we...well...anyway. I did not realize what I was saying. Or what I was doing."

"I didn't realize what you were saying, either, although I was pretty sure what you were doing." Alicine smiled awkwardly. "I thought you were saying we were committing a sin. That's what made me realize we were. I'm glad you said it."

"Is that what you thought we were doing? Sinning?"

Alicine lowered her eyes. "It's a sin for a boy and a girl not married to touch each other like that."

"I see. Well," Reiv said, "I would never want to lead you into sin, Alicine. You are far too important to me."

Alicine placed a hand on his arm. "Reiv, what you said earlier. Did you mean it?"

"Of course." He looked at the hand resting upon his arm and felt a tingle. "Goosy bumps," he said.

"What?"

"Dayn once said something about goosy bumps. I did not understand what he was referring to. It was not an expression I was familiar with."

Alicine ran her fingers across the tiny bumps blanketing his arm. "Oh, you mean goose bumps. So I give you goose bumps, do I?" She had an unusually mischievous tone, and her expression left Reiv somewhat unnerved.

"Yes, you do," he said, pulling his arm away, "but that must be as far as the bumps go until you no longer feel it is a sin." He turned and took a step. "I think I will go find Dayn. The clans will have questions." Then he disappeared into the blur of the encampment.

The meeting between the Tearians and the Jecta took place where the battle had been fought. All the clan representatives attended, including Torin who had received the message about the meeting in the middle of the night. He had arrived with little time to spare, but the Shell Seekers would have been represented even without him; Reiv would have stood in his place if need be. All the conditions set forth by the Jecta were met without protest. They asked for nothing more than the rights the Tearians had always enjoyed. It was understood that the adjustments would be difficult; old habits and prejudices were hard to break. While they realized much work lay ahead, there was an air of giddy excitement within both camps. A new age had begun for all.

Reiv, Torin, and Dayn arrived back at the encampment in a festive mood. Brina, Alicine, and Nannaven had prepared a simple, but in their minds lavish, feast of beet and venison stew, flat breads, and wine. Dayn, who had once hated beets, seemed to have forgotten his previous disdain for them and was working on his third helping. Reiv sat beside him, staring into a mug with distaste.

"What's wrong with it?" Dayn asked. He leaned over and peered into Reiv's mug as if expecting to find a bug swimming in it.

"Wine no longer suits me," Reiv said.

"I'll take it, then," Dayn said, holding out his hand. "I seem to have acquired a taste for it since becoming a Jecta."

"Perhaps we need to have a talk, little cousin."

Dayn laughed. "Some of us can just hold their spirits better than others."

Reiv scowled in playful irritation, then shoved his mug into Dayn's outstretched hand.

Torin plopped down beside the two boys with a plate full of stew in hand. "Have you told him yet?" he asked Reiv between chews.

"No, but I guess now is as good a time as any," Reiv said. "Dayn, I will be going back to Meirla with Torin in the morning. Everything is going well here and I think it is time I went home."

Dayn choked on a swallow of wine. "Back to Meirla? Tomorrow?" He glanced around for Alicine who could be seen huddled with the women, chattering away. His face grew solemn. "Have you told Alicine yet?"

"No, but I will. Maybe after we finish eating."

"Well," Dayn said, "if you tell her now, I'll be assured of another helping. She won't have any appetite once you tell her." He forced a laugh, though he clearly did not find it all that amusing.

When they finished eating, Reiv rose and made his way over to the women. He stood there awkwardly then said, "Alicine, may I talk to you privately?"

Brina regarded him with knowing eyes, for he had told her earlier of his planned departure. She stepped aside and hooked her arm through Nannaven's, then ushered the old woman away.

Reiv stared at the ground for a moment and stabbed his toe at the sand like a boy having to confess an indiscretion. He folded his arms. "I am going back to Meirla with Torin in the morning," he finally said.

At first Alicine's expression seemed curiously distant, but then a weak smile formed on her lips. "I knew you would eventually. I wish it wasn't so soon, but I guess I understand."

Her words put him at ease and he released a slow breath of relief. "I was worried you would be angry."

"I can't be angry with you about that anymore. Meirla is your home. We'll still see each other...at least..." She turned her face away in an attempt to hide the tears pooling in her eyes.

Reiv took her chin and turned her face back toward his. "Of course we will see each other again. It is not so far away and..." She lowered her eyes, giving him the impression there was more to it. "Is there something you are not telling me, Alicine?"

"Dayn and I will be leaving soon. I don't say that to spite you. Not like I did before. But it's time for us to go home too."

Reiv felt as though the wind had been knocked out of him. He had thought of his departure to Meirla as a temporary separation, but now...His eyes shot over to Dayn, who was still seated next to Torin beneath the canopy. Dayn must have felt his attention upon him because he looked up at Reiv, then swallowed guiltily and turned his head away.

"When are you going?" Reiv asked, struggling to keep his voice steady.

"Maybe in a week or so, when we're sure Brina is all right. Dayn hasn't told her yet. I doubt she'll handle it well."

"She must come to Meirla, then," Reiv said. He worked to draw some saliva into his mouth, then grabbed a nearby mug of wine and swigged it back. "Come to Meirla before you go," he said after he had swallowed, "and bring Brina with you."

Alicine nodded and Reiv excused himself, claiming the need for a moment of personal privacy. He didn't know where he was going as he headed away. His feet were moving one in front of the other, but they were not in his control. His mind was too wrapped up in other things to concern itself with destinations.

The next morning Reiv prepared to leave for Meirla with Torin. The two of them didn't have any possessions to gather up, so preparations were more mental than physical. Reiv made excuse after excuse to delay their departure. He hated the thought of saying goodbye to Dayn and Alicine, even though he knew it was inevitable.

Earlier that morning he had said farewell to Alicine privately. The sun had not yet risen when he motioned her from the tent and away from the sleeping others. He had not been able to sleep at all, and apparently she hadn't either. The two of them slipped into the filmy gray of pre-dawn, but when they stopped to face each other, their tongues grew still. To break the awkward silence, Reiv gathered Alicine's hands into his and mumbled something. He recalled refusing to say the word "goodbye." There would be time enough for that when she and Dayn left for Kirador. Regretfully, he did not attempt a kiss, and after some time Alicine turned away, claiming the need to go check on the fever patient. But Reiv knew the sadness in her eyes was not for the child.

The sun was high in the sky now, and Reiv could come up with no more excuses to linger. Alicine had not returned, he had not really expected her to, and Torin, having already said his goodbyes to Brina, Dayn, and Nannaven, had gone to bid farewell to Mya and her children. Reiv was to meet him at the crossroads and knew he was probably already waiting for him there. Reiv could risk no more delay; he was going to get a dose of Torin's temper as it was.

Brina was kneeling over the cooking stone, scraping up the last of the flatbreads she had insisted Reiv take with him. Dayn sat cross-legged nearby, quietly sharpening a knife, refusing to meet Reiv's eyes. Nannaven was rummaging in her bag of personal items, muttering to herself, as was her habit. She pulled out the tome she kept hidden there and hobbled over to Reiv. The book and an old burlap sack were clutched in her hands.

Nannaven ushered Reiv from the tent, glancing from side to side. Even though there was no longer a need to keep the book secret, she clearly did not want anyone witnessing her conversation with Reiv.

"You must take this with you," she said, thrusting the book into his hands.

Reiv ran his eyes over the strange runes chiseled into the leather cover. "But, Spirit Keeper, I do not know how to read it. It is written in symbols I do not understand."

"You must learn the words, Reiv, but more importantly, you must learn the meaning."

"How? I will be in Meirla and you will be here."

"There is no time for doubt, boy. You have work to do. Don't forget, a serpent sheds its skin to be born again." She drew his gaze to hers, her meaning clear.

Reiv nodded, swallowing hard.

Nannaven held the bag out to him and Reiv dropped the book into it. She smiled and wrapped her thin arms around him. "Goodbye, Reiv," she whispered.

"Goodbye," he said. And he knew it was.

# 28

# Departure

The morning sky was brilliant blue, but Reiv would have preferred a rainy day. Not only would it have better matched his mood, but it would have erased any chance for visitors. It had been several days since his return to Meirla, and with each new dawn he had awoken in fear that Dayn and Alicine would arrive. He knew he should be happy at the thought of seeing them again, but he also knew their arrival would mean only one thing—departure.

He sat at the workbench inside the hut, trying to keep busy with a drilling tool. He didn't have enough skill to make fine jewelry, the scars on his hands hindered his dexterity, but the concentration required to drill holes and string shells at least kept his mind off of other concerns.

Kerrik bounded in. "Reiv! Reiv! Guess who's here!" Even the boy's splinted arm and bandaged ribs could not stop his youthful gyrations.

"Who?" Reiv asked, but he already knew.

"Brina's here, and Dayn, and Alicine!"

"Oh, are they now?" Reiv set the crafting tool aside and rose from the bench. He wiped his hands down the cloth wrapped around his hips. "Well then, let us go greet them."

Kerrik skipped out while Reiv took a calming breath and followed him through the doorway.

Dayn, Alicine, and Brina could be seen coming up the road, all three of them on horseback. Brina, Reiv noticed, was riding Gitta. He could not help but grin. Dayn waved and Reiv returned the gesture as he advanced to meet them. Alicine was dressed in her Summer Maiden gown, its golden material clean, but wrinkled. Dayn had on his Kira-dyn wool bottoms and moss-green tunic, but was not wearing his boots.

Dayn jumped off his mount, took hold of Brina's reins, and helped her down while Reiv placed his hands around Alicine's waist and lifted her off. They walked toward the hut in silence.

When they arrived, Jensa was there to usher them in. "Kerrik, go find Torin," she said as the guests entered.

They gathered on the floor around the fire pit while Jensa poured them each a cup of honey sweetened water. Reiv passed a basket of palm nut to Dayn with an unsteady hand. "How long will you be staying?" he managed to ask.

"Not long," Dayn said. "We need to be getting on."

Reiv nodded and noticed that Brina's eyes were red with tears. She didn't say a word and for a long moment no one else did either.

Torin arrived and Kerrik danced in behind him. The man brightened at the sight of the visitors. "We're so happy to see you," he said. The downcast expressions on every-one's faces indicated they did not agree.

They partook of the refreshments with a spattering of small talk, then Reiv rose and asked Dayn to follow him outside.

"What route will you be taking?" Reiv asked. "You are not planning to attempt the cave again I hope."

"No," Dayn said, "that's out of the question. I'm not really sure, but I guess we'll figure it out."

Reiv pointed in the direction of the mountains. "Take the road that runs northeast of here, then follow the river toward the first peak beyond the tallest one there. There is a pass between them that will take you into a valley. Once you have crossed it, you will find passage to the other side. You can make your way down from there."

Dayn cocked his head. "How do you know this?"

"Let us just say I have seen it."

Dayn nodded, then slanted his eyes toward the hut. "Alicine's anxious to go home, but she's a mess about it." He studied Reiv's face for a moment. "I'll fetch her for you."

Dayn left, while Reiv waited. He stared toward the mountains in the distance, trying to picture Kirador in his mind. Then he felt Alicine's presence at his back.

"I guess this is goodbye," she said softly.

Reiv swallowed hard as he turned to face her. "I suppose it is."

"You do understand, don't you? Dayn and I never had a chance to say our goodbyes to Mother and Father before we left. They must be frantic. Besides, we're worried about what may have happened there, what with the earthquake and the smoke on the mountain and all. We have to go back."

"I know."

She raised an inquisitive brow. "Where's your kohl?"

Reiv realized he was not wearing it, just as he had not since the day he arrived back. "I did not know when you would be coming and I knew how much you hated it."

"I don't hate it."

He crossed his arms and stared at the ground. "Well, anyway, now you can remember me without it." He glanced back at the hut. "Could you excuse me for a moment?"

"Oh...sure," Alicine replied, looking a bit disappointed.

Reiv sprinted back to the hut where everyone was still visiting, and headed straight for the trinket box he kept by his bedroll. He tipped back the lid and retrieved the shell bracelet he and Kerrik had worked so hard to perfect. Voices hushed. Reiv could feel the eyes of everyone on him. He glanced up and his face went hot at the knowing smiles aimed in his direction.

"Well, I have to give it to her sometime, don't I?" he said. Then he grinned and headed out the door.

He resumed his place before Alicine, and stood in silence for a long, clumsy moment. It occurred to him that she might not like the bracelet, that she might actually reject his token of affection.

"What do you have in your hand there?" Alicine asked, interrupting his thought.

"Something I made...for you."

"Well, let me see it."

"Of course. Here." Reiv opened his fist and thrust the bracelet out to her.

A soft gasp whispered from her throat. "Oh, Reiv. It's beautiful. You made this?" She took it from his hand and held it up, admiring its iridescent pink and gray swirls in the sunlight. A glistening came to her eyes as she pulled it over her hand and adjusted it at her wrist.

"Of course, I made it," Reiv said. Then he added hastily, "Well, Kerrik helped me...but I was completely in charge."

"As always," she said with a laugh.

Reiv gathered her hands in his, then stammered, "Would you—would you allow me to sin one more time?"

Alicine's blush rose to match his and she nodded, then raised herself on tiptoes and tilted her face to his.

He kissed her on the lips, not hard and passionately like he had the time before, but gently and with a sweetness reflective of his feelings for her. She returned it, and he felt as though his heart was soaring. How in the world could such a beautiful thing be considered a sin?

"Be happy," he whispered.

"I will," she said as she wrapped her arms around him. *Every time I think of you.*

Dayn watched from the doorway as his sister and cousin said their goodbyes. He glanced over his shoulder at Jensa who was busying herself in the kitchen. "Jensa," he said, "can I talk to you for a minute?"

She walked toward him, drying her hands on her skirt, and followed him outside and away from the hut.

Dayn shifted his weight and folded his arms. "About what happened outside the cave..."

"Don't give it another thought," she said.

"But I wanted to thank you."

"Thank me? Whatever for?"

"Because I'll remember it for the rest of my life. You're one of the most beautiful girls I've ever seen and I felt honored that you even wanted to—with me I mean."

Jensa smiled. "The honor was all mine, Dayn. I've grown up being stared at and groped by men, but you're...well...different."

"I am?"

"Yes. You're sweet."

"Oh...sweet," he muttered.

"I'd hoped we could get to know each other better," Jensa said, "but I guess it was not meant to be."

"You know, if I'd planned to stay, things might have been different, but the fact is, I'm going back to Kirador for a reason other than to take my sister."

"Your parents?"

"No."

"Ah, this other girl then?"

Dayn smiled. "Falyn means everything to me, and I'm going back for her."

"Well, Dayn, you go back and find this girl and don't let go. She'd be a fool not to love you."

"Well, I don't know, but I guess I have to find out."

Then Jensa leaned in and whispered in his ear, "Just kiss her the way you did me and she'll be yours forever."

Dayn's eyes widened and he looked at his feet bashfully. But as they walked back toward the hut, he had a new-found bounce in his step.

They all congregated by the horses, hugging and saying their farewells. Brina found it particularly difficult and could not seem to pry her arms from around Dayn's waist. He gave her a kiss on the cheek, the first he had ever given her, and gently squirmed from her grasp. But his expression reflected regret at having had to do so.

Dayn and Alicine mounted their horses and gathered up the reins.

"Remember what I told you about the valley," Reiv said.

Dayn reached down and clasped Reiv's hand in his. "I'll remember. Thanks, cousin, for everything."

Alicine looked at Reiv one last time, but said not a word, then turned her horse and headed slowly up the road.

Dayn glanced over his shoulder toward his sister, then back down at Reiv. "We'll meet again, Reiv."

"Of course we will."

Dayn kicked his heels and urged his horse up to Alicine. They headed into the distance as the others stood silently watching. Jensa and Torin excused themselves while Brina stood with her body leaned against Reiv's. He put his arm around her and held her tight. A sob burst from her throat and she pulled away to run back to the hut. Reiv and Kerrik were then left alone to watch the fading images of Dayn and Alicine.

Kerrik tugged at Reiv's arm. "Are they going very far away?"

"Not so far," Reiv replied.

"But they're coming back sometime aren't they?"

"We will meet them again."

"Good! Come on, let's go. You can't even see them anymore."

"I can see them."

Kerrik twisted his face and narrowed his eyes toward the horizon. "No you can't. Come on!"

Reiv sighed with exasperation and looked at the antsy boy. "Very well. Now, was there something we were supposed to do today?"

Kerrik jumped up and down excitedly. "Yes! You were going to teach me to fight with the dirk. You've been promising me *forever*."

"It has not been forever, Kerrik."

"Yes it has. Gods, I'm almost eight. How long do you expect me to wait?"

Reiv laughed. "Well, you still have some healing to do and may not be strong enough yet."

Kerrik lifted his good arm and flexed his muscle. "Stronger than you," he declared.

Reiv looked him up and down. With one arm splinted and the other barely able to lift a weapon, the boy with the crooked foot did not look much like a warrior. But the determination that beamed in his eyes erased all doubt. Reiv smiled. "Perhaps you are stronger than me," he said. "Perhaps you truly are."

Reiv wrapped his fingers around the tiny arm, finding plenty of room to grow. He took Kerrik's hand in his. It was time for the lesson to begin.

# END

# OF

# BOOK

# TWO

FOR A PREVIEW OF BOOK THREE . . .

Preview of

*The Taking of the Dawn*

Book Three

The Souls of Aredyrah Series

# 1

# Oblivion

Dayn stood atop a rocky outcrop, silhouetted against a palette of molten fire. As far as he could see, a glowing danger
stretched, a great flood of lava from which sparkling channels
crept down the mountain in bright braided patterns. Trees in the
paths of melted rock ignited like thousands of flaming candles.
Some evaporated into white-hot oblivion; others were left as distorted figures, eternally posed.

Dayn clutched Alicine's hand, squeezing it so tight the tips of
her fingers turned white. But she didn't complain. She probably
didn't even notice.

"Have you ever seen such a thing," Alicine whispered. "Now
what are we going to do?"

"I don't know," Dayn replied. "I must've taken us the wrong
way. We'll have to go back."

"*All* the way back?"

"No. I don't know. But we sure can't go this way."

"But Reiv said—"

"Well, he obviously didn't know about this...or maybe I misunderstood him. Don't worry, we'll get home. I probably just didn't take us far enough east or something."

Dayn pulled in a deep breath, then released it slowly. It didn't matter whether his cousin Reiv had told them wrong. It didn't matter whether they had gone too far one way or the other. The vale before them was impassable, or would be by the time they reached it. Turning back was not a difficult decision. Where they went next was.

The wind shifted in their direction, wrapping them in a veil of vapor that reeked of sulfur and smoke. Dayn covered his nose with his free hand and pulled his sister along with the other.

"Come on," he muttered. "The horses are getting nervous."

Dayn scrambled his bare feet down the slope. A sudden stab at his heel sent him hopping. He cursed the ground, the rocks, and anything else he could think of at the moment. His feet were already aching, and this was yet another in a long series of attacks upon them. It was time to put his boots back on, and he dreaded it.

Where he was from, no one ever went without their boots. And for the past fifteen and a half of Dayn's sixteen-year-old life he hadn't either. The terrain in Kirador was mountainous, and the temperatures almost always cool, if not downright frigid. To go barefoot was something no sensible Kiradyn would do. But Dayn had not worn his boots in months now, preferring to go barefoot. That was what the Jecta of Tearia did. And that was what he considered himself now—Jecta.

He pulled up his foot up to inspect it, finding a deep indention where a tiny white pebble had lodged. He picked it out, then limped to the horse, grumbling as he yanked a bundle from its back.

"Don't tell me," Alicine said with amusement, "you're actually putting them back on."

"Well, I have to some time, don't I? I'm tired of having to dance around every time I get off the horse. It's a lot rockier here than back home—I mean, back in Tearia."

"A lot rockier and a lot colder. I'm surprised your feet aren't blue." Alicine scolded him with her eyes, once again acting as if she were the older, then tightened her shawl around her shoulders. It was the last defense she had against the decreasing temperature, other than the ratty blanket she had been using as a bedroll.

Dayn glanced at his sister, noting the cold-swept features of her face and the stiffness of her body. The dress she wore should have been warmer; it was long sleeved and high collared, its full skirt reaching her ankles in yards of gold-colored material. But the fabric had been selected for its beauty, not its practicality. It was a dress embroidered with hundreds of tiny white flowers, a dress for a Summer Maiden, not a girl trudging through the mountains. No, the weave of the decorative material wasn't enough to stave off this kind of cold. Even the molten fire on the other side of the ridge did little to warm their surroundings.

"Where's your coat?" Alicine asked.

"In my pack. But one thing at a time. Boots first...coat later," Dayn said.

Alicine sighed. "Suit yourself, but that tunic of yours is not going to keep you warm for long."

Dayn shrugged his shoulders against the rough, green wool of his tunic. At one time he had worn it in comfort, but it felt itchy to him now. For too many months in Tearia he had gone bare-chested, with nothing against his skin but a kilt around his hips. Now he had on long sleeves and thick trousers, the scratchy material pressed against every part of his body.

He pulled the boots from his pack and plopped to the ground, then stared hard at his feet. They were stained and rough with calluses from months of going barefoot. But the boots, he knew, would bring blisters to his toes no matter how tough his feet had become. He scowled and yanked on his socks, then the brown leather boots, shiny new when he left Kirador, now scuffed with travel. He snaked the long laces up his calves without regard to pattern and tied them in a knot, then stood up and groaned. The things were miserable.

Alicine laughed. "You loved those boots when you first got them. Couldn't wait to wear them as I recall. Worked extra chores at home and helped Jorge out in the smithy to earn the coin to buy them. And now…"

Dayn cocked a brow. "And who is it that keeps tugging at her collar? Hmmm?"

Alicine arched her neck and ran her finger beneath the scratchy lace of the collar that stopped just below her jaw line. Ever since she had donned the dress for the return trip home, she had tugged and fidgeted in the material almost as much as Dayn had his.

"I don't know how I ever thought this dress was comfortable," she said, "but I guess we'd better get used to dressing like Kiradyns again. I doubt the climate of the mountains *or* our neighbor's icy attitudes will allow us to go around showing our arms and legs."

Dayn turned away and checked the strapping of the packs on the back of his horse. "There's a lot of things we won't be allowed," he muttered.

"What did you say?" Alicine asked.

"I said, won't Father and Mother be pleased that we're bringing two horses back with us?" He stepped over to Alicine and lifted her onto her horse. "Come on, let's get going. There isn't much daylight left and I want to get us as far away from here as possible before we set up camp for the night. I'd hate to wake up and find us in the path of all that," he said, motioning to the glow of roiling fire on the other side of the ridge.

Dayn mounted his horse, a broad-backed chestnut with a patch of black on its face. It was a beautiful animal, nothing like the old hag of a horse their father owned. But then again, their father probably didn't own a horse anymore. Alicine had ridden out of Kirador with the only one he owned when she'd come looking for Dayn the day he ran away. They'd left the animal grazing near the cave that took them to the other side of the world, and it was doubtful the old gray had managed to find its way home. The poor beast was probably still wandering the mountains somewhere, or else dead by now. Regardless, Father would be pleased to see his children riding home after all these months. Maybe the horses would settle the man's temper once the joy of the reunion had faded and the reality of what Dayn had put him through set in. But it wasn't likely.

# THE SAGA CONTINUES

Don't miss the next book in

The Souls of Aredyrah Series!


Coming in 2008

Book Three

The Taking of the Dawn


Dayn and Alicine return to Kirador to find things very different from when they left them. Their home has been ransacked, their parents missing, and disturbing evidence speaks of spell-work done at Dayn's expense. Frightened and confused, they go to the nearest place they know of for answers, the homestead of their uncle, Haskel, a man who has never been accepting of Dayn's differences, and even less so of his own son's.

Back in Meirla, Reiv has settled into the quiet life of a Shell Seeker. But while the rhythm of his routine is calm enough, the primal beatings of his heart are not. Sulking over his love life, he turns his attentions to Cora, an eye-catching girl who has also attracted the amorous intentions of Lyal, a man with more than his share of women. But romance is the least of Reiv's worries. A terrible plague is spreading across the land, thousands are dying, and their friend Mya and her son have fallen ill.

While Reiv holds things in check in Meirla, Torin heads to Pobu, determined to be by Mya's side. Upon his arrival, he finds himself facing a secret long kept hidden, and a loss from which he might never recover. Surrounded by death and decay, Torin is further mortified to learn that Whyn, Tearia's beleaguered King, has gone through some transformations of his own: The Priestess has become so firmly entrenched in the young monarch's psyche, it is difficult to tell where one begins and other ends.

While Reiv and his friends face annihilation by Tearia's increasingly brutal King, Dayn faces challenges of his own. His disappearance from Kirador months before not only ended the life he once knew, but started a witch hunt that threatens his safety and the very existence of his clan. Will the Fire and the Light of the Prophecy be snuffed out by the darkness that is descending upon the land? Or will Reiv and Dayn unite and fight with a power that only they, as one, possess?

# Glossary

Aredyrah *(Air-uh-DEER-uh)*—An ancient island world, divided geographically by a range of volcanic mountains.

Agneis *(AG-nee-us)*—Goddess of Purity. Supreme deity of Tearian culture. The Priestess is said to commune with Agneis through the act of Transcension.

Alicine *(AL-uh-seen)*—Kiradyn. Daughter of Gorman and Morna of the Aerie clan. Sister of Dayn. Alicine is gifted in herb lore and medicinals.

Brina *(BREE-nuh)*—Tearian. Sister of Queen Isola. Birth mother of Dayn. Maternal aunt of Ruairi (Reiv) and Whyn. Estranged wife of Mahon who is the Commander of the Guard.

Cinnia *(SIN-ee-uh)*—Tearian. Daughter of Labhras. Wife of Whyn, who is the future King of Tearia. Cinnia was once betrothed to Ruairi, King-heir of Tearia. When he was disowned, she was lured by the Priestess into marrying Whyn, Ruairi's brother.

Crymm *(Krim)*—Tearian. Former bodyguard to Ruairi. Crymm blames Ruairi for his demise within the royal household. Dismissed as his bodyguard, Crymm was later demoted to the Guard, where he used his position to persecute Ruairi, now called Reiv. Crymm was eventually promoted within the ranks, but continues to work against Reiv.

**Daghadar** *(DAG-huh-dar)*—Also called The Creator. The one true God of the people of Kirador.

**Dayn** *(Dane)*—Kiradyn, Tearian, and Jecta. Adopted son of Gorman and Morna of the Aerie Clan of Kirador. Brother of Alicine. Only child of Brina and Mahon of Tearia. Cousin of Reiv and Whyn. Believed by some in Tearia to be "The Light" of the first Prophecy. In Kirador, Dayn is considered demonkind due to the paleness of his hair and eyes.

**Eben** *(EH-ben)*—Jecta. Potter of Pobu. Childhood friend of Jensa and Torin. Husband of Mya. Father of Farris, Nely, and Gem. Executed by the Guard for possession of an illegal tome.

**Eileis** *(I-luss)*—Kiradyn. The Spirit Keeper of Kirador. Alicine's teacher in the craft of herb lore and medicinals.

**Eyan** *(EE-yun)*—Kiradyn. Son of Haskel and Vania. Eyan is considered "not quite right," though no one knows why. He is kept hidden from family and friends at his parents' farm.

**Falyn** *(FAL-un)*—Kiradyn. Daughter of Lorcan. Sister of Sheireadan. Object of Dayn's affections. Falyn is friends with Alicine, but is forbidden to see Dayn. Her brother Sheireadan acts as her bodyguard, assaulting Dayn at every opportunity. She has affection for Dayn, but turns a blind eye to her brother's treatment of him.

Farris *(FARE-iss)*—Jecta. Son of Mya and Eben.

Gair *(Gare)*—Jecta blacksmith. Member of the rebel movement. Dayn's employer in Pobu.

Gem *(Jim)*—Jecta. Daughter of Mya and Eben. Siser of Nely and Farris.

Gitta *(JIT-uh)*—Reiv's horse when he was Foreman over the Jecta who worked Labhras's fields.

Gorman *(GOR-mun)*—Kiradyn. Member of the Aerie Clan. Adopted father of Dayn. Father of Alicine. Husband of Morna. Defied his fear of demons to seek a cure for his wife's inability to bear children. When he discovered the infant Dayn in a cave, he believed the child to be a gift from Daghadar, the Creator. But he also believed the child to be demon-kind.

Haskel (HASS-kuhl)—Kiradyn. Brother of Mahon. Husband of Vania. Father of Eyan.

Isola *(Iss-O-luh)*—Tearian. Wife of King Sedric. Mother of Ruairi and Whyn. Sister of Brina. Loyal to her husband, but has had little interest in motherhood.

Jecta *(JEK-tuh)*—The name given by the Tearians to anyone considered "impure." The Jecta primarily live in the city of Pobu, but many work within the walls of Tearia as slaves or servants. Their impurities include (but are not limited to) dark coloring, scars or other bodily imperfections, tainted blood, family ties, and criminal activity.

Jensa *(JEN-suh)*—Shell Seeker. Sister of Torin and Kerrik. Member of the rebel movement.

Jorge *(Jorge)*—Kiradyn. Elderly blacksmith in the city of Kiradyn who befriended Dayn when no one else would.

Keefe *(Keef)*—Dayn's Tearian birth name.

Kerrik *(KARE-ik)*—Shell Seeker. Adopted younger brother of Jensa and Torin. Discarded in infancy by Tearian parents because of his deformed foot. Kerrik longs to be a Transcendor, a legendary hero who will do great deeds and save the world.

Kirador *(KEER-uh-dore)*—Region north of the mountains on the island of Aredyrah. Its northernmost shore is plagued by eddies, jagged rocks, and the belief in sea monsters. The rest of Kirador's borders consist of a vast mountain range where it is said the demons make their home.

Kiradyn *(KEER-uh-din)*—Primary city in the region of Kirador. Also refers to any person living in Kirador.

Labhras *(LAB-russ)*—Tearian. Wealthy land owner. Father of Cinnia. Best friend of King Sedric. It is Labhras's home that was burned to the ground by Ruairi, and it is against him that Dayn and Alicine were accused of thievery.

Lorcan *(LORE-kun)*—Kiradyn; father of Falyn and Sheireadan; Head of the Council, the governing board of Kirador.

Mahon *(Man)*—Tearian. Husband of Brina. Uncle of Ruairi and Whyn. Birth father of Dayn (Keefe). Commander of the Guard.

Meirla *(MEER-luh)*—Shell Seeker village on the southern coast of Aredyrah.

Memory Keeper—A historian. The term generally refers to members of a covert group that came into being after the Purge which banned all documents belonging to the Jecta. The Memory Keepers are dedicated to preserving all forms of writing.

Morna *(MORE-nuh)*—Kiradyn. Dayn's adopted mother. Alicine's birth mother. Wife of Gorman. A sickly woman, Morna lost many infants at childbirth. Alicine is her only living child by blood.

Mya *(MY-uh)*—Jecta. Widow of Eben. Friend of Jensa and Torin. Mother of Farris, Gem, and Nely.

Nannaven *(NAN-uh-vin)*—Jecta. Elderly Spirit Keeper of Pobu. Was the daughter of a Memory Keeper. Nannaven recently recovered a tome that contained the Prophecy and evidence that Dayn and Reiv are major players in it.

Nely *(NELL-ee)*—Jecta. Youngest daughter of Mya and Eben. Sister of Gem and Farris.

Pobu *(POBE-ew)*—Jecta city to the south of Tearia.

Priestess—Title of the supreme leader of the Temple. Known by no other name. The Priestess is the true power of Tearia.

Reiv *(Reev)*—Jecta. Name given to Ruairi when he was disowned by his family. Banished from the palace after an injury that left him scarred and impure, he was given a job as Foreman over the Jecta who work Labhras's field. He was later accused of thievery, but rather than death, was sentenced to fade away in the Jecta city of Pobu. Rejected there on a number of levels, he left with Jensa and went to Meirla to learn how to seek.

Ruairi *(Rue-AW-ree)*—Tearian. Reiv's birth name. Means "Red King." Was believed to be the second coming of a king of old who carried out the first Purge. Ruairi's name was taken from him when he was disinherited.

Sedric *(SED-rik)*—Deceased King of Tearia. Husband of Isola. Father of Ruairi and Whyn.

Seek—The term used for hunting shells beneath the waters.

Seirgotha *(Seer-GOTH-uh)*—Legendary sea serpent. The Shell Seekers believe the slayer of Seirgotha will gain great knowledge from the gods.

Sheireadan *(SHARE-uh-den)*—Kiradyn. Dayn's nemesis in Kirador. Son of Lorcan. Brother of Falyn.

Shell Seekers—A community of Jecta who live in the coastal village of Meirla. The Shell Seekers are known for their skills at diving and hunting the waters for food and shells. They are also excellent craftsman, using shells to make jewelry and decorative vessels. Their wares are highly desired by the Tearians. Though the Shell Seekers are respected for their skills, they are still considered Jecta.

Spirit Keeper—Title given to a healer. This title is con-sistently used by all the residents of Aredyrah.

Tearia *(Tee-AIR-ee-uh)*—Great city-state to the south of the mountain range of Aredyrah. All navigable land on this side of the island is known as Tearia. The city itself is a walled metropolis of elegant architecture, fountains, colorful gar-dens, and art. It is home to a race of people who strive for purity, as dictated by their gods and defined by Temple law.

Tenzy *(TIN-zee)*—Jecta. Was the daughter of a Memory Keeper. Kept prisoner by the Priestess to interpret forbidden texts.

Torin *(TORE-un)*—Shell Seeker. Older brother of Jensa and Kerrik. Member of rebel movement. Torin has no wife or known offspring, but is close to Mya and her children.

Unnamed One—Person spoken of in the Prophecy. Depending on the interpretation, he can be either savior or threat.

Vania *(VAN-yuh)*—Kiradyn; wife of Haskel; mother of Eyan

Whyn *(Win)*—Tearian. Fraternal twin brother of Ruairi. Son of King Sedric and Queen Isola. Prince and future King of Tearia. Husband of Cinnia.

Will of Agneis—The Tearian term that refers to the custom of killing infants who are not considered pure.

# Character Portraits

## by Annah Hutchings

### ALICINE
**Age:** 15
**Parents:** Gorman and Morna
**Siblings:** One older brother, Dayn
**Home:** Clan region of Kirador
**Character Traits:** Gifted in herb lore and potion-making. Protective of her brother Dayn; quick-tempered and opinionated; conservative in her religious beliefs.

### BRINA
**Age:** 33
**Marital Status:** Married to Mahon, who is Commander of the Guard
**Children:** One son, Dayn
**Other Relations:** She is sister to the queen and aunt to Ruairi and Whyn
**Home:** City-state of Tearia
**Character Traits:** Estranged from her husband; bitter toward Tearian customs; has secret agendas; especially fond of Reiv (is like a mother to him).

271

## CINNIA

**Age:** Fifteen
**Parents:** Father Labhras, Mother
    *(name not indicated)*
**Marital Status:** Married to Whyn, Prince and future King of Tearia
**Siblings:** None
**Home:** City-state of Tearia
**Character Traits:** Ambitious; well aware of her own beauty; manipulative

## DAYN

**Age:** 16
**Parents:** Gorman and Morna
**Siblings:** One younger sister, Alicine
**Home:** Clan region of Kirador
**Character Traits:** Gentle nature; self-conscious; fearful of social situations; skeptical; hopelessly in love with Falyn.

## FALYN

**Age:** 15
**Parents:** Father Lorcan, mother deceased
**Siblings:** One older brother, Sheireadan
**Home:** City of Kiradyn
**Character Traits:** Oblivious to Dayn's affections; seems to turn a blind eye to her brother's bad behaviors; there is more to her than meets the eye.

## JENSA

**Age:** 23

**Parents:** deceased

**Marital Status:** Single

**Children:** None

**Siblings:** Older brother Torin; adopted brother, Kerrik

**Home:** Meirla, the Shell Seeker village south of Tearia

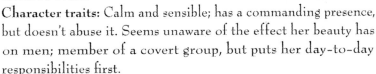

**Character traits:** Calm and sensible; has a commanding presence, but doesn't abuse it. Seems unaware of the effect her beauty has on men; member of a covert group, but puts her day-to-day responsibilities first.

## KERRIK

**Age:** 7

**Siblings:** Older brother and sister (by adoption), Torin and Jensa.

**Home:** Meirla, the Shell Seeker village south of Tearia

**Character Traits:** Energetic and good-natured. Childish awe of Tearian royalty. Helpful and generous. Wants to save the world.

REIV (former heir to the throne of Tearia; the Red King; Ruairi)

**Age:** 16

**Parents:** King Sedric and Queen Isola

**Siblings:** Fraternal twin brother, Whyn

**Home:** City-state of Tearia

**Character Traits:** Cocky, stubborn, frustrated, angry. Firmly entrenched in the customs of Tearia, yet miserable as a result of them.

## TORIN
**Age:** 25
**Parents:** deceased
**Marital Status:** Single
**Children:** Maybe
**Siblings:** Sister, Jensa; adopted brother, Kerrik
**Home:** Meirla, the Shell Seeker village south of Tearia

**Character Traits:** Strong and loyal where his family is concerned; hates Tearians, especially the royal family; member of a covert group; quick-tempered and stubborn.

## WHYN (Prince and second heir to the throne)
**Age:** 16
**Parents:** Sedric and Isola
**Siblings:** Fraternal twin brother, Ruairi
**Home:** City-state of Tearia
**Character Traits:** Loyal to Tearia; conservative in his beliefs; obedient to his father and accepting of his royal duties.

# About the Author

Tracy A. Akers is a former elementary school teacher who taught students with language learning disabilities. She grew up in Arlington, Texas, but currently makes her home in the rolling hills of Pasco County, Florida. She resides with Marv, her husband of twenty-seven years, and four naughty pugs. As a child, Tracy gravitated to books about ancient worlds and mythologies, but until recently did not realize she had stories of her own to tell. Believing herself to be a teacher, not an author, she graduated from the University of South Florida with a degree in Education. Though Tracy loved teaching and working with young people, she began to feel restless in the classroom. She left the field to explore other avenues, but found mostly dead-ends, until one day, as if by magic, she discovered the world of writing.

Tracy feels blessed to have found her true calling, and gives credit to the spirits that led her there. When she is not putting words to paper, she draws, reads, listens to music, and studies the writing craft. She has done numerous presentations at schools, libraries, and writers' conferences, and has participated in author panels at Literary Festivals and Fantasy/Science Fiction Conventions. She is an active participant in Florida Writers Association, was the 2005 FWA Tampa group leader, and is the founder and group leader of FWA Young Writers of East Pasco. She holds memberships in PMA, the Independent Book Publishers Association; the Society of Children's Book Writers and Illustrators; and the

Florida Publishers Association. She was also on the steering committee for Celebration of the Story, a literary event held at Saint Leo University.

Ms. Akers' debut novel, *The Fire and the Light*, Book One in the Souls of Aredyrah Series, was published through her own publishing business, Ruadora Publishing. It has earned numerous awards and recognitions for its contribution to Young Adult Literature. *The Search for the Unnamed One*, Book Two in the series, is published through Aisling Press, which is also the publisher of the companion Curriculum Guides for *The Fire and the Light* and *The Search for the Unnamed One*. Ms. Akers was recently named a member of the Aisling staff as the Editorial Director for both Young Adult Literature and Curriculum Guide development.

Ms. Akers is available for book signings, speaking engagements, and fund raisers. She can be reached at taakers@msn.com. For more information about Ms. Akers and her series of books, please visit www.soulsofaredyrah.com.